FOUND SHADOWS

A NOVEL

PT HYLTON

Copyright © 2019 P.T. Hylton

All rights reserved.

This is a work of fiction. Any resemblance to actual persons living or dead, businesses, events, or locales is purely coincidental.

Reproduction in whole or part of this publication without express written consent is strictly prohibited.

Thank you for supporting my work.

Published by Six-String Books, LLC

PROLOGUE

Eric Partin saw his first ghost when he was twelve. It happened twenty days after they kidnapped him.

The house where they kept him was set back from the road, just out of the reach of the streetlights in a pool of darkness. Eric's room was on the third floor. He had one window, and it looked out on a patch of woods behind the house. He'd tried to break the window on his second day, but it was made of some hard plastic that he couldn't even dent. It let light into the room, but the outside world looked hazy through its pane, like seeing the world through a thick, dirty pair of glasses. The room smelled strongly of sawdust and cleaning solution, though his captors hadn't so much as mopped since he arrived.

After nearly three weeks, all the notions he'd entertained of escape were long gone. There was no way out of this room except through the door, and that was triple bolted on the outside. They'd removed everything that could possibly be used as a weapon. The toilet in his small attached bathroom had neither a seat nor a lid on its tank. The only piece of furniture was a mattress on the floor. The pathetic bed had no sheets, as if he could use those against his captors somehow, just a thin blanket and a caseless pillow. There wasn't much to do except stare out the dingy window at the trees and wonder how his life had turned so awful so quickly.

Twenty days ago, he'd been walking home from another day of sixth grade when a van had pulled up beside him. Two men had jumped out, and the next thing he knew he was speeding away from his old life. They'd drugged him, and sometime later they'd arrived here and thrown him in this room.

His captors hadn't been cruel since that van ride. They hadn't been particularly kind either. Mostly, they'd ignored him, only entering the room to bring him meals. That somehow made things worse. He had no idea why they'd taken him. Were they trying to get ransom money from his parents? If so, they'd be disappointed. The Partins could hardly afford their car payment let alone a sack of cash for kidnappers.

Eric did, however, know that he wasn't the first kid they'd taken. He knew it from the casual ease with which they were handling the situation and the way they seemed to have all the kinks worked out in their little system. But he also knew it from the initials scratched into the baseboard next to the mattress. *M.N.* His best friend Matt's initials, a strange coincidence that both comforted him and made him feel even more homesick.

He wondered how the kid had scratched his initials into the plaster. Had he had a tool of some kind? Or had he simply done it with his fingernails?

A familiar click came from the door, followed by a second, then a third. Eric froze, filled with a sudden powerful terror, the way he always was when the door opened. They'd only brought him meals so far, but he knew someday they would come for some other purpose, and then he'd find out why they'd taken him.

The door opened, and a man Eric had never seen before stepped into the room. He was tall and thin, and younger than the others. Eric guessed he was in his thirties. He carried a folding chair under his arm.

As soon as he stepped inside, the door closed behind him and the three locks clicked shut.

Eric's breathing sped up and he pressed his back against the wall.

"It's okay," the man said. "I just want to talk."

Eric doubted that very highly, but he said nothing.

The man slowly unfolded the chair, set it two feet in front of Eric's mattress, and sat down. "I'm sure you have lots of questions."

He paused.

Of course Eric had questions. He had dozens of questions. Hundreds. Why had they taken him? Would he ever see his family again? What were they going to do with him now?

But sitting under the gaze of the thin man's cool blue stare, he couldn't give voice to any of these questions. His tongue felt too big in his mouth, and he wasn't sure he'd be able to speak if he tried.

The thin man didn't look surprised at Eric's lack of response, but neither did he seem happy about it. "All right then. Let me start by addressing something I'm sure you're wondering about. I assume you've heard them?"

He paused, and again Eric said nothing.

"The noises in the night?"

For the last twenty days, all the fear within him had been compressed into a tight cold ball in his stomach. The worst had happened. The thing parents and teachers had warned him about in frightened, urgent tones for as long as he could remember. The most unfair part, the thing that bothered him above all else, was that he hadn't done any of the things they'd cautioned him against. There was no candy from a stranger or seemingly kind adult trying to lure him into a car. He'd been minding his own business, walking home from school like it was any other day, and they'd dragged him into their vehicle.

Ever since, he'd been waiting for what would happen next. His parents and teachers never talked about that part. Their instructions were all about avoidance, not what to do if you were taken. Kidnapped. Was it still called kidnapping when the victim was twelve years old? He didn't know, and it didn't much matter.

He'd spent almost three weeks alone in this room, but at night... sometimes it was as if he *wasn't* alone. Sometimes he felt something brush against his cheek, something prickly that seemed to whisper to him. Sometimes he thought he saw it out of the corner of his eye, a flicker of light, there one moment and gone the next.

But what bothered him most were the noises.

He didn't have a word for the strange sounds. They weren't human, that much he knew. It was as if air were being forced through a disfigured throat and words were being formed by a mouth without lips and only the stub of a tongue. That's how he pictured it in his mind during the long hours when he couldn't push the bad thoughts away.

Sometimes in those dark hours, he wondered if maybe the things in the darkness were the reason he'd been taken from his family. Maybe he was meant to be a sacrifice to them.

But then the morning came. As the dawn broke and

light cascaded through the plastic window, thoughts of creatures hiding in the dark started to seem silly. Surely it was just his strained, sleep-deprived mind beginning to break under all he'd been through. It wasn't real. It couldn't be.

But now, hearing the thin man say the words aloud, giving voice to his fears, it seemed just as real as it did in the wee hours before the sun rose. The ball of icy fear in his stomach grew spikes that sent chills through every part of him.

The thin man watched him for a moment, a knowing look in his eye. Then he leaned back and rubbed his chin as if trying to decide where to begin. "The first thing you should know about them is that they won't do any real damage to you. They can't."

"Why not?" His voice was a scratchy whisper, and he barely recognized the sound of it.

The thin man smiled, his lips curling up at an odd angle. "That's a good question. Very good, in fact." He rubbed his chin again. "I guess you could say it's beyond them. *We're* beyond them, me and the others who live here. You are too. You live here now, after all."

Eric looked away, trying to hide the tears that sprang into his eyes. *You live here now*. It sounded rather permanent.

The thin man followed Eric's gaze to the door and its three deadbolts. "It won't be like that forever. Just a temporary measure to give you time to get used to things. It's a period of adjustment."

Eric looked back at the thin man. There was something in the corner of the man's left eye. A speck of dirt, maybe. As he watched, the small black speck... it almost seemed to be growing.

The thin man adjusted in his seat as if he realized he'd

made a misstep somewhere along the way and was trying to reset the conversation.

"Listen, son. There are certain things here, things with which you'll have to come to terms. I'm not saying it's easy. It's pretty far from easy. Few will ever know the truth of what we've been through, people like you and me."

You and me? That gave Eric pause. Was it possible that this man was like him? That he'd been taken from his home, that he'd been ripped away from his life like Eric had? It didn't seem likely.

"Okay, let's try this. A little test. I want you to look into my eyes." The thin man put a finger to his nose, directing Eric where to look. "Good. Now stay here. Focus. Ignore everything else in the room. Whatever you hear, whatever you sense, stay focused on me. If you can do that, you'll be safe."

"Safe from what?" Eric choked out the words in a voice that didn't quite sound like his own.

"Think of it as practice for the rest of your life."

The statement was so strange, so unrelated to Eric's question, that he wasn't sure how to respond. So he focused on that black speck in the thin man's eye. The one that seemed to be growing.

He stared for a long moment, trying to drown out the rest of the room as he'd been instructed.

From behind him, he heard a door creak.

Eric knew that sound only too well. He heard it every time he opened the bathroom door, and it always made him flinch, He'd cursed the noisy hinges a hundred times, cringing at the thought of the attention they might bring from his kidnappers. The bathroom door moved only reluctantly, groaning to give voice to its displeasure when he pressed against it.

There was no one pressing against it now; that much he knew. The only people in the room were him and the thin man. He'd seen the bedroom door open just long enough for the thin man to step through. There was no way anyone else could have followed.

And yet the sound of the bathroom door opening was unmistakable.

Someone was back there. Behind him. Crossing over from the bathroom to the bedroom and creeping toward Eric's back.

The thin man didn't seem to notice. He remained perfectly still, his forefinger erect and touching the tip of his nose.

Eric resisted the growing urge to turn and see what was behind him. He stayed focused on the black speck in the thin man's eye. As he watched, he realized that the speck wasn't just growing; it was pulsating. Every three seconds it contracted ever-so-slightly, before expanding to a size just a bit bigger than before. The black mark had been the size of a speck of dirt when Eric had first spotted it, but now it was at least four times that size. It reminded Eric of the mark on the die in a Monopoly game, bold against the white of the eye.

Behind him, he heard the floorboards creak.

It could have been a natural noise, the sound of the house settling maybe, but Eric knew it wasn't. In the three weeks he'd been there, he'd only heard that sound when he walked across the room.

"Focus," the thin man muttered, his voice barely a whisper. "Stay with me."

Eric watched the pulsating black spot with growing dread. Was it a stain on the man's eye? Or was it a hole? And if it was a hole, would something emerge from it?

He didn't know what scared him more: the black mark or the sounds coming from behind him.

There was a click, like a heel coming down on the floorboards. Then another, closer this time.

"Focus," the thin man repeated.

The sounds behind him were coming faster now, a footstep, a popping sound like an ancient bone moving in a way to which it wasn't accustomed, a soft groan.

All the while, the black mark in the thin man's left eye grew until the mark and pupil were like twin black suns.

Eric realized he was trembling. Not just his hand or his lip, but his whole body. Never had he been so overcome with fear, not even when they'd thrown him in the van with the hood over his head and he'd felt them speeding away from everything he'd ever known.

That had been terrifying, but this? This was primal.

Something brushed against the back of his neck, and every tiny hair stood on end. It took him a moment to realize what he was feeling on the back of his neck was a breath.

He tore his gaze away from the black mark and whipped his head around.

And he gasped.

Until he turned, there was a possibility he'd been imagining everything, the bathroom door, the floor creaking, the breath on his neck. But the small semblance of doubt in his instincts quickly fled as he saw the being behind him.

The being's feet floated three inches above the ground. The light coming through the window passed through it, revealing a hint of the wood paneling on the wall beyond.

It was as if seeing the being somehow made it real. The air filled with a sickly-sweet odor that reminded Eric of rotting vegetables. It poured into his nose and down his throat until he could taste it.

But that wasn't the worst for Eric. The thing that pushed his mind to the edge—the thing that made him question his own sanity—was the way the being looked.

It looked exactly like the thin man.

The thin man leaned back in the chair, his expression impossible to read. "We know the truth now, Eric. I was wrong. You don't belong here. Not yet."

The ghostly version of the thin man reached out its hand, and its fingers stretched to impossible lengths. Then they wrapped around Eric's throat.

PART I

SOMETHING IN THE WATER

1

Thirty years later.

"She's dead, boss."

Eric Partin frowned, put his hands on his hips and let out a weary sigh. On today of all days. "You've gotta be kidding."

Donovan shook his head. "I don't know what happened. She's been kicking fine all week. But now... well, unless you plan on burying her in the field back there, we'd better load her onto the truck."

Eric stared at the glistening metal body at his feet. So young. So beautiful. Even cracked open with her innards showing for the world to see, she looked like she might just get up and start running at any moment. Sadly, if Donnie said that wasn't going to be the case, it wasn't happening. There was nothing to be done about it. At least not here.

Today of all days.

"All right," Eric said. "Let's load her up."

Donovan shifted the old girl into neutral, and they pushed her up the ramp and onto the trailer.

The machine in question was a 2010 John Deere Max Ztrack 777 commercial mower. She could zip along at up to eleven miles an hour, execute a zero-turn like nobody's business, and cleanly cut just about any yard they could throw at it. Best of all, she'd been more dependable than any employee Eric had ever had, excepting maybe Donovan, and that was a hard maybe.

And now, the one day he most wanted her to run smoothly, she crapped out. Somewhere, the gods of lawn care were laughing at Eric Partin.

"I can't hand her over like this. We gotta get it taken care of."

Donovan raised an eyebrow. "Don't you have to head out soon?"

Eric set his jaw as he glanced at his watch. As usual, Donnie was right. It was a twenty-minute drive to the lawyer's office, and he was supposed to be there in twenty-five minutes. Still, it didn't sit right with him, leaving the mower in non-working order. Not only that, they were leaving the Millers' property three-quarters mowed. The Millers were among E&J Landscaping's oldest customers, and there was no way Eric was going to have them come home from work and find their yard in such a state. After so many years, after they'd taken a chance on a twenty-three-year-old Eric Partin whose upstart lawn care company had consisted of one man, a standard push mower, and a Black and Decker weed wacker, there was no way he was going to let them down. Not on today of all days.

"Griff and his crew should be wrapping up on Rugger Street in an hour or so." Eric pulled his phone out of his pocket as he spoke. Griff and his two-man crew were what Eric thought of as the E&J second unit. He gave them the less demanding jobs. The simple lawns that didn't require much in the way of finesse but were still the bread and butter of the company. Today, Griff's crew was working on a subdivision on the south side of Mequon, an upper-middle-class neighborhood where E&J had more than a dozen customers. While the crew generally spent the full day in the subdivision every Tuesday, Eric knew full-well that their day involved plenty of jaw wagging. If he called and told them to double-time it, they could surely swing by and finish the Millers' estate-like property before the owners got home.

Eric started tapping the keypad on his phone, but Donovan cleared his throat.

"Hey, do you think maybe I should make the call?"

Eric pushed away the tinge of annoyance that crept up inside of him. "By my watch, I'm still in charge. At least for the next hour or so."

Donovan ran a hand over his stubbly chin. "No argument there. And I don't want to see you go a moment sooner than you have to."

"All right then." Eric scrolled through his contacts for Griff's number.

"Still...it might mean something if you let me make the call."

It took Eric a moment to understand what his friend meant. But only a moment. As of three o'clock, Donovan would be taking over running the day-to-day operations of E&J. That meant he was going from being Griff's peer to being his boss. If Eric could show his support by letting Donovan call a few shots before the reins were officially passed, it might help ease the transition.

Eric slipped his phone back into his pocket and nodded. "Make the call."

Donovan fished out his own phone and dialed.

Eric put his big hands against the small of his back and stretched, feeling the tension in every disc and muscle. A part of him was reluctant to give up the business he'd spent the last nineteen years building, but another part—a smaller but increasingly vocal part—was looking forward to not putting the strain on his forty-two-year-old body. The last nineteen years of pushing himself were finally catching up with him, it seemed.

Being in his forties was strange. Some days he felt like he was still twenty-five. His tall, lean body felt strong most of the time. He still had all his dark brown hair, though more gray seemed to appear daily. His blue eyes still held the spark of youth, or so he liked to think. Other days, he felt stiffness in his joints and pain in his back. Thankfully, those days were the exception, not the norm. At least so far.

Donovan put his phone away and grinned at Eric. "Griff bitched a little, but he'll get it done."

Eric nodded and looked around, wishing there was something else for him to do. Some other task he needed to take care of. But there wasn't. Which meant there was no avoiding getting in his truck and driving downtown.

He held out his hand to Donovan. "I guess this is it. Take care of her for me?"

Donovan nodded solemnly.

There was plenty more they could have said. Donovan could have thanked Eric for hiring him despite his less than stellar record, for teaching him the ropes and giving him the opportunity to work his way up. Eric could have thanked Donovan for being the best damn employee he'd ever had, for being the one guy he could always count on to show up and do the work with artistry and care.

But they weren't those kinds of people. For better or for worse, they weren't the types who could say what was in their hearts. So they just shook hands and went their separate ways.

Eric made it downtown three minutes after the meeting was scheduled to start. That wouldn't have been so bad if not for the parking situation. Mequon, Wisconsin was a small town just north of Milwaukee, but it had recently become a fashionable place to live for urbanites looking to escape the city and start a family. That had been very good for the local economy, including lawn care businesses, but all the new, hip restaurants and shops hadn't done much for the downtown parking situation.

It turned out that there weren't any empty spaces on the same block as the lawyer's office. Nor the next one over. Nor the one after that. He finally found a spot near a bridal shop four blocks over. He had to wedge his pickup in between a Prius and a Malibu, but he'd had plenty of practice easing his vehicle into tight spaces. Once he was done parallel parking, he climbed out of the truck and jogged to the law office. He made it in less than five minutes, which wasn't bad when you factored in all the pedestrians and strollers he'd had to dodge.

The receptionist showed him to the conference room and ushered him inside. Immediately, he wished he'd taken Donnie's advice to shower and change clothes before the meeting. Between the grass-stains on his pants, the fresh layer of sweat on his face, and the dirt under his fingernails, he felt more than a little out of place in this nicely appointed law office.

Jennifer, Bill, and their lawyer sat on the right side of the table. The lawyer's face was scrunched up in something bordering on disgust. Whether it was caused by Eric's attire or his tardiness, Eric didn't know.

Eric's lawyer sat alone on the other side of the table. He clapped his hands together, a wide smile on his face, as Eric entered.

"Ah, there he is!"

Eric sheepishly returned the smile. "Hi everyone. Sorry I'm late." As he took his seat, he looked at Jennifer and Bill. "Hey, sorry about this, but there was a problem with one of the mowers. Donovan's going to be the rest of the day fixing it. I hate leaving you with a broken mower, but Griff's crew is going to finish up at the Millers."

Bill waved a hand in front of his face, dismissing the apology. "Don't even worry about it."

"Donnie's sure he can fix it?" Jennifer asked.

"He says he can."

Bill nodded. "Then that's good enough for me."

Eric felt the familiar old annoyance that threatened to appear whenever Bill spoke. Part of the annoyance was that Bill seemed like a genuinely nice guy. The fact that he was so hard to hate somehow made Eric dislike him even more.

Jennifer, on the other hand, he couldn't seem to hate no matter how hard he tried. Even two years ago when their marriage had been falling apart, even in the lowest moments, he'd never hated her. Truth was, he had a harder time understanding why she'd married him in the first place than why she'd left him. Eric wasn't sure it was possible to truly be friends with an ex-spouse, but he and Jennifer were about as close as it came. It wasn't like they were going out for beers on the weekend, but they shared a closeness, a connection. And they could still make each other laugh.

Jennifer and Bill's lawyer straightened the stack of papers in front of him. "Shall we begin?"

For the next fifteen minutes, they reviewed the terms of the sale. There were no surprises. Eric's lawyer had walked him through the details the previous week. While the lawyers had negotiated a few of the finer points of the deal, the big picture, the part that mattered most, they'd agreed upon almost immediately. Bill and Jennifer would buy Eric's fifty percent ownership in E&J Landscaping. Eric would be paid enough money that work wasn't going to be strictly necessary for the next couple years, and in return, he agreed to stay out of the lawn care business for at least ten years. It wouldn't have made sense for them to buy the business if Eric could just start a new company and steal all their clients.

Once they'd finished reviewing the details, the lawyer slid a stack of papers to Eric and handed him a pen.

He looked down at the papers for a long time, surprised at how calm he felt. He was about to sign away the business he'd spent his life building.

But that wasn't totally accurate. He hadn't built the business alone. If it had been just him, he would have been satisfied keeping it a one-man operation with just enough clients to keep him afloat. It had been Jennifer who'd grown his idea into a real business. She'd marketed the hell out of E&J, and she'd encouraged happy customers to leave online reviews long before that was the norm. She did the accounting, the scheduling, the payroll, and so much more.

Yes, he was the one with the eye for landscaping, but she had the mind for business. It only made sense that she would be the one to run things. They had plenty of employees who could do the dirty work.

He drew a deep breath and signed and initialed where

they told him to. He'd spent nineteen years building the business, but it took less than two minutes to sign it away.

And just like that, it was over. For the first time in his adult life, he was unemployed.

A hearty round of handshakes later, he walked out of the office, cashier's check in hand.

He almost made it to the street before he heard a voice behind him.

"Eric, hold up a minute."

He turned and saw Jennifer hurrying down the stairs. He couldn't help but smile as he watched her.

She reached him and stopped. "I just wanted to... I wanted to make sure you're okay."

He crossed his arms and chuckled. "Yeah. I mean, it's a lot. Big change, but I'm good. How about you? You and Bill up for keeping the ship running?"

"You kidding? E&J's a well-oiled machine." She paused, then course-corrected. "Without you, it'll be harder. I just meant—"

"I know. It's fine." He met her eyes and saw something there. Something she wanted to say to him. He had something he needed to say first. "You want my advice? Give Donovan a raise. Before he asks for it. He's the key to the operation."

"Noted."

She got that look in her eye again, like there was something she wanted to say but wasn't sure if she should. So he waited.

She broke eye contact, her gaze drifting to the floor. "Listen, I know it's none of my business."

"You can say it."

She nodded slowly, looking up at him. "The money

you've got? It's enough to start something new. Maybe you want to go somewhere else."

A slight smile grew on his face. "You trying to get rid of me?"

"No, not at all. I'd miss the hell out of you. It's just... you need something new. You have for years. The things you used to care about so much, our marriage, E&J..."

That caught him off guard, and a bit of annoyance crept up inside him. "Hang on. Are you saying I didn't care about our marriage? Or the business I've worked my ass off building for nearly half my life?"

"No. I'm just saying there was a time when you would have fought for them. And you gave up both pretty damn easy."

He started to speak, but she held up a hand.

"Like I said, it's none of my business. But I care about you. And I hope whatever you do next, it helps you find it again."

He swallowed hard, pushing down the hurt her words caused him. "Find what?"

"The passion. The thing that made you a force of nature. You can be that again. Do whatever it takes and find it."

With that, she turned and walked back up the stairs to where her husband was waiting for her.

Eric wandered back to his truck in a daze. Jennifer's words had hurt, but that didn't mean they weren't true. It probably meant they were. He was so lost in thought he didn't notice the Jeep circling the block, its driver carefully watching Eric each time it passed.

2

Eric woke at two in the morning, shivering.

He climbed out of bed and stumbled to the closet. It didn't take him long to find a sweatshirt, even in the dark. Through the haze of sleep, he didn't think about the oddness of being cold in early August, the most sweltering time of the year in Wisconsin. If he'd stopped to listen, he would have noticed the air conditioning wasn't running. All that was far from his mind, which was consumed with the need for warmth and the lingering remnants of the dream he'd just been having. While he didn't remember the details, he did remember the setting: a cold room with an opaque plastic window and three locks on the door.

He thought of the place occasionally, usually in the wee hours of the morning, but he couldn't remember ever dreaming about it. He didn't look back on it with fear. It was just something that had happened to him when he was a kid. Something terrible and unexplained, yes, but still only a half-remembered experience, almost like a childhood illness that had left scars.

As he emerged from the mental fog, he wondered if being suddenly unmoored from his business had sent his mind reeling back to another time he'd been lost.

He was standing in the doorway of his closet, rubbing his arms through his sweatshirt to warm them, when he heard the sound. A scratching noise, like a chair being dragged across the floor. And it was coming from his bedroom window.

He blinked hard, trying to figure out what could be causing the noise. Deep inside, something in his brain flashed danger like a neon sign, but Eric quelled that instinct. Just because he didn't know what was making the noise didn't mean it was bad.

He waited until the scratching came again. It seemed a bit quieter this time, and for a moment he thought he had it figured out. It was a branch, probably swaying in the wind, lightly scraping the glass of his window as it moved.

But there was no tree outside his window. His bedroom was on the first floor.

The scratching came again, louder this time.

The neon danger sign flashed again, and this time he didn't ignore it—not completely. But he didn't give in to it either. The danger sign wanted him to jump back into bed and pull the covers over his head like a frightened child until the scratching stopped. He wasn't about to do that, so he slowly made his way across the room to the window. The creak of the floorboards seemed amplified to his heightened senses, another indication his barely awake mind was making more of this than it should have. Still, he paused at the window a moment before parting the curtain and peering out.

His front yard was still and empty. It looked exactly as

he'd expect it to at two in the morning. The full moon illuminated the single oak tree that stood on the other side of the yard, its branches nowhere near this window or any other in the single-story home. His eyes scanned the lawn, looking for any sign of something out of place. But there was nothing. His carefully manicured grass, the bushes, the sidewalk in front of the house, it all looked perfectly normal. The only thing remotely unusual was a green Jeep parked across the street. Though he couldn't recall seeing that vehicle before, it was hardly cause for concern.

He stared out the window for a long time, letting the danger light in his mind dim naturally. When it had faded to nearly nothing, he let the curtains fall shut and turned to walk back to bed.

Another sound came from the window, much louder now. Not a scratching sound. His breath caught in his throat as he realized what it was. It was tapping. Something was tapping on the window.

The danger sign was back, flashing brighter than before, threatening to drive out all logical thought. His gaze darted to the bedside table and the phone resting there. Then his eyes went to his closet where he kept his revolver.

Great idea, Eric, he thought. *You're so spooked you'd probably shoot the damn window out just because a woodpecker thought two in the morning was a great time to go to work.*

He turned back to the window and slowly raised his hand. His fingers were only inches from the curtain when the sound came again. *Tap, tap, tap.*

That was no woodpecker.

Before he lost his nerve, he grabbed the curtain and pulled it open.

A face stared at him, inches from the glass.

Eric gasped and staggered backward.

The man was impossibly thin; his cheekbones stood out like boils, offsetting his sunken eyes in the moonlight. His wild, dark mane of hair jutted in every direction, and he wore a ragged white tee shirt and threadbare shorts.

He leaned closer to the window and smiled, revealing two rows of teeth that looked too big for his mouth. "Eric."

The man spoke in a whisper, but somehow it carried through the glass.

Eric wanted to run to the closet and grab his revolver, to show this lunatic he was capable of defending himself. But he found he was frozen, transfixed by the man's crazed stare.

"Eric. It's time to come home."

Eric's mouth fell open at the strange statement. Whose home? He was home. Or was the man saying it was time for *him* to come home?

He blinked hard, breaking the strange spell, disgusted that he'd been trying to decipher the words of this lunatic instead of taking steps to defend himself. His throat felt dry, but he forced himself to speak. "You can't be here. You have to go."

The words sounded lame even as he said them, but at least he'd spoken. It was a step in the right direction. Now to get his gun.

Just as Eric was about to turn away, the man flickered.

It was as if he were there one second and gone the next. Eric could see the tree behind the man, then he was back again. The strange man was flickering in and out of existence.

The effect was so disconcerting, Eric felt a phantom pain in his eyes, as if it were easier for his mind to believe his senses weren't working properly than to believe the laws of physics were being so blatantly disregarded.

A familiar smell filled the air, and something deep inside Eric went cold. The smell was somehow worse than the strange flickering man just outside his window.

A sweet sawdust smell, the same one he'd smelled when his father cut the two-by-fours to build his treehouse. And under that, a pungent chemical odor—a cleaner his parents never used.

It was the room. Somehow, after all these years, the smell of the room had found him. He recognized it immediately, his muscles tensing and his heart rate increasing wildly. His mind knew he was a forty-two-year-old man in his home in Mequon, Wisconsin, but his body felt differently. To his body, he was once again a twelve-year-old boy being held in a room with three locks on the door.

The man outside the window blinked out of existence for nearly a full second, then reappeared. His mouth gaped open and the cords on his long neck stood out. He was screaming. Though Eric had heard him speaking clearly through the glass moments ago, he heard nothing now. Whatever was pulling him out of reality was swallowing his voice as well.

The man flickered at a faster pace now, alternating between there and not there for fractions of a second. His hand reached into his pocket and pulled out a large folding knife.

Eric stood frozen, transfixed by the strange sight as the man unfolded the blade. It was like watching a poorly rendered stop-motion animation or a movie with most of the frames missing. Once again, he felt the phantom pains in his eyes.

The stranger reached down and grabbed the bottom of

his shirt. He disappeared for a moment, and when he came back, he'd pulled the shirt up to his sternum, revealing an emaciated torso. With his other hand, he brought the blade to his stomach.

"No," Eric muttered. Even in the relative darkness, he could see the scars crisscrossing the man's body. He knew what was going to happen next.

The stranger pressed the edge of the blade against the left side of his stomach and drew it across, a mask of pain replacing the silent scream.

As blood began to seep from the wound, the flickering slowed. The man let his shirt fall back down, and the blood almost immediately soaked through, creating a red line on his dingy white shirt. The line blossomed as the red stain spread.

But the flickering had stopped.

The stranger tilted his head to the side, as if cracking his neck. His jaw was set, the pain clear on his face. "Eric, you need to get Agent Baughman. He'll show you where we are. It's not too late to fix this."

The words and the familiar name of Agent Baughman seemed to break whatever trance Eric had been under. He stumbled his way back across the room toward the closet, keeping his eyes on the stranger bleeding outside his window.

How the hell did this guy know Baughman? What did Baughman have to do with any of this? Eric hadn't so much as spoken to the man in over a decade. He wasn't even sure the guy still worked for the Bureau.

All those questions could wait until later. The more pressing matter was the crazy, knife-wielding man outside his window.

Eric slowly eased the closet door open. "Okay. We'll talk to Baughman. Whatever's going on, I'm sure he can help."

He risked a glance into the closet. In the darkness, he could just make out the shelf where he kept the revolver, jammed under a stack of sweaters. Not the safest place for a gun, maybe, but he lived alone.

The stranger let out a low sound that might have been a laugh. "No man, you don't understand. Baughman can't help. He's in danger too. Just like the rest of us. Thanks to you."

The stranger placed his hand against the glass.

The window was locked, Eric was almost sure of it, but that didn't mean the man couldn't break the glass. The growing splotch of red on his shirt testified to the fact that he didn't mind hurting himself.

"Come to Wakefield," the stranger said. "See for yourself. Make it right."

The man lifted the knife so its handle was pointed at the window, then drew back his hand.

Eric couldn't wait any longer. He had to act.

He rushed into the closet and jammed his hand under the stack of sweaters. For a terrible moment, he didn't feel the gun. Then his fingers brushed something hard and cold. The weapon was further back than he'd expected. He had to stand on the tips of his toes to reach it.

Finally, he pulled the weapon free, knocking two sweaters onto the floor. He stepped out of the closet, the revolver raised. He hurried to the window, taking long strides, the revolver held in a two-hand grip. As he reached the window, he heard an engine start, and immediately the Jeep sped away.

The stranger was gone.

Eric stood at the window for a long time, staring at the moonlit street, trying to understand what he'd just seen and wondering what that man had to do with Agent Baughman, the FBI agent who'd investigated his kidnapping thirty years earlier.

3

Morning came gradually, the sun creeping over the eastern horizon just behind the police officer taking Eric's report.

Eric held back nothing, stating the facts plainly and honestly, even the ones that made him look a bit less than sane. When the police officer suggested maybe the light had been playing tricks on him, he didn't object even though he knew that wasn't the case. He was a rational man, and he understood the skeptical reactions. Expected them even.

The one area he did not accept any hedging was in terms of Agent Carl Baughman. If a crazed, knife-wielding psycho said the FBI agent was in danger, it could very well be the case. Most likely, the peeper *was* the danger.

The police officers assured Eric they'd contact Agent Baughman's office to let him know about the threat. Eric intended to do the same later in the day, just to be sure.

Thankfully, no matter how skeptical the officers were about Eric's claims, there was enough physical evidence for them to be sure someone had been there. The peeping cutter had left blood behind, and the grass was trampled outside Eric's window. Eric was confident there were fingerprints on his window—the stranger had pressed his hand against it after all—but the officers didn't seem too keen on dusting for the prints. They said they'd send a tech by later to handle it.

By the time they finally left, the sun was fully up, and Eric was feeling the aftereffects of the adrenaline and a nearly sleepless night. Although this wasn't the way he'd expected to start his post-E&J Landscaping life, he was mighty glad he didn't have anywhere to go today. After checking the locks on all the doors and a few windows, he stumbled back to his bedroom, fell into bed, and slept deeply and dreamlessly for three solid hours.

He woke with a start, certain he'd heard something that required his attention but with no idea what that something might be. He lay there in a strange state halfway between sleep and wake until the sound came again.

The doorbell.

He glanced at the clock on the bedside table. 10:18 a.m.

With a sigh, he climbed out of bed and shuffled to the door. The face he saw on the other side of the window in the door surprised him. There were lines on the man's brown face and his hair had gone silver, but it was unmistakably the man who'd spent so many hours working with Eric and his parents after the kidnapping.

Agent Baughman.

Eric smiled as he opened the door. "Wow, Agent Baughman. That's what I call service."

The FBI agent stared back, a quizzical look on his face.

"It's only been three hours since I made the report. How did you even get here so fast?"

Baughman smiled weakly. "The report?"

That caught Eric off guard. If Baughman wasn't there

about the report, why was he there? "I suppose you'd better come in."

Baughman's face broke out in a wide smile. "How've you been, Eric?"

The two men shook hands. Seeing Agent Baughman brought up complicated feelings for Eric. The man had been there during the worst times of his life, but he'd been a calming presence. "I'm not working for the government, so I guess I'm doing better than you."

Baughman came inside, careful to wipe his already spotless shoes on the matt before entering.

Eric gestured to the couch. As Baughman settled in, Eric took a seat in the rocking chair across from the couch.

Baughman rubbed his hands together as he took in the room. Jennifer had taken most of the decorations when she left, so the place was pretty sparse. "How's the glamorous world of landscaping treating you?"

Eric knew Baughman was just trying to be friendly, but this was just about the last topic he wanted to discuss. "Actually, it's not. Jennifer and I... she was the real brains behind the operation. So we agreed she and her new husband would buy the business."

"Ah." Baughman's face made it clear he knew how much he'd stepped in it with that question. "Figured out your next move yet?"

"Still working on that. Is the Bureau hiring?"

Baughman barked out a laugh. "You know there's a background check, right?"

There was an awkward silence as Eric tried to figure out if this was a social visit or something else. The odds of Baughman just passing through Mequon were slim, but what was the other option? What possible FBI business could involve Eric?

When he was twelve years old, Eric had been kidnapped. His captors had driven him across the country in a van, held him in a locked room in an unknown location for three weeks, and then—inexplicably—dropped him off in front of a post office in Cary, North Carolina.

A ransom was never demanded. Eric was never molested. They'd just taken him for a few weeks and then returned him. The motives remained a mystery and the kidnappers were never caught.

It was a traumatic and bewildering experience for Eric. Baughman had been the FBI agent in charge of the case. Despite his lack of results, his calming and matter-of-fact demeanor had been a comfort to Eric and his parents, mooring them to reality during a time when it would have been all too easy for them to lose their minds.

Even after it was clear the case was growing cold, Baughman had stayed in touch with the Partins. He'd grown to be good friends with Eric's father, and he'd attended both Eric's parents' funerals. Still, it had been a long while since he'd dropped by to say hello.

"So what's this about a report?" Baughman asked.

"It's a bit of a long story," Eric said. "A guy came around here looking to pass you a message last night."

Baughman's face grew serious as Eric recounted the events of the previous night. A couple times, he looked like he wanted to interject something, but apparently he thought better of it and kept his mouth shut.

When Eric was finished, he stayed silent for a minute, letting Baughman process what he'd just heard. Finally, he said, "I asked the police to contact you, so naturally when you showed up at my door—"

"You thought that's why I was here," Baughman finished

for him. "It's not... but in a strange way, I suppose it sort of is."

Eric frowned. It was too early and he was too tired for riddles. "You're going to have to walk that back for me, Agent Baughman."

Baughman looked at the floor for a long moment. Finally, he met Eric's eyes and spoke. "Had you heard of Wakefield, Tennessee, before last night?"

Eric thought a moment, then shook his head. "Should I have?"

Baughman rubbed his hands together again. "I don't know, son. I just don't know. The last thing I want to do is waste your time or bring you into something that doesn't involve you. Especially with everything you've got going on."

It was all Eric could do not to laugh. Truth was, for the first time in his adult life, he had absolutely nothing going on.

"Well, Agent Baughman, the weird disappearing man outside my window leads me to believe I'm already involved, whether either of us likes it or not."

Baughman nodded slowly, clearly deep in thought.

In the silence, Eric realized something. He'd told Baughman the full story, just as he'd told it to the police. But something had been different: Baughman's reaction. Unlike the police, he hadn't made any suggestion that maybe the moonlight had been playing tricks on Eric. In fact, he hadn't looked all that surprised.

Eric ran a hand over the stubble on his face, a nervous habit that emerged when he had a couple days growth going and would get even worse if he didn't take a razor to his whiskers soon. "You know something about this guy, don't you? About what he said. And about his disappearing act."

Baughman chuckled. "If only I did. I've seen hints. Clues and insinuations. But nothing that makes any damn sense."

"And yet, you don't seem entirely surprised about the flickering man cutting himself outside my window."

Baughman looked Eric in the eye, and the fear was evident on the FBI agent's face. "I'm not, God help me. I'm afraid there's very little that surprises me these days." He paused. "You heard about what happened in Rook Mountain, Tennessee, a few years back?"

Eric blinked hard, surprised at the non-sequitur. "Sure. The thing with the cult leader. The tabloids went nuts with conspiracy theories. You couldn't go grocery shopping without five ridiculous Rook Mountain headlines staring you in the face."

"I was one of the first agents on the scene after everything went down with the regulations and whatnot. I'll tell you, I'm not sure those tabloids were entirely wrong."

Eric fought to keep the surprise off his face. He'd always thought of Baughman as a level-headed guy. He'd never expected him to buy into this unexplained phenomena stuff.

On the other hand, after what Eric saw just last night, he wasn't one to judge. "What's Rook Mountain have to do with the man at my window?"

"Nothing at all, except for the fact that Wakefield, Tennessee, is only forty miles down the highway from there. My point is that there are things in this world that can't be explained." He leaned forward and smiled, hands on his knees. "But that doesn't mean we're going to stop trying to explain them."

Now Eric chuckled. That was an idea he could get behind. "You want to tell me why you really came here this morning?"

The smile faded from Baughman's face. "It's about your kidnapping."

"I kinda figured. After all this time, you're still working on that case?"

"Not actively, no. But there has been a development."

"A development." Eric leaned back and crossed his arms.

"Yesterday a woman called my office and asked to speak to me. Said she had some information on a cold case."

"And that case was mine," Eric guessed.

"Not just yours. Multiple cases. She said they were all tied to her town. Wakefield, Tennessee."

Eric suddenly very badly wanted a glass of water.

Baughman paused, clearly uncomfortable. "Eric, there were some things about your case we left out of the public record. We didn't even tell you and your family. You weren't the only kid taken that day."

"What the hell are you talking about?"

"There were five other twelve-year-old kids taken that day in a manner similar to your own. One in Oregon, one in New Mexico, one in Texas, and two in Maine. All disappeared about one in the afternoon, local time. Not all my colleagues agreed with me, but I believed the six cases were connected. I think the same people were behind all six kidnappings."

For the second time in less than twelve hours, Eric felt like the room was spinning. It was as if everything he understood about the world was slipping out of his grasp.

"That's insane. It can't be true."

"I wish like hell it wasn't, but I'm almost certain it is."

Eric drew a deep breath. The tightness in his chest made it more difficult than it should have been. "The other kids... did they get home like me?"

Baughman shook his head. "You were the only one who

made it back to his family. The other five were never heard from again."

"Jesus."

Baughman nodded slowly. "My thoughts exactly. But this woman, she had a claim. It's an absurd one, and I would say she must be a crank except for the details she knew about the kids."

"What did she say?"

"She claimed that the kids are all still alive. And that they are all living in Wakefield. She said that she could tell me their names, even introduce me to them if I wanted. But she had a condition."

Eric's mouth felt so dry he could barely get out the words. "What condition?"

"She said she'd only give the information in person. And that she'd only give it to you."

4

TWO DAYS LATER, Eric headed for Milwaukee, bound for an early morning flight from General Mitchell International Airport to the tiny regional airport closest to Wakefield, Tennessee. Agent Baughman had gone back to Milwaukee after their conversation, and Eric was meeting him at the airport. It was Saturday, and Donovan had agreed to drive him.

They'd been on the road for ten minutes when Donovan said, "You're awfully quiet this morning."

Eric couldn't argue with that. Ever since the flickering man had appeared outside his window, he'd been in a strange, unsettled mood. It wasn't just the unexplained things he'd seen, though that was certainly part of it. There was something deeper, something that shook him at the core of his being, and he couldn't put his finger on it.

He still wasn't exactly sure why he'd agreed to this little trip. Granted, he didn't have much going on and that idea of getting away from Mequon for a few days sounded good. And then there was the curiosity factor of why some woman in a town he'd never heard of wanted to have a personal conversation with him and only him.

But another part of him, a deeper part, knew there was more to this than just a simple conversation. In helping with this investigation, he was stepping into murky waters, and he had no way of knowing how far down they went. Or what lived down there.

"You okay, man?" Donovan asked.

Only then did Eric realize he hadn't responded to his friend's last statement. "Yeah, sorry. I'm a little distracted this morning."

Donovan shook his head sadly. "Three days out of work and your mind's gone soft already. Sad state of affairs."

Eric chuckled. "Speaking of soft minded, you didn't have to drive me. I appreciate it and everything, but I could have driven myself and parked in short-term parking at the airport."

"You kidding? And miss the chance to borrow your truck for a few days?" He paused. "I can borrow it for a few days, right?"

The truck was a dilemma Eric had been thinking about for a while. It was only two years old and it still had the E&J logo stenciled on its side. He was loath to paint over the logo, and even if he did he'd always know it was there hiding underneath the fresh coat. This truck was too associated with the business. As much as he loved the thing, he didn't want the constant reminder of his former business.

"Maybe we can do better than a few days," Eric said. "Make me an offer."

Donovan glanced at Eric, the skepticism clear in his eyes. "For the truck?"

"For the truck."

Donovan thought for a long moment before speaking again. "Honestly, man, I couldn't scrape together more than twelve grand, and we both know this truck's worth three times that."

Eric nodded slowly. "Okay, then. Let's call it ten."

Donovan raised an eyebrow. "Ten thousand? For this truck? That's... why the hell would you do that?"

"Look, I just had a pretty good payday, and the way I see it, you should get a little something out of it. You worked for me twelve years. Helped me build this thing into what it is. Honestly, I truly believe if it wasn't for your hard work, the business wouldn't have been worth what Jennifer and Bill paid me."

Donovan shook his head, clearly dumbstruck. "Dude, I don't know what to say."

"Say you'll take care of her."

They drove for twenty more minutes, most of it in silence before Donovan broke out in a grin. "I should have said I could only scrape together five grand."

"Yeah, you should have," Eric agreed.

After Donovan dropped him off, it didn't take Eric long to get through security. He was traveling light. A single small duffle bag with a change of clothes, a beat-up old paperback to keep him occupied on the plane, and a few toiletries. The airport was oddly quiet, especially for a Saturday, but Eric wasn't about to complain. He made his way to the gate where he found Agent Carl Baughman.

Baughman sat as far from the gate as one could while still reasonably expecting to hear the gate-related announcements. He was dressed in gray slacks and a tucked-in polo shirt, which qualified as the most casual Eric had ever seen him. He had a manila folder open in front of him, and he was so engrossed in it he didn't notice Eric standing there for a full ten seconds.

Eric grinned when Baughman finally looked up. "Still have the keen law enforcement instincts, I see."

Baughman chuckled. "Sadly, this is about as keen as my instincts ever were."

The two shook hands, then Eric plopped down in the seat next to him. "So, I don't want to be rude, especially to an older man like yourself."

Baughman raised an eyebrow. "I already hate where this is going."

"I'm just a little surprised you're still on the job. Thirty years is a damn long time. How long's the average FBI agent's career?"

"Both too long and not long enough." Baughman closed the folder and leaned forward in his seat. "Look, your case was my first as lead agent. Do I think about retirement? Hell yeah. More every day."

"But you want to solve the one that got away. Is that it?"

The FBI agent smiled wryly. "Not even close. If I waited until I closed all my open cases from over the years, they'd be burying me at my desk."

Eric held up a finger. "Ah, but I didn't say all the cases. I said this one."

Baughman shrugged. "I'm not gonna lie. The weird way this went down... it always stuck in my craw. It's a tough one to move past."

"You and me both." Eric nodded to the manila folder. "Case related?"

"Yeah. I'm reviewing the details on the other five kids who went missing." He flipped through the pages for a moment before finding what he was looking for. "This one's interesting. A boy named Casey Sunup. From Oregon. As far as we know, he's the only one whose abduction was witnessed. Neighbor heard a shout and glanced out the window. He saw two men grab Casey and toss him into a green van. One guy grabbed him under the arms, and the other grabbed his legs. Picked him up like he was nothing and had him in the van in two seconds. The vehicle was moving before the door was even shut. That sound familiar?"

Eric felt a chill. "Yeah."

He didn't remember his own kidnapping in vivid detail, but he did have some sensory recollections. He'd been walking home from school when the van pulled up. His van had been sky blue, not green. The side door flew open and two men hopped out.

Eric didn't remember the men's faces. When he tried, he only saw a fuzzy blur. But he did remember the way their rough hands felt when they grabbed him and the way the world had suddenly tilted as they picked him up. He remembered the cold, hard metal of the van's floor as they threw him inside and the overly sweet smell of coolant. And the rough feeling of the coarse rope on his wrists and ankles as they tied him. And the sudden prick of a needle in his arm as they injected him with something.

He remembered waiting. Lying tied on that van floor for so many hours, a blindfold over his eyes. No one speaking, no one responding to his countless cries and pleas. He'd faded in and out, shifting between a drug-induced sleep and a dreamlike, surreal wakefulness. At some point, he'd pissed himself, but that had been the least of his worries.

He'd had no sense of time, no sense of place.

After what might have been hours or days, they'd finally opened the van door and picked him up again. They'd carried him somewhere new. Up a flight of stairs. Then they set him on something soft and took off his blindfold. He'd blinked hard against the painful sudden brightness. He'd heard a door close and three locks clicking shut.

And then he was alone.

There was no need to repeat the story for Baughman; he'd been the first person Eric had told it to in full. Eric had recounted the story to Agent Baughman in his living room, his still shell-shocked parents listening in horrified silence. He'd told the story to Baughman at least two more times. It could have been three, it was difficult to remember. They all blended together. But he remembered the anguished expression Baughman couldn't quite hide as he listened, trying to decipher some clue that might help him find the culprits, but hearing none.

"Here's what's bugging me about this," Eric said. "Aside from the flickering man and this woman mysteriously knowing my name and asking for me."

Baughman leaned back and crossed his arms, a slight smile on his face. Clearly he'd worked this thing through in his mind dozens of times, and was a bit amused watching someone else do the same.

"You said six kids were kidnapped at roughly the same time in six different parts of the U.S."

"Yep."

"Let's say each kidnapping team consists of three guys."

"Sounds reasonable," Baughman agreed. "Two to grab the kid, plus the driver."

"Exactly. So we're talking eighteen guys. Minimum."

"Or gals. Let's not be sexist."

"Right." Eric ran a hand over his still unshaven face. "A kidnapping ring of eighteen people working throughout the country, coordinating their efforts. We're getting into serious conspiracy theory territory here."

"You're not wrong." Baughman flipped to the first page in his folder. "And that's not even the half of it. Most serial kidnappers had something specific they're after, right? A type. But in this case? Age is just about all the kids have in common. Boys. Girls. Black. White. Asian. Rich families. Poor families. Middle class."

Eric thought a moment. "Okay, so let's assume they were working out of one centralized location. They're all from Wakefield, Tennessee."

"An assumption I'm not ready to make, but okay."

"How are they choosing their victims? What's special about these kids? I mean, even if they want to spread it out a bit to avoid suspicion, why not take kids from throughout the southeast?"

Baughman chuckled. "Man, that's the big question. One of them, anyway."

"And what are the others?"

"Why did they let you go? And was this the only time they've done something like this?"

The first question was one Eric had been mulling over since Baughman told him about the other five kids. It had kept him awake long into the night, in fact. But the second question caught him off guard. He hadn't considered that this could have been more than a one-time event.

"Truth is," Baughman continued, "dozens of kids go missing every day. It's been that way as far back as the Bureau's been keeping track. The fact that we managed to tie those six kidnappings together was nothing but dumb luck. It could easily have happened before. Or since."

"Jesus, Baughman. What the hell are we walking into?"

It was a very good question, but one without an answer.

With the call to board, Eric glanced at his ticket and

grabbed his duffle bag. He smirked at Baughman. "You guys couldn't have sprung for Comfort Plus, huh?"

Baughman just shook his head. "Son, you're riding on Uncle Sam's dime. You're lucky we're not going by Greyhound."

The first leg of the flight went by quickly, with Eric sleeping through most of it. He dreamed fitfully, and while he didn't remember most of it, a few images stuck with him after he woke. An old woman with a basket filled with bees. A lake with a terrible darkness living in its waters. A man with a device that could turn off his enemies' ability to see, rendering them blind.

None of it made sense, but it left him feeling groggy and discombobulated when they landed in Atlanta. They only had forty minutes before their next flight was scheduled to depart, so they had to hurry through the crowded airport, taking the tram from Terminal A to Terminal T, where the smaller regional flights were routed. The plane was boarding when they reached the gate. Agent Baughman had to check his roller suitcase at the door. Though it was carry-on sized, this regional jet didn't have standard-sized overhead compartments. He was given a tag and told to drop his bag off on the walkway. The lady at the counter gave Eric's duffle bag a long look, but it narrowly made the cut and he was allowed to carry it on.

Eric glanced out the window and frowned when he saw the plane. "Uh, Baughman? I can't help but notice our plane has propellers."

"That is an accurate assessment," he answered with a chuckle.

"Where the hell are you taking me?"

Baughman clapped him on the back as they started down the walkway to the plane. "This is nothing. You should see some of the puddle hoppers I've been on. One time in Montana, we were flying through this thunderstorm and—"

"Let's save the scary flying stories for later, okay?"

Baughman gave Eric an appraising look. "I didn't take you for a nervous flyer. All I'm saying is be glad this plane is three seats wide. They make them smaller."

That didn't do much to calm Eric's nerves. "Three seats? Like, across?"

"Yep. Two on one side and one on the other. They'll probably move us around to make sure the weight is distributed properly. Just hope you get lucky and end up in the one-seat row. No neighbor."

Eric did not get lucky. On most flights he'd been on, row six would have been near the front of the plane. That was not the case here. Row six turned out to be just behind the wings. He had the aisle seat, and his row-mate, a man who looked to be in his late fifties, was already seated when he arrived.

As the plane rolled down the runway, Eric made some nervous conversation with the man. His name was Claude—old family name—and he was returning home after two weeks spent traveling for business. He lived in Redding, a town twenty miles north of Eastern Tennessee Regional Airport.

"How about you?" the man asked. "From your accent, I'd say you're from Michigan."

"Wisconsin, actually." Eric stifled a smile. He'd never thought of himself as having an accent. It was people in other parts of the country who didn't talk right.

"Ah. What brings you to the beautiful mountains of Appalachia?"

Eric thought a moment and realized he had no idea

how to answer that question. He wasn't about to go into the details of his kidnapping and everything that had happened afterward, but he didn't know how to summarize it either. There was no shorthand for visiting a woman who will speak only to you in regards to a federal investigation from the 1980s. At least, there wasn't one that wouldn't end with him having to spend the rest of the flight filling in the details. So he went with the vaguest version possible.

"I'm visiting someone. In Wakefield."

Claude's expression darkened. It was a long moment before he spoke again. "You look like the outdoorsy type. What's your poison?"

The plane was picking up speed now, racing down the runway in preparation for takeoff.

"I'm sorry?" he asked.

"Your sport. What do you like to do outside? You hunt? Fish?"

Eric gripped his armrest hard as the plane's engine reached a higher pitch, the nose of the plane angled upward, and the ground fell away. Now that they were in the sky, he immediately felt a bit better. The anticipation was over and now he just had to survive the forty-five-minute flight.

He turned his attention back to Claude's question. In truth, he hadn't done much in the way of outdoor recreation in recent years. E&J Landscaping had kept him too busy. But there had been a time. A time when he'd through-hiked the Superior Hiking Trail in northern Minnesota. A time when there wasn't a weekend you wouldn't find him on some hiking trail or another, everything he needed to survive strapped to his back. And most weekends, Jennifer had been right by his side.

"I'm a backpacker," he said. "Or, I was once. It's been a while."

Claude's eyes lit up. "Ah, you've come to the right place, my friend. You know the Appalachian Trail passes through this area, right?"

Eric shook his head. "I never thought to look."

"Some of the best sections in the south, too. You've got the Great Smoky Mountains, the Rook Highlands, and Hot Springs, North Carolina all within a few hours of where we're landing." He slapped his armrest as if remembering something. "You know what else? Just over the border in Virginia, there's a place where herds of wild ponies graze along the trail. They'll eat right out of your hand. Cutest thing you've ever seen."

Eric had to admit that sounded pretty cool. He wasn't sure why he hadn't thought of it before, but now that he was unemployed, he could get back on the trail.

Claude leaned closer and his voice was quiet when he spoke again. "Listen, I know you didn't ask for my advice, but I'm going to give it to you anyway. Pick one of those places I mentioned. Doesn't matter which one. Have your friend meet you there. Walk the trails. Take care of whatever business needs taking care of. But don't do it in Wakefield."

Through the window behind Claude, Eric could see Atlanta getting smaller and smaller. "Yeah? Why's that?"

There was such a long pause that he wasn't sure if Claude was going to answer. Finally he did. "Appalachia gets a bad rap sometimes. There are plenty of lovely towns, places with culture and community and wonderful people. Wakefield isn't one of them." He paused and looked away. "Wakefield's a dying town. It's a slow death that's taken decades. The only people left are the ones too stubborn to leave. They don't much like each other let alone people from outside. There's nothing there but misery. Best thing you can do is stay away and let it die."

They didn't speak again for the rest of the flight. Apparently Claude had said his piece, which hadn't done much to settle Eric's stomach.

5
―――

Eric was grateful the flight from Atlanta to Eastern Tennessee Regional Airport was so short. They had a window of all of five minutes at cruising altitude. Then they were heading back down and preparing for landing.

After climbing down a rolling staircase and walking to the gate, they headed to the rental car desk and picked up a sedan. Ten minutes after landing, they were on the road. Eric supposed small regional airports had something going for them after all. It took a scary-small plane to get to them, but things went quickly once you arrived.

He threw his duffle bag into the trunk and climbed into the passenger seat.

Baughman tapped away at his phone, finding the directions. "Looks like we've got about a half hour drive to Marsha Crawford's house."

"Uh-huh." Now that they were on the ground, the bizarre situation seemed more real to Eric. "So what, we just show up and she's going to solve five outstanding kidnapping cases for us?"

"That's the plan." Baughman started the car and pulled out of the lot.

"And then what happens?"

Baughman glanced at the map on his phone, then turned left onto the road. "Well, it all depends on what she tells us. Best case scenario, she tells us about the kids, and we're out of there in an hour or two. Then I investigate further while you spend the evening luxuriating at the Wakefield Motor Inn, the motel where I've secured us rooms for the evening."

"And what's the less-than-best case scenario?"

Baughman adjusted his hands on the steering wheel, his head bobbing back and forth as if he were deciding how best to explain. "The type of people who make demands before sharing information? They can be greedy. She might see I gave in to her first request by flying you out here and want more."

"More what? Money?"

"Maybe. Some want that. For others, it's immunity from prosecution of some crime. Or it could be information. Or, I don't know, it could be she wants a scoop of fudge mint chip cookie dough ice cream. It's impossible to say. Point is, folks like her are happy to dole out the information a morsel at a time until they're sure they've gotten everything they can."

"So you're saying this could be a wild goose chase."

Baughman shrugged. "Could be. We're going to find out. That's the job."

Eric raised an eyebrow. "That's *your* job. I'm unemployed. Doing this out of the kindness of my heart."

"And because you want to know."

"There is that."

They drove in silence for the next few minutes. Eric stared out the window, taking in the rural surroundings.

Coming from a place where things were flatter, the rolling hills were a beautiful change of pace. Everywhere he looked he saw vibrant, green life. In the distance, he saw mountains, but with all the hills of various sizes, it was impossible to get a good sense of their true size or distance.

Something else caught his attention: many of the hillsides were covered in what seemed to be leafy, green vines. They blanketed the hills, hiding anything underneath from view.

"Checking out the kudzu?" Baughman asked.

Eric glanced back at him. "Yeah. I've never seen this much of it."

He chuckled. "You haven't spent much time in this part of the country, have you?"

"Never been." He thought a moment, then quickly corrected himself. "Well, there was that one time my kidnappers dropped me off outside a post office in North Carolina."

"I seem to remember something about that." Baughman nodded toward one of the vine-covered hills. "Anyway, kudzu is everywhere in these parts. It comes from Japan. It was brought over here and sold as an ornamental plant you could use to shade your porch on those sunny days."

"Yeah?" Eric asked. "How'd that work out?"

"Pretty well for the kudzu. Turned out it spreads much more easily than anyone anticipated. It's officially classified as a weed now, and, as you'll notice, it's damn near everywhere. There are all kinds of legends about it. Kids say it hides tangles of exotic snakes that will bite if you dare stick a hand inside. Other folklore says it's the plant itself that's the danger. That it'll grow on anything it touches. You brush up against it, you might wake up to find a vine growing out of your hand tomorrow."

"Huh." Eric had to admit, the strange vine did have an eerie-looking quality to it.

About halfway to Wakefield, they came upon a Shell station. Baughman flicked his turn signal on.

"I gotta hit the head."

Eric clicked his tongue in disapproval. "Kids and old people. You should have gone at the airport."

Baughman shot him a look. "I'll make it worth your while. You like Red Vines?"

Eric stayed in the car while Baughman went inside. As he waited, he pulled out his phone and opened his photos app. He swiped until he found the one he was looking for.

It had been taken at least fifteen years before, in the early days of E&J with an honest to God film camera. Eric liked the picture so much he'd had it digitized and kept it on his phone. For many years, it had been his background photo. He'd changed it after the divorce, but he hadn't had the heart to delete it.

In the picture, Jennifer sat atop their brand-new John Deere commercial mower. The first of many. She had her blond hair tied back and she wore a bikini top and cutoff jeans. With one hand, she gripped the wheel. She held a beer in the other, using it to salute the camera.

Once upon a time, this photo had represented everything he wanted in life. He remembered seeing it the first time, his heart practically bursting with pride. The woman he loved and the means to forge their own future together. He hadn't been able to imagine he'd ever be unhappy again.

And yet, here he sat, his wife and his business both gone, helping an FBI agent dig up things that might be better off staying under the dirt.

As he looked at the picture, he thought about what Jennifer had said after the contract signing. That he hadn't fought for his marriage or the business. Was that true? He certainly hadn't wanted to lose either of them, and now that they were gone, he felt unmoored in a way he'd never anticipated.

But had he really fought for them? Either of them?

Sitting in the rented sedan, thinking back over the past few years, he couldn't truthfully answer that question.

He didn't want to think about it anymore. Not now. Not when he had a job to do. There would be plenty of time to mope and pore over the mistakes of the past when he got home. He locked the phone and slid it back into his pocket.

He looked up and saw Baughman coming out of the gas station, a plastic bag in his hand. The promised Red Vines, no doubt. As Baughman approached, Eric noticed a blur of motion out of the corner of his eye.

A moment later, Baughman collided with the blur. It was a woman, and she bounced off Baughman like he was a stone wall. She fell backward, dropping the grocery bag she'd been carrying. The contents spilled out on the pavement.

"Shit," Eric muttered. He jumped out of the car and trotted over to help.

The woman was frantically gathering her items. Eric grabbed a can of beans that was rolling away and put it in her bag.

"Thanks." She glanced up and Eric got his first real look at her. Her dark brown hair fell in curls that framed her pretty face. She looked to be about Eric's age, and when her brown eyes met his, he felt something inside him stir.

Baughman dropped to his knees and starting helping pick up the fallen items. "Ma'am, I'm so sorry. I didn't see you coming."

She gave him an easy smile. "Don't worry about it. If

there's a speed limit for walking, I was probably over it." She put the last item—a carton of yogurt that had somehow survived the fall—into the bag and touched Eric's arm. "Thank you both for your help."

With that, she picked up her bag and walked to a blue Nissan parked by one of the fuel pumps.

"She seemed nice," Eric said as she drove away.

Baughman shot him a look. "We're here for the day. Don't go making lady friends."

He stood up and stretched. "There's nothing wrong with making friends. I'm a big fan of making friends."

"Uh-huh. You make a lot of friends since the divorce?"

Eric chuckled. "Not a one. I'm overdue."

Baughman walked to the car. "Yeah, well, just make sure your friends don't get in the way of our..." He trailed off, patting his jacket. "You gotta be kidding me."

"What?"

He patted his pants, his expression quickly morphing from surprise to annoyance. "My wallet is gone."

Eric tilted his head. "Did you leave it in the gas station?"

"I most certainly did not." He thought a moment. "I'm an idiot. Your new friend was carrying groceries. You see a grocery store around here?"

Eric did not. The Shell station was the only business in sight. "They don't sell food in there?"

"In the Shell station? Come on."

"Okay, sorry." Eric patted his own pockets. He was relieved to find his wallet still present. Then he noticed his jacket pocket was empty. His heart sank. "She got my phone."

Baughman sighed. "Well, she's good. I'll give her that."

They spent the next half hour sitting in the parking lot of the Shell station making calls on Baughman's phone.

Baughman called his bank and his credit card company and Eric called his cellphone provider to report the theft.

When they were finally finished, Baughman sighed and started the car.

"This is wildly disappointing," Eric said. "You're an FBI agent. I feel like we should be chasing down the perp instead of calling banks."

"Perp, huh?"

"I'm just saying…" Eric looked out the window. "She touched my arm. It's not like I was going to marry her, but I thought maybe…"

"You thought you'd made a lady friend."

"Yeah. But it was just a distraction to steal my phone."

"Don't feel bad. I fell for the bump and grab. Oldest pickpocketing move in the game." Baughman chuckled. "I gotta admit, she was good though. Most couldn't have pulled that on me."

"Somehow that doesn't change the way I feel about it at all. So, what's our next move?"

Baughman brought the map up on his phone once again. "Our next move is we keep our date with Marsha Crawford."

"All right then." Eric thought a moment. "Hey, are you going to be able to get on the plane out of here without your ID?"

"Nope. I guess I live here now. Keep an eye out for any nice houses for me."

As they drove, the anger Eric felt at having his phone stolen faded and his sense of adventure began to return. As much as he hated having someone take advantage of him, was losing his phone really such a bad thing? He was completely out of touch with his old life now. If Jennifer or Bill wanted to ask him a question about the business, if

Donovan wanted to call to share his most recent relationship drama, too bad.

He was unreachable. He didn't know when that had happened last. It felt like starting over. It felt like freedom.

A few minutes later, Baughman nodded to a sign along the road. "Looks like we made it."

Eric took in the sign.

Welcome to Wakefield. Population 1,129.

Based on the rust around the sign, it was a few years overdue for a refresh. If this town really was shrinking at the rate the man on the plane had indicated, Eric wondered how accurate the population was. How many people lived in the town now? Less than a thousand?

Still, as they entered town, Eric was surprised by what he saw. It wasn't the rotting wasteland he'd expected from the man on the plane's description. These were homes that wouldn't have looked out of place in the middle-class neighborhoods E&J Landscaping worked. Granted, there were a few yards that made the lawn care professional in him want to smack the owners upside the head, but that was the exception rather than the rule.

Overall, he was surprised to see it was an incredibly nice town. It had the look of an affluent suburb, not a failing rural community.

"This is not what I expected," Eric said.

"You and me both."

Baughman looked troubled as he drove. What Eric took as a pleasant surprise, the FBI agent seemed to interpret as something darker.

"What's the problem?" Eric asked.

Baughman didn't answer immediately. His eyes scanned the houses along the road. "There's money here."

"Sure seems that way."

"That's not what I mean." He turned the car onto a side street before continuing. "A town of a thousand people. No major cities in a two-hour drive in any direction. No major employers as far as I can tell. Where's the money coming from?"

Eric couldn't disagree. It seemed odd. "Well, we know they're good at kidnapping. I imagine that can be profitable."

Baughman turned on him, fire blazing in his eyes. "Don't even joke about that."

Eric held up a hand. "All right, sorry. As the guy in the car who hasn't been kidnapped, you're awfully sensitive about the whole thing."

Baughman didn't answer, but Eric immediately regretted the second joke. It was true that Baughman hadn't experienced a kidnapping firsthand like Eric had, but the man had been an FBI agent for more than thirty years. He'd probably seen more horrible things than Eric could imagine.

"This is it," Baughman said, breaking the tense silence.

He pulled the car into the driveway of a beautiful colonial-style home. Large white pillars adorned the large porch, and the lawn was immaculate, even by Eric's exacting standards.

"Money, indeed," Eric muttered.

Baughman shut off the car and turned to Eric. "You are here as a civilian assisting in this investigation only to the extent required. That means you let me do the talking. She asks you questions, you answer. But beyond that, keep it locked down. Let me handle this, and with any luck, you'll be home tomorrow.

Eric opened his mouth to respond, but Baughman was already getting out of the car.

Baughman pressed the doorbell, and the two men waited on the porch.

Eric wondered how the two of them must look to any of the neighbors who happened to be peeking out their windows. A fifty-seven-year-old black man dressed in a polo shirt, a blazer, and dress slacks, and a forty-two-year-old white man who looked like his clothes had just been pulled out of a hamper and he hadn't shaved in a week.

It didn't take long before the door opened, and a woman in her sixties stood before them, a bright smile on her face.

"Marsha Crawford?" Baughman asked.

The woman nodded. "You must be Agent Baughman." She turned to Eric and her smile widened. "And you. Eric Partin. I've been waiting a very long time to meet you. Please, come inside."

6

Becky Talbot was a thief, and a damn good one.

She hadn't intended to rob anyone that day. She rarely did. The problem was that she was very good at spotting marks, and once she spotted them it was very difficult for her to pass them up. It was like something in her brain latched onto the opportunity, and it needled at her like an uncomfortable tag in a shirt until she took care of the situation.

She and Mikey were pretty much always scraping their last two nickels together, but that wasn't why she did it. It wasn't about money; it was about power.

When she saw the rental car with the out-of-state license plates in the parking lot, she'd quickly succumbed to the desire to relieve them of their valuables. She'd been on the way back from the grocery store in Kingsport, so she had a nice misdirect that would give her quick hands plenty of time to do what needed to be done.

All told, she'd taken a wallet, an iPhone, and a watch from the sweet but gullible idiots. She'd immediately turned off the phone to deactivate the Find Your Phone feature, but she hadn't had a chance to look through the wallet yet.

The watch she'd identified while it was still on the older man's wrist. An Omega Speedmaster. It wasn't in perfect condition, but not beat to hell either. Clearly worn by a man who took care of it. She figured she could get two grand for it no questions asked. Maybe twenty-five hundred. That money would go a long way. It could get her and Mikey across the country. Maybe Colorado, like they'd always talked about when they were kids.

Part of her thought that was nothing but wishful thinking. There were things tying them to Wakefield, things that wouldn't be easy to get clear of. But if they ever managed to pull it off, if they somehow did the impossible, Becky promised herself she'd put this town in the rearview and never come back. She'd be gone for good, this time.

She turned right onto Falcon Street, then took a quick left onto Wilmore. She pulled into the parking lot of Wilmore Avenue Baptist and waited. Any vehicles following her would have seen the second turn but not her pulling into the parking lot, so they'd be hustling to catch up.

After watching for thirty seconds, she was confident no one was on her tail. Only then did she open the wallet.

She knew most of the contents would be worthless. Most likely the guy had already called his credit card companies to let them know the cards were stolen. There was no way she'd risk using them. So it came down to cash and whatever other random stuff was in there. Probably nothing, but you never knew until you checked. The watch had been the real prize and the iPhone was a solid score, so whatever was in the wallet was just a bonus for a job well done.

She pulled out a small stack of cash and counted it, flicking quickly through the bills with the speed of an experienced bank teller. That had been a long time ago, but some skills stuck with you.

Sixty-seven dollars. Not exactly a windfall, but a helluva lot better than nothing. These moments gave her a dopamine hit like few she'd ever experienced. Maybe it was the ability to control something in a life where she controlled so little.

She stuffed the money in her purse and looked through the rest of the wallet. A couple credit cards. A Wisconsin driver's license for one Carl Adam Baughman. A savers club card for a grocery store called Cub Foods.

Her fingers snatched a small stack of cards out of the last pocket in the wallet and she froze. They were business cards for Special Agent Carl Baughman of the Federal Bureau of Investigation.

"Damn it, Becky," she muttered. "You sure know how to step in it."

A tap on her window made her jump. She looked up, her hands already frantically searching for the gear shift, when she saw who it was. Her panic quickly morphed into annoyance.

"Becky?" the man said through the closed window. "It's been a while! How are you?"

She forced a smile and nodded. "Doing well. Nice to see you."

He moved his hand in a small circle, the universal request to roll down the window.

Becky considered just putting the car in drive and getting the hell out of this parking lot. But something stopped her. Jim's family had moved to Wakefield when Becky was in high school, and they'd been classmates for three years; a minute or two more of small talk with him wouldn't kill her.

"How you been, Pastor?"

He looked mildly embarrassed. "You don't have to... Jim's fine." He cleared his throat. "I've been good. Keeping busy as always. Just wrapped Vacation Bible School, so things will slow down a little now."

She nodded politely, not sure where to take the conversation from here. The stolen items sat on the passenger seat next to her, openly in view. The phone could easily be hers, but the man's wallet and wristwatch would be a bit harder to explain. Not that he'd give her trouble about it—he wasn't the confrontational type—but it wasn't a conversation she was eager to have at the moment.

"Um, how's Mikey?" Jim asked. "I heard he was ill?"

"Yeah, he's not feeling his best. But he'll bounce back. He always does."

"Is it the flu or..." He trailed off when he saw the expression on Becky's face. It was definitely not the flu. Jim Vogel had lived in Wakefield long enough to know there were some questions you just didn't ask. "Sorry, I didn't mean to pry."

Becky shrugged. "No worries. I should probably—"

"Of course. I didn't mean to keep you. It's just... I'd love to grab dinner with you. Catch up on old times and all that."

It was everything Becky could do to avoid rolling her eyes. Still, she couldn't blame the guy. He was single, and the pickings in Wakefield were beyond slim.

She started to answer, but something behind Jim caught her eye, stopping her. There was a shed near the back of the parking lot, an older building, probably used for storage. In the shadow cast by the structure, she could just make out the shape of a man.

"Maybe some time," she said absently, her eyes still fixed on the shape.

"Fantastic? Are you free tonight? I make a mean risotto. I could cook up some salmon to go with it. Unless you'd feel more comfortable in a restaurant. The Stir Fry Café in Kingsport has a new chef, and he's really quite excellent."

Becky was barely listening. Even though the shape hadn't moved, she felt a familiar sense of dread looking at it. Any moment now, it would step out of the shadows. She knew who she'd see when that happened.

She muttered a silent prayer. *Not today. Please, not today.*

She glanced back at Jim and noticed he was frowning at her.

"What do you think?" he asked.

She blinked hard. "Sorry... what do I think about what?"

"Dinner. Tonight."

She started to answer, but before the first word passed her lips, the shape stepped out of the shadows.

He was a big man, six-foot-four and stocky. Though he lived only half a mile from her, Becky made it a point to see him as infrequently as possible.

His name was Caleb Bloom, and he worked for the man who had ruined her life.

"Becky?" Jim asked.

Caleb rushed toward them, his walk boarding on a run as he made his way across the parking lot.

A powerful fear gripped Becky, and she found that she couldn't speak. Couldn't move. Couldn't do anything but stare at the man marching toward her. Then it was as if the knots holding her in place had suddenly disappeared. She could move again. She grabbed the shifter and threw the car into drive. Her foot slammed down on the gas pedal, and the car lurched forward, driving through the patch of grass in front of the parking lot. There was a jolt as the front tires hopped the curb and landed on the pavement. In a moment all four wheels were on the road, and she was speeding away from Wilmore Avenue Baptist.

She risked a glance at her rearview mirror, and what she saw caused a lump to form in her throat. Jim stood where she'd left him, a bewildered expression on his face, but Caleb was gone.

"Hello, Becky."

Becky flinched at the sound of the voice so close to her ear. She didn't want to look, but she had to. Hesitantly, she turned her head. Caleb Bloom sat in her passenger seat.

"If you're not careful," he said in a low, growly voice, "I might get the impression you're avoiding me. I'm liable to get offended."

Becky wanted to shout. To scream at this man. She'd been shackled to Caleb since the age of twelve. Lewis and Mikey too. Not to mention poor Nancy. And she was starting to believe she'd never be rid of them. Merle had all of them under his thumb. The difference was Caleb seemed to like it there.

She eased off the gas and let the car roll to a stop. No use running anymore.

Caleb leaned over, putting his weight on the armrest between the seats. "Merle's been trying to get a hold of you. Told me you were dodging his calls."

"One call. He called once, and I just hadn't gotten around to calling him back."

Caleb clucked his tongue disapprovingly.

"What's the Bible verse say? Raise up a child in the way he should go, and he will not depart from it? That hasn't been my experience. Not with you two, anyway. The Talbot kids defy the very wisdom of the scriptures."

Becky gripped the steering wheel. "What's so important, Caleb? What's Merle want from us now?"

"It's getting worse for Mikey, isn't it?" Caleb asked. "He's losing his grip. It won't be long."

Becky felt her lips curl into a snarl. "Don't worry about my brother. He's got his method, just like the rest of us. He'll be fine."

Caleb shrugged. "Maybe. But he won't be fine forever. None of us will."

"That's the way it is for every living thing on the planet."

Caleb frowned. "Don't get cute. You know what I mean."

"You going to tell me what Merle wants, or should I head over to the lake?"

"I'll tell you." He shifted in his seat, still angled toward her but sitting more casually now. "There's someone in town looking for information on us. An FBI man."

Becky concentrated on keeping her expression blank. She hoped Caleb didn't notice the business cards strewn all over the floor near his feet, knocked there along with the watch, the wallet, and phone when he'd appeared. "That so?"

"Indeed. Seems somebody's been talking to the law."

"What's Merle going to do about it?"

"Depends on how it plays out. But the FBI man brought somebody with him, and that's the part Merle's most interested in."

"Who?"

"Eric Partin."

Becky didn't speak for a long moment. Eric Partin. She'd heard about him for so long. The one who got to go home. The one who passed the test the rest of them didn't. And she'd touched him. Stolen his phone.

"How is that possible?"

"Don't know. But if you see either Partin or the FBI man, you call me. Don't answer their questions. Got it?"

"Yeah. I got it."

"Good. Because if you get any ideas about talking to them... Well, Merle might just send you to join Nancy."

Becky's head snapped around, and her eyes bore into him. "Don't even joke about that."

"I'm not joking." He reached out and put a hand on her knee. "Be a good girl, Becky. We'll get through this the same way we've gotten through everything else. Together."

And then Caleb was gone.

He reappeared a moment later, on the sidewalk ten feet away from her car. She could hear him softly whistling as he moseyed down the road.

A wave of relief swept over her. She noticed pain in her hands and realized how tightly she'd been gripping the wheel. She loosened her grip, and her hands began to shake. The tremors spread up her arms and into the rest of her body until she was shaking uncontrollably.

Parked on the side of the road, she finally rolled up her window. She tried to control her breathing. Then she glanced onto the floor of the passenger's side and saw the items she'd stolen less than a half hour before. The watch. The wallet. The phone.

Tears formed in her eyes as she stared at the items. She was forty-two years old and still pickpocketing strangers. How had this become her life? How had things gotten so off track?

But she knew the answers to those questions. It all started with one man, a man who was currently in Wakefield. If she could find Eric Partin, maybe she could set things right.

7

Marsha Crawford led Eric and Agent Baughman into her living room. The place was immaculate, and while that might have been for their benefit, Eric got the idea that this was status quo for Mrs. Crawford. The living room was crowded with antiques—old maps on the wall, end tables that didn't match, yet somehow went together perfectly, and a coffee table made of beautifully aged wood. Every item felt like it had been carefully selected and thoughtfully placed by someone with an eye for interior design and altogether too much time on their hands.

She gestured to the couch. "Please, have a seat. Can I offer you a glass of tea?"

"No, thank you," Eric said automatically. In his line of work, homeowners occasionally offered him a beverage, perhaps out of some vague guilt about not caring for their own lawns. Accepting such a drink obligated you to a solid ten minutes of conversation, which could easily throw off the schedule for the rest of the day.

Baughman gave her an easy smile. "Yes, ma'am. That sounds lovely."

Eric was a bit surprised by that, but then he considered it a moment. In lawn care, it was important to get the job done and move on. In Baughman's line of work, extending conversations would be essential. The longer you sat with someone, the more likely they were to spill something useful. Accepting the tea probably came as naturally to Baughman as turning it down had to Eric.

They sat in silence while they waited for Mrs. Crawford to return. When she did, she was carrying a tray with a glass of tea and a small plate of Hydrox cookies. She set the glass in front of Baughman and nodded toward Eric. "Please, help yourself to the cookies."

"Thank you." He felt obligated to take one, and he munched on it carefully, trying not to get crumbs on her immaculate furniture.

"I appreciate you coming all this way. I'm sure it was an inconvenience." Mrs. Crawford sat down in the rocker across from the couch, her eyes never leaving Eric.

He swallowed the last of the cookie, suddenly wishing he hadn't turned down the tea. "It's all right. Good excuse to get myself down to this part of the country. I haven't been here in many years."

"No, I guess you haven't," Marsha said, her face darkening.

Baughman took a long pull off his tea and let out an exaggerated sigh of contentment. "That's the stuff right there." He carefully set the glass down on the coaster in front of him and leaned forward. "Now Mrs. Crawford, why don't you tell us about the kidnappings that happened thirty years ago."

For a long moment, it seemed she hadn't heard him. Her eyes were still focused on Eric, and her expression was unreadable. Finally, she spoke,

"My husband wasn't a bad man. In fact, I'd say he was a good one. But he did fall in with a bad crowd." She chuckled. "Listen to me, making excuses for him like he's a teenager who stayed out past curfew. A grown man should be able to own up to his decisions."

Baughman folded his hands across his lap and said nothing, letting her find her rhythm.

"He passed nearly twenty years ago, my Henry. Went in his sleep. Heart attack, they said."

"I'm sorry for your loss," Baughman said.

She nodded. "Thank you. Recently, I started going through Henry's old things in the attic. There's a yard sale coming up, and I wanted to see what I could sell. Last week I ran across a notebook with some details on what happened thirty years ago. It was a list of six names. Addresses too. A little Googling led me to realize these were all kids taken from their homes on the same day. It had the children's names, along with another list. It took me a bit to figure it out, but I eventually determined these were their new names. The names they were to go by in Wakefield, with their new families. Understand?"

"I understand." Baughman's voice sounded casual, as if they were discussing directions to the airport rather than five missing kids.

Eric, on the other hand, was finding it much harder to hide his discomfort. He'd already considered how many kidnappers would need to be involved to pull off a crime of this magnitude, but for the first time he was really understanding the scope. Families would need to take in the abducted children. Teachers and neighbors would need to somehow look past the sudden appearance of five new children in town. How deep did the lies go?

He suddenly remembered the words of the man next to

him on the plane. *Wakefield is a dying town. Best thing you can do is stay away and let it die.*

Eric knew he'd promised to keep his mouth shut, but he couldn't help himself. "What was mine?"

Marsha tilted her head. "What do you mean, dear?"

"My name. What was my name supposed to be?"

"Thomas. You were supposed to be Thomas."

"Thomas," he repeated. The name tasted bitter in his mouth, as if it carried with it all memories of an alternate life, one where he hadn't been returned to his parents. One where he'd stayed in Wakefield, an eternal prisoner.

Baughman softly cleared his throat. "Mrs. Crawford, do you have that list for me now?"

She nodded slowly. "You'll get your list, Agent Baughman. God help this town, but you'll get your list." She paused a moment, her eyes on her hands. "My Henry never did anything else like this, before or after. Never so much as ran a red light. But I remember the week it happened. He told me he had to go out of town for a few days, and he wouldn't give me any details no matter how hard I pressed. He got surly about it too, which wasn't like him. And he was out of sorts for weeks after."

"Do you have any idea why they did what they did?"

"No. But that's the way of things in Wakefield. People look the other way. They don't ask too many questions." She looked up at Eric. "That's why I wanted you here today. To apologize. I didn't know what was going to happen to you, but if I'd pushed a little harder rather than trying to ignore what was in front of me, perhaps I would have. Maybe you wouldn't have gone so long looking for answers."

"Thank you," Eric said, though the words felt cold as they passed his lips.

She turned back to Baughman. "As I promised, I'll hand over the list. But I have one more request first."

"Mrs. Crawford, I don't think—"

"Please. It's a simple one. I'll give the list to Eric. But I need two minutes alone with him first."

Baughman's brow creased with annoyance. "Eric is here at my request. I don't think leaving him alone with you would be wise. No offense, but I have to ensure his safety."

"It's fine," Eric said quickly. He'd come on this trip almost on a whim. He had the free time, and he was happy to help Baughman with his investigation. But now that he was here, now that he was speaking to this woman whose husband may have been involved in his kidnapping, it all felt more real. He had the sense that this woman was holding back. Whatever it was she had to say to him alone, he wanted desperately to hear it.

Baughman shook his head. "Eric, it's just not a good idea."

"It's not your decision. I'm doing it."

Baughman hesitated, then nodded. "Fine. Two minutes. I'll be on the front porch."

Mrs. Crawford watched silently as he stood up and walked out of the room. She waited until she heard the front door close, and then she reached into her pocket and pulled out a folded piece of paper.

"This is the list. I'm going to give it to you. I expect that once you give it to Agent Baughman, he'll want to see you on your way back to Wisconsin. And you can do that if you want."

Eric couldn't help but smile. "I take it you have another option in mind for me."

She nodded. "Eric, I don't know why my Henry would help kidnap a child. I have no idea why he and his friends did such a thing. I have no idea why every one of those kids except you stayed in this town. And I don't know why they all grew up to be such troubled adults."

Eric felt a twinge of annoyance at that. "I'm thinking being kidnapped and being forced to live under a false identity might have had something to do with it."

"Sure, but why haven't any of them gone public? They're adults now. There's nothing stopping them."

"Okay. Still not sure what you want me to do about it."

Mrs. Crawford thought a moment before answering. "There's something wrong with this town. I've been swimming in the tainted water too long. I barely notice the taste of it anymore. If I were to talk to those kids, they wouldn't tell me anything. And the kidnappers... if I were to approach them, something worse might happen to me."

"Look, Baughman's going to investigate all that. That's why he's here."

Mrs. Crawford chuckled. "People will close ranks so fast it'll make his head spin. The people in this town aren't going to talk to him. But you..."

"Uh, I think you've got the wrong idea. I'm just a guy who cuts grass for a living."

"You're one of them," she said, her voice insistent now. "Whatever's wrong with this town, it's infected them too. But I think you could help. And you could finally find the answers to what happened to you. And maybe you could help me ease my mind about my husband and who he really was."

Eric suddenly wondered if Marsha Crawford might be a crazy person. If the names she was offering him were nothing more than a random collection pulled from the phone book. So far, she'd offered no real evidence.

"I understand you're not a lawman. I'm not asking you to

go on stakeouts and dig for clues. I'm just asking you to talk to a few people. Ask a question or two."

Eric could just about imagine how that would go. *Hey random stranger, an old lady said we might have been kidnapped by the same gang. Want to grab a drink?*

She gave him a long look. "I can see you're not convinced. Do me one favor then. Go to the house at 125 Barker Street. See if it looks familiar. If you want to go home after that, I can't stop you."

She also couldn't stop him from going home before that, but he felt like that was a point he didn't need to make while she was still holding the list.

"What's at 125 Barker Street?" he asked.

She held out the folded piece of paper, offering it to him. "It's the house where they held you captive for three weeks."

He took the piece of paper with a shaky hand. "Mrs. Crawford, I'm not sure what you think I—"

"You'd better go," she said. "Your friend is waiting outside."

8

Eric and Agent Baughman walked to the car in silence. When they were inside, Baughman held out his hand, and Eric gave him the folded piece of paper. The FBI agent slowly unfolded it, his breathing a bit heavy. Smoothing it on the steering wheel, he stared at it for a long while.

Finally, he said, "Unbelievable."

"You didn't think she'd give it up?" Eric asked.

Baughman shook his head. "I figured getting you down here was an opening gambit. I assumed there would be more requests." He looked up at Eric, his eyes wide. "Guess she really wanted to talk to you."

"Guess so."

"So you going to tell me what she wanted?"

"She thought I should stay in town and talk to the folks on that list. She's under the impression a guy like me might have more luck getting them to open up than an FBI agent."

"That would be a very bad idea. The last thing I want is you sticking your head in this hornet's nest." He turned back to the piece of paper.

Eric shifted in his seat uncomfortably. He was surprised

to find he had no intention of telling Baughman about the address Crawford had given him. Not yet, anyway. He hadn't decided on whether he wanted to go to the house. If he did go, he wanted to go alone, though he couldn't articulate why. Perhaps because he'd been so alone in that house, it only felt right to go back the same way.

Or maybe he just liked the thrill of keeping a secret from an FBI agent.

He nodded toward the piece of paper. "Think those names are legit?"

Baughman carefully folded the paper and stuck it in his jacket pocket. "I don't know, but I aim to find out." He started the car but didn't shift it into reverse just yet. He gave Eric a long look. "I'll make the arrangements to get you back home. We'll put you on the first flight out tomorrow. I just wanted to say, what you did, coming all this way... it means a lot. It's not something most people would have done, and it's going to help me finally put this thing to bed."

Something about the way Baughman said the words irked Eric, even though he knew the agent was genuinely grateful. The way he said it made it sound like Eric was a random concerned citizen who'd passed along a tip rather than the victim of a terrible crime who wanted answers himself. He did his best to push these feelings down, but still they bubbled up, burning his throat like acid.

"Yeah, well, happy to help," Eric said.

"Let's get back to the motel. We can grab some dinner later after we get settled in."

"Sure."

The ride to the motel was short. The Wakefield Motor Inn was older, but it appeared clean and mostly empty. As Baughman was checking them in, Eric spotted a twenty-year-old computer and printer set up in the corner. A plaque on the wall optimistically declared this the Business Center.

Baughman handed him a key and grabbed his suitcase. "Looks like we're both on the third floor. Meet back here in twenty minutes?"

Eric glanced down at the piece of metal in his hand. He wasn't sure when the last time was he'd stayed in a hotel that used physical keys. "Let's make it an hour. I'm a little tired. Might grab a quick nap."

Baughman had no objections.

Eric trotted up the exterior stairs, his bag slung over his shoulder. When he let himself into room 331, he was pleased to find it clean and surprisingly spacious. It seemed the Wakefield Motor Inn gave its customers their forty-two dollars' worth. He spent a moment or two considered unpacking, but decided against it. He'd be checking out in just over twelve hours. Instead, he threw his bag on the desk and sat down in front of it. Before he knew what he was doing, he found himself picking up the phone.

He had no idea how much the motel charged per minute for long distance, and he didn't much care either. As far as he was concerned, Uncle Sam could pick up the tab for a single phone call, especially after one of their agents had gotten Eric's cell phone stolen. He only hesitated for a moment before dialing a number from memory.

The phone rang twice before Jennifer picked up. It was a bit of a surprise that she didn't ignore the call coming from an unknown Tennessee number, but her voice was cool and business-like when she spoke. "Hello?"

"Hey, Jen. It's Eric."

"Oh, hey. Is everything all right?"

The question stung a little. Time was, she would have been delighted by a call from him, no matter the reason.

Anytime one of them was out of town, they'd talk for hours on the phone, catching each other up on the minutia that had occurred while they were apart. "Yeah, I'm good. I just wanted to let you know I'm out of town for a couple days. You know, in case anything comes up with the business."

"Donovan mentioned something about that. Though he wasn't big on the details."

"I didn't give him many. I just needed to get away for a few days."

"Good for you." She sounded like she meant it, too. "Listen, enjoy your time away. We've got things under control, Eric. You don't have to worry about the business anymore. It's off your plate."

"Yeah." He hesitated and swallowed hard, suddenly racked with emotions. "Jen, you know that thing you said the other day? About how I didn't fight for our marriage?"

She sighed. "Yeah, I'm sorry about that. It was a shitty thing to say."

"No. I've been thinking about it. A lot, actually. And I think you're right. I lay down and gave up, and now I feel like a damned idiot."

"Eric, you don't have to—"

"Yes, I do. I owe you an apology. I'm sorry I didn't fight for our marriage."

"You couldn't have... I mean, it's nobody's fault. It just ended. These things happen." There was a long pause. "I appreciate you saying it, though."

He swallowed again, pushing down the lump in his throat. "All right, I gotta go. See you... when I see you."

"Bye, Eric."

He kept the phone pressed to his ear long after the click told him he was no longer connected. Something about the goodbye felt even more final than signing the papers for the business had. There'd been something in Jennifer's voice—a hint of sadness. Calling and bringing up the past upset her. She was trying to move on with her life and he needed to let her. He promised himself he wouldn't call her again. At least not for a long time.

As he placed the handset back in its cradle, he noticed something else on the desk—a thin phonebook. He picked it up and flipped through it, back-to-front, and saw more advertisements than actual listings. When he reached the beginning, he stopped at a page that caught his attention. It was a map of Wakefield.

Looking it over, he quickly located the Wakefield Motor Lodge. And Barker Street was only a half-mile away. Considering he wasn't willing to bring Baughman in on this, walking would be the only way to see the house at 125 Barker Street.

He considered that a moment. He'd told Baughman he'd meet him in an hour, and that had been ten minutes ago. Plenty of time to walk half a mile, reminisce about the bad-old days, and walk back. He tore the page out of the book, grabbed his key, and headed for the door.

BAUGHMAN STOOD AT HIS WINDOW, looking out as Eric headed down the stairs toward the parking lot. He kept watching as the man headed west, occasionally glancing at the piece of paper in his hand. Baughman briefly considered following. It had been years since he'd tailed a target, but he was confident he could pull it off, especially with an unsuspecting target like Eric. In the end, he decided against it, not because he thought he couldn't do it, but because he had an important phone call to make.

Still, it bothered him. The Crawford woman had talked to Eric alone for a reason. The way Eric had hesitated when Baughman asked about it gave away the fact that he'd held something back. But what? What could a stranger tell him that he'd keep from Baughman?

He sighed and turned away from the window, pulling out his phone. There'd be plenty of time to pry the truth out of Eric over dinner. He opened his contacts and tapped Albert Wilson.

A voice came on the line just after the first ring ended. "Did she give it to you?"

Baughman smiled, suddenly wondering if he wasn't charging enough for this particular job. "She did."

"And?" The voice sounded desperate, like that of a starving man who can see a loaf of bread but can't quite reach it.

Baughman thought about drawing out the moment, but he wasn't cruel enough to actually do it. "Becky Talbot."

Wilson drew in a sharp breath. "Becky Talbot." Baughman heard the clicking of keys, probably the man Googling the name.

"I didn't find much about her online," Baughman said, "but I'll do some digging. I'll have her background for you tomorrow."

"Yeah, okay." The man's voice sounded distant. "What happens now?"

Baughman eased himself down onto the bed. "First off, maybe we thank God that it all went so smoothly. Even in my most hopeful moments, I didn't think she'd hand over the list that easily."

"Already done," Wilson said with a chuckle. "What else?"

Baughman thought a moment. "Next thing is getting

Eric Partin out of here. I don't want him wrapped up in this any more than he has to be."

Bringing Eric into this had been a risk, but a calculated one. Baughman felt a little guilty about it—and about not being entirely honest about his motives—but in the end it was for a noble cause.

In fact, if there was a theme to Carl Baughman's life, it was noble causes. That was why he'd joined the Bureau. It was why he'd stayed so long. And it was why he'd agreed to help Albert Wilson.

"Fine," Wilson said. "You get Partin gone first thing in the morning. Then you go talk to... to Becky. You tell her it's time to come home."

9

The walk to 125 Barker Street only took Eric ten minutes, but in that time he managed to cross into two different worlds. On the drive to the motel, they'd stayed on the main road, Highway 42. Marsha Crawford's place had been just off that road. Eric had been surprised at the apparent money on display. Now he ventured off Highway 42 and saw a different side of Wakefield. Walking down Apple Lane, he passed homes in decidedly worse condition than any he'd seen so far in town. One ranch-style house particularly concerned him; its roof sagged at such a dramatic angle that it gave the structure a saddle-like appearance. It was unclear if anyone lived in these homes. There were vehicles in a few of the yards, but they were old and rusted, and Eric doubted any of them were functional. It could be that these were the abandoned homes of the people who'd fled Wakefield, the ones the man on the plane had told him about. At least, Eric hoped so. The alternative—that someone was living in these dilapidated shacks—was grim.

Two blocks later, he entered yet another stratum as he passed a massive factory, this one definitely abandoned.

Grass grew tall through cracks in the pavement on the other side of the chain-link fence that still protected the industrial building, and few windows remained. Perhaps this place had once been a source of employment in Wakefield, but now it was nothing but a rotting corpse.

As he walked, Eric mulled over what he knew about the kidnappings. Six children, age twelve, taken from their homes in the early afternoon of March sixteenth. According to what the woman had told them, they'd all been brought to Wakefield. The kidnapping would have had to involve at least eighteen people, not an insignificant portion of this town's population. If Marsha Crawford could be believed, her husband had been one of the kidnappers, and he'd been a law- abiding citizen both before and after the kidnapping. Which raised an important question for Eric—what could possibly make a normal guy take part in a kidnapping?

Eric sighed and kicked at a small rock, sending it flying across the road, rolling to a stop when it hit the curb on the other side. He supposed he could add this question to the ever-growing list. Why had he been released, and the others had not? Why those six children in particular? Why Wakefield? Eric wanted answers, but his curiosity was like a dull light, one easily ignored. He was perfectly happy to let Baughman and his FBI colleagues finish their investigation. The only urgent need he felt was to see the house.

He crossed a set of railroad tracks and once again found himself in a residential area, this one as dilapidated as the last. Consulting his map, he saw that Barker Street should be the next block up. When he reached the faded street sign that confirmed it, he folded up the map, shoved it into his pocket, and turned left.

His recollection of the exterior of the house was limited. When they'd dragged him out of the van and into the house, he'd been in a drug-induced stupor. It had taken nearly all of his concentration to simply put one foot in front of the other. When they'd brought him out three weeks later, he'd been blindfolded. Perhaps they'd been more careful on that trip knowing that he'd be released. But there was one thing he did remember very clearly—the woods behind the house. The warped image of the trees and the path leading through them was burned into his mind, probably his clearest memory of the entire experience.

Now, looking down Barker Street, he was certain he was once again looking at that same forest. Even from a block away, it looked dense and foreboding. And in front of it stood a large Victorian-style home draped in shadows.

Eric covered the remaining block to the house in something like a daze. Though he hadn't thought he'd be able to remember the house, the sight of it now hit him hard. It was as if a half-remembered dream had suddenly come to life. He recalled with almost alarming clarity the rough, calloused hands of his kidnappers as they grabbed his arms and hauled him out of the van. He remembered the sound of his feet scuffling along the pavement as they led him to the house. He recalled the sweet, almost pungent aroma of the forest and the way the thick pollen had brought tears to his eyes.

These senses were stronger than any memory he'd ever experienced. His upper arms ached in sympathy for the boy where the kidnappers had grabbed him. The sound of his shoes was the same as it had been then, and the smell in the air was identical, though it was now late summer instead of early spring.

He paused when he reached the end of the road, stopping at the cracked sidewalk that led up to the house. The bushes grew wild and untamed below the wrap-around porch, and the white paint had come off in great flakes, leaving the wood beneath exposed and rotting. But in Eric's mind, he saw the house as it had been—a great, well-maintained maw that had swallowed him for three weeks.

His eyes drifted to the third floor. There was only a small window on this side of the house, but he knew what that floor held. A makeshift bedroom, twelve paces by fourteen, and a tiny bathroom. And a door with three locks.

Eric stared up at the house for a long time. His hands began to hurt, and he realized he was clutching them into tight fists. He'd long considered his kidnapping a weird blip in an otherwise unremarkable life. A speeding car that had narrowly missed him. He'd been taken, yes, but he'd been released. Tragedy had been averted. Now he realized he might not have gotten away from this house as cleanly as he'd assumed. That terrified little boy still lived inside of him, and, looking at the house, that boy was screaming.

How had the experience affected his life? How many unconscious impacts had it made on him? It was impossible to say.

He tore his eyes away from the house and slowly uncurled his fists. Silently, he reprimanded himself for being so affected by the sight of an old house. Whatever had happened here, it was ancient history. It couldn't hurt him now.

He started to turn away, but then he remembered there was one more thing he wanted to see. The woods behind the house. The path. He'd spent so many hours staring at it through the plastic window that he wanted to see it clearly one time. Based on the way the house was maintained, the path would be overgrown by now, but he still wanted to take a peek. Wondering where that path led had been one of his few diversions in the upstairs room.

Drawing a deep breath, he stepped over the curb and onto the sidewalk. He was walking through the long grass in the lawn when he heard a voice calling to him.

"Help me!"

The sound was so distant, so quiet, that for a moment he thought it must be another part of his memory returning. After all, hadn't he called for help from that upstairs room? Hadn't he shouted for days? But then the sound came again.

"Help me!"

The voice was louder now, and the desperation in it was clear.

He looked up at the house, his heart suddenly racing. He didn't see anyone in the windows. He glanced back at the street. If he'd had his phone, he might have called for help, but that pickpocket had taken it. The voice sounded young; was it possible they were still holding children up there all these years later? If so, he wasn't going to let that kid suffer a moment more than he had to. Going back to the motel to get Baughman might give the kidnappers enough time to move the kid and destroy the evidence. No way in hell was that going to happen.

His decision made, he raced around to the back of the house.

When he reached it, he paused, momentarily distracted by the forest. The path stood in the center, leading from the woods to the yard, as wide and clear in reality as it had been in his memory.

Then the voice shouted again. "Please! Help me!"

Eric spun toward the house, his eyes going to the third floor.

A dark shape stood in the window. The shape slowly raised a hand and placed it against the window, its fingers splayed wide.

"Damn it all," Eric muttered. He trotted toward the house, carefully making his way up the rotting steps that led to the back door. When he reached it, he realized it wasn't fully closed. It was open just far enough to stop the latch from catching. He gently gave it a push, and it swung open, giving him a clear view of the kitchen.

To his surprise, the inside of the house looked completely different than the outside. While he wouldn't have called the kitchen modern, it was clean and clearly maintained. Papers lay on the counter, and a set of men's work boots stood inside the door on a small rug. Someone was living here.

He cleared his throat and hesitantly called through the open door. "Hello?"

The only response was another call from the child. "Please! Hurry!"

Eric gritted his teeth and stepped over the threshold.

10

THE MOMENT ERIC'S foot touched the floorboard, he felt a jolt running from his toes all the way to the top of his head, something between a shiver and an electrical shock. Whether it was his imagination or his body's visceral reaction to returning to the site of his childhood trauma, he did not know.

He walked into the kitchen, leaving the door wide open behind him. He didn't know what the hell he was about to encounter, but he wanted to give himself the clearest possible path of escape. Heart thudding in his chest he walked gingerly, hands stretched out and fingers spread as if he were walking on a balance beam.

He drew a deep breath, pausing and forcing himself to relax. Yes, something bad had happened to him here, and yes, the distinctive smell of cleaning solution he remembered from his childhood was assaulting his nose, cutting through the musty overtones. But he was no longer a child. He'd survived this place once before, and he'd survive it again. What's more, there was a kid here that needed his help. He'd be damned if he let that child suffer as he had, alone and afraid for who knew how long.

His fear suppressed for the moment, he glanced around the kitchen, hoping to get some clue to the house's occupants. A crumbled dish towel lay on the small table near the door. There were a few dirty dishes in the sink. Beyond that, the room was pretty tidy. It was almost as if the residents were avoiding putting down permanent roots here. There were no magnets on the fridge or pictures on the wall.

"Help me!" the cry came again.

At the high-pitched, desperate sound of that voice, all his fear returned in one crushing wave. The pain in that voice... it was like hearing his own terrified shouts echoing down through the years. Eric clenched his fists and forced himself forward, moving out of the kitchen and into the room beyond.

He stepped into the living room and experienced the same strange feeling that this place was both lived in and abandoned. The room was clean and well arranged, but the furniture had to be thirty years old. Again, not a single item was out of place. This might as well have been a museum seeking to preserve life in the 1990s.

A large staircase stood to Eric's left, its hefty oak banisters carved with elaborate swirls. And to his right was the front door. The exit called to him like a pool of water calls to a thirsty man. Thirty years ago, he would have given anything for a chance at that door. Now it stood eight feet away, its small window providing a tantalizing glimpse of the world beyond this house, the world where things made sense.

He tore his eyes away from the door, silently cursing himself. No more dawdling. There was a kid up there who needed his help. Giving himself no more time to second-guess his situation, he put a hand on the rail and started up the steps.

The stairs creaked under his feet and the chemical cleaner smell grew stronger, but he ignored these things, pushing them away. He didn't stop when he reached the second floor; he knew the room he was looking for was higher. He followed the stairs upward to the third floor.

The staircase ended, depositing him in a short, dimly lit hallway. To his right was a small window that looked out over the street. The evening sunlight cast the wood-paneled hallway in a sickly yellow hue. And to his left was the door with three deadbolts.

His shirt clung to his sweaty chest as he walked toward it. Reaching up with a shaky hand, he touched the top deadbolt and turned the knob. The lock disengaged with a click, and the distinctive sound made the memories come rushing back.

He's sitting on his mattress on the floor, and a man is on a chair in front of him. There's something wrong with the man's eye. It has a black speck that isn't a speck at all. It's a hole. Or maybe a door. Yes, that feels right. It's a door. And that door is opening, pulsing, growing larger. Eric knows he's supposed to keep staring at it, but he doesn't want to. If he stares at it long enough, something might step through that door. And he doesn't want to see what might come through a door like that. He thinks that if he sees it, he might go mad.

Eric pushed the thoughts away. In the thirty years since his kidnapping, he'd gotten very good at not thinking about that time. Especially the man with the speck in his eye. He'd not thought about it in so long that he'd almost forgotten. He reached for the second deadbolt and turned it. It clicked.

There's a noise behind him. Someone is coming! The man wants him to keep looking at his eye, but there is something creeping out of the bathroom toward him. He has a terrible thought: maybe it isn't a door in the man's eye. Maybe it's a key. Maybe it's opened a door behind Eric, in his bathroom. The man's telling him not to look, but he can't stop himself. There is a monster behind him, worse than anything he's ever imagined. It's going to grab him and tear him apart unless he finds a way to stop it. He can't stop it unless he looks at it. So he turns and—

Eric gritted his teeth, trying to focus. There was a child who needed his help. Taking a trip down that particular memory lane was probably a bad idea at the best of times, but now? It was downright crazy. The last thing he needed was to be unnerved by thinking about what he saw—or thought he saw—way back then.

But it was already too late. His hands were shaking badly now and his arm felt heavy as he lifted it.

"Please! Help!"

The voice was right on the other side of the door, and the fear in that voice shook something free in Eric. He grabbed the final deadbolt and turned it hard. *Click.*

The creature behind him isn't some monster as he'd imagined. It looks just like the man in the chair, which is somehow even more terrifying. The doppelganger reaches out, grabbing Eric by the throat. But it doesn't choke Eric, it just holds him there. Eric notices one difference between the man grabbing him and the one in the chair. This one doesn't have the black speck in his eye.

Eric beats at the arm holding him, but it doesn't budge. Its sinewy muscles hold fast. Finally, Eric grabs the arm with both hands, holding tight, hoping to pry it away.

Then something strange happens—the man begins to fade. Eric can see the wall behind the man. A moment later, his fingers slip through the man's arm and his hands close into fists. The man is gone.

Eric stands in shocked silence.

Then the man behind him, the one in the chair, speaks. "Good. You're strong, Eric. I think you'll do."

The lights seem to flicker, and for an instant, the man appears in front of him. Just as quickly, he disappears. A cold wind slams into Eric's face, rushing into his mouth and up his nose. His mouth fills with a bitter, acrid taste and he's cold, colder than he's ever been. Ice seems to fill his veins. His eyes widen in terror, and just when he can't take it anymore, the feeling is gone.

The man folds up his chair and leaves without another word.

An hour later, they put Eric in a van and drive him three hours to a post office in Cary, North Carolina.

It had been so long since he'd thought about those memories. In fact, he wasn't sure he'd ever thought about them, not since that day. How strange was that? With all the times he'd been over the story with his parents, with Baughman, with police officers, and he'd never once spoken about the strange disappearing man. It wasn't as if he'd purposefully left it out. It had simply not occurred to him. Even when he'd seen the fading man at his window, he hadn't made the connection. It was as if the memory had crept into the back of his brain and shrouded itself in the shadows, and only the sound of those three clicking deadbolts was enough to expose it.

He turned the doorknob and eased the door open. As he did, the cry came again. "Help me!"

Eric blinked hard at the sight of the room. For some reason, he'd expected it to be exactly as it had been during his stay—a mattress on the floor, a thin blanket, a plastic window. But, unlike the rest of the house, this room had been transformed. A queen-size bed sat against the far wall, an end table next to it. Curtains hung open over the window, and even from the doorway, Eric could tell it was made of glass now. There were a desk and chair in the corner, and a laptop sat closed on the desk. A pile of dirty clothes lay next to the bed. Unlike the rest of the house, this room felt lived in.

And there was a figure in the bed.

Eric stepped into the room, and the figure didn't move.

"Please, help me."

The voice sounded different now that Eric was in the room. There was a grating quality to the yelling, which was just as loud as it had been when Eric was outside. Which raised the question, how had he known Eric was out there? Had he been watching at the window in case someone wandered down this dead-end street? If so, why had he gotten back into bed and covered up?

"I'm here," Eric said. "I can help you."

The figure turned over and faced Eric, who let out a soft gasp.

It wasn't a child. This was a grown man, maybe in his late thirties or early forties. His hair was thin and what was left of it was buzzed short.

"Please, help me," he repeated, shouting just as loudly as before.

Eric took a step back, moving instinctively away from the man. "I don't understand. What do you need?"

The man began to laugh. It was a high, wheezy sound, and it shredded Eric's nerves like a hundred knives. He wanted nothing more than to run out of this room, lock those three deadbolts, and go back to the motel. He could still meet up with Baughman for some pizza and beers.

Then he'd stay in his room until morning, get on the first flight out, and never come back to this creepy little town.

And yet, this guy *had* been locked in this room. Maybe he was suffering from some mental illness and was being abused and held against his will. Maybe he really did need help.

On the other hand, the way he was laughing at Eric made that seem unlikely.

He took a deep breath and tasted the sharp tang of chemical cleaner. There was another option, one he probably should have taken from the beginning. He could go back to the motel and call the cops. He'd call from the lobby, give an anonymous account of what he'd seen, and leave it up to them. They could investigate whether there was anything illegal going on here. That was their job, not his.

And yet, he was standing here, and they were not.

Eric was just about to speak again, to offer his help one last time, when the man flickered. Eric might have thought he imagined it, but when the man disappeared, the blanket covering him flattened. When he reappeared, he was on top of the blanket, still grinning his strange grin.

Eric took another step back and almost stumbled, catching himself on the doorframe. There was no denying what had just happened. This wasn't some two a.m. occurrence he could write off as a dream or a half-remembered childhood memory. This was real and right in front of him. A man had ceased to exist before his eyes and returned a moment later.

Reality, as Eric understood it, had just shifted forever.

Eric was so taken aback that he didn't hear the footsteps coming up the stairs behind him. He didn't even realize anyone was there until he heard the voice.

"Turn around. Slowly."

Eric turned and was shocked at what he saw.

It was the woman from the gas station. The one who'd picked his pocket. And she was pointing a pistol at his chest.

She glared at him, fury in her eyes. "What the hell are you doing to my brother?"

11

CARL BAUGHMAN SET down his phone, reached into his bag, and pulled out a moleskin notebook. Its original light brown had grown darker over the years, and it was spotted with the evidence of at least three coffee spills, but that didn't matter. What was inside mattered.

Baughman started a new notebook for every major case he worked. While many of his colleagues had transitioned to notetaking apps, he still preferred the feel of a nice pen curving and sweeping over paper. The sensation, the smell, they calmed him somehow. It was a meditative experience that often brought him clarity. His organizational system probably would have been nonsense to anyone else, but he found it the only logical way to catalog the case. The latter half of the notebook was reserved for interview notes and outstanding questions. The front half he used to document things he knew for certain. Sometimes he returned to this section and drew a line through a fact that had proven to be a false assumption. But not often. He was rather stingy in what he considered certain.

He was on his third notebook for this particular case.

He'd labeled the first notebook *The Eric Partin Kidnapping*. The second he'd called *May, 1989 Mass Kidnapping*. This last notebook—and he was certain it would be the last for this case—he'd titled *The Wakefield Five*. He found the name more satisfying, more accurate. True, there had been six children taken on that day thirty years ago, but Eric had been returned. He hadn't grown up in Wakefield like the rest of them, so Baughman didn't include him in the tally.

He flipped to the page of names. Then he took the piece of paper Mrs. Crawford gave Eric and set it next to that page. He wasn't ready to write the names in his book; they were far from confirmed. Still, it felt good to see them there, alongside the names he'd been looking at for so long.

He started at the top with Rachel Wilson. He always started with Rachel. Now he had another name for her. Her Wakefield name. If Mrs. Crawford was to be believed, this was the name she'd used throughout her teenage years and was still using today. Rachel Wilson was Becky Talbot. His fingers itched to write that name in his book, but he couldn't. Not until it was confirmed. Instead, he moved down the list.

Matt Soule was the next victim, the first of those taken back in May 1989. According to the list, his new name was Caleb Bloom. Then Sandy Thorne, who apparently now went by Nancy Evans. Casey Sunup was now Lewis Keller. Colin James was now Mikey Talbot. Same last name as Becky. Had these two been raised as siblings? Cousins, maybe?

Baughman tapped his pen anxiously on the paper, considering how best to handle this. He needed to approach Becky first. She was the first name on his list, after all. He'd have to come up with a cover story, a reason to approach her that wasn't *I know you were kidnapped thirty years ago and are still living under a false identity for some reason.*

That was the real question, wasn't it? These people hadn't been young kids when they were taken. They'd almost been teenagers. They remembered their parents and families. Their entire lives had been taken from them. And yet, not one of them had attempted to contact their families, even after they came of age. Every one of them was still living under their new names, and they all remained in the town where they'd been held.

He shut the notebook, leaving Mrs. Crawford's paper as a bookmark on the page with the names. There would be time enough for all of these concerns tomorrow. He expected he'd be in Wakefield for some time working on this mess. The last thing he wanted to do was make an error just because he was anxious to have this over and done with.

Tonight, he would enjoy a nice meal, try to put all this out of his mind, and pick it back up tomorrow. The case had been open for thirty years. One more night wouldn't hurt anything.

Besides, he had a greater responsibility: Eric.

The original case he'd been assigned thirty years ago was the Eric Partin kidnapping. That's what it said on the first page of his original notebook, and he took that very seriously. He considered Eric's safety his primary responsibility, even above his responsibility to Albert Wilson. Bringing Eric to Wakefield had been a risk, though it was a calculated one. He'd feel much better about things once Eric was on a plane back to Wisconsin.

Even having Eric walking around town made Baughman nervous. Of course, it would be impossible that anyone would recognize him as the boy they'd kidnapped thirty years ago. But Baughman couldn't shake the feeling that this town wasn't safe for him. Somehow, it had sucked the other five into its abyss and refused to let them go. He felt it would do the same to Eric if given the chance.

He sat for another full minute, staring out the window before he grabbed his keys and stood up. He'd spent long enough waiting. It was time to go find Eric.

Eric stared wide eyed at the gun. Behind him, the man in the bed was still giggling.

"I'll ask you one more time," the woman said. "What the hell are you doing to my brother?"

Eric swallowed hard, trying to find his voice. He'd never had a firearm pointed at him. "Hey, look, I'm not doing anything. I was just—"

"Trespassing?" she interrupted. "Attacking a sick man in his home?"

"No. It's not like that. It's a little hard to explain."

The woman's eyes bore into him now. She was furious, not a great quality in someone with a handgun. "Well, you'd better try. And do it fast. Pretty sure I'm within my rights to shoot you, seeing as you broke into my house and all."

"I didn't." To Eric's surprise, he found that anger was rising up in his stomach, slowly overtaking his fear. "And you want to talk about crimes? Where's my phone? Can I have that back or did you hock it for drug money already?"

The confidence on her face flickered. "That's not... Let's stay on topic. What did you do? Follow me? How'd you know I live here?"

"I didn't. Think maybe you can put the gun down and we can have a rational discussion?"

"I really don't. Keep talking."

Eric wanted to shout. Being in this malevolent house again and stumbling upon this creepy brother who apparently got his kicks by impersonating a child and calling for help brought Eric to the edge. Was the brother's act a regular occurrence, or did Eric just get lucky enough to witness a rare performance? More unnerving was the way he'd *disappeared*. Eric didn't even want to think about that; if he did, he was afraid it would consume all his other thoughts. He needed to focus on staying alive and bullet-free.

This pickpocket was pointing a gun at him, threatening to pull the trigger if he didn't dance to her little tune. He needed to find a way to deescalate the situation, and quickly. "Look, I'm sorry I came in uninvited. I was walking by and I heard your brother calling for help. I thought it was a child. And I didn't have my phone, as you are all too aware. I was trying to help."

"Uh-huh." From the look in her eyes, it was clear she was buying exactly none of this story. "Just happened to be wandering by a house on a dead-end street?"

Before Eric could answer, the man in the bed let out a loud moan. There was pain in that voice, a deep and abiding pain that sounded barely human.

"Shit," the woman muttered. "Mikey, you okay?"

He answered with another moan; this one sounded even worse.

The woman gripped her pistol tighter and glared at Eric. She gestured toward the corner with her head. "Get over there. I want you on your knees. Put your palms against the wall where I can see them. Understand?"

Eric let out a short, desperate laugh. "I'm not—"

"Do it now, or I'll shoot you dead. I swear to God."

Eric hesitated, then he walked to the corner and

kneeled. The rough, uneven floorboards pressed into his knees, causing his left one to ache. It gave him problems now and again, and the wood cutting into it intensified the dull pain. The chemical smell was stronger here, causing bile to rise in Eric's throat. He swallowed, forcing it down. The woman with the gun looked pretty stressed already. If he threw up, it probably wouldn't improve his chances of getting out of this.

Behind him, he heard footsteps as the woman moved to the bed.

"Mikey, we're going to have to clear the Fade, understand?"

The man let out another moan.

"Look, I know it sucks," she said, "but you've got to do it. There's no choice here."

"But the man..." He was on the verge of tears.

"Don't worry about him. Focus on me. You've got this. Just like last time."

There was a long pause during which Eric cursed his own stupidity. He should never have come here. This house was evil. He'd been lucky to make it out the first time, and he'd been an idiot to come back. His eyes drifted up toward the window. From his angle, all he could see were the tops of a few trees and a relentlessly blue sky.

Finally, the man in the bed answered. "I can do three."

"That's not enough, and you know it. We gotta do seven."

"Becky."

"Don't Becky me. You want to stop hurting? We got to do seven."

Mikey drew a deep, wheezy breath. "All right. I'll try."

"You'll do better than try. Muscle through. You'll feel much better in seven. Ready?"

"Yeah." He sounded anything but.

"Set," Becky said.

Eric kept his eyes on the window and the hypnotic way the leaves swayed in the wind.

"Go." She paused. Her voice was low when she spoke again, like she might not even know she was speaking aloud. "One Mississippi."

Eric felt the sudden, almost irresistible urge to turn and look, knowing full well that doing so might get him shot.

"Two Mississippi. Three Mississippi." She sounded like she was barely holding it together.

Eric flashed back to that moment in this very room when the man in the chair hadn't wanted him to look behind him. As much as he'd tried to obey, the urge had been too strong. Something had called to him. Not with words, but with something much deeper. He'd felt that something inside him needed to see. He felt the same way now.

"Four Mississippi."

Ever so slowly, his hands still pressed against the wall, he turned his head.

Becky knelt at the side of the bed, which was now empty. She had her hands raised as if she was preparing to grab something. The gun lay on the floor next to her. Mikey, the man in the bed, was gone. This wasn't like the flicker. He was truly gone.

"Five Mississippi."

Becky's attention was so focused on the bed that Eric was almost certain he'd be able to get up and sprint for the door before she had time to react. He might even be able to grab the gun off the floor. But he didn't. His attention was focused on the bed as much as Becky's was. He needed to see this. It was important, and he had no idea why.

"Six Mississippi."

Eric craned his neck around farther, wanting to have a clear look at what would happen when she got to seven.

"Seven Mississippi."

As soon as she spoke the words, Mikey flickered back into reality. Her hands shot downward, grabbing him by the shoulders. His body lay so straight and stiff that for a moment, Eric thought he might be dead. Then he gasped and began to flail. His arms whipped in the air, as if he were swatting at invisible bats around his head.

"You're here!" Becky shouted. "It's okay, Mikey. You're home. You're safe. I have you."

Mikey was startled at the sound of her voice, a look of confusion on his face. Then his body relaxed and he let out a sob.

"Was it bad?" she asked.

"Yeah. It was bad." His voice sounded different now. It no longer had the crazed, hysterical tone. He lay back on the bed, breathing heavy. His face was slick with sweat.

"You feel better now, though. Tell me I'm wrong."

"I feel gross, dirty, but no pain," he admitted. "I just hope the next one's not too soon. If I could just have a couple weeks..." He paused as he spotted Eric staring at him. "Becky."

She saw him looking and snatched her pistol off the floor. In an instant, she had it pointed at Eric again. "What the hell? I thought I told you to look at the wall!"

Eric didn't answer. He wasn't sure he could.

"Becky," Mikey said, "when I was out, I felt him. Same as I feel you."

She blinked hard, her expression blank.

"He's like us."

"I know." That hung in the air for a long moment. Then

Becky stood up, keeping her gun trained on Eric as she shakily got to her feet. "You're him. You're Eric Partin."

Eric met her gaze. "I am. What does that mean to you?"

Becky scowled. Before, she'd looked at him like he was an invader. Now she looked at him like he was absolute scum. She ignored his question and reached into her back pocket with her free hand, pulling out a cellphone.

"What are you doing?" Mikey asked.

"I'm calling Caleb. I think it's time for a little class reunion."

12

Becky handed Mikey the pistol and left the room to make the call. He was sitting up on his bed now, looking entirely composed, a stark contrast from the cackling madman he'd been when Eric had first seen him.

"You can turn around," Mikey said. "Feels kinda odd with you kneeling against the wall."

Eric slowly did so, turning and sinking into a sitting position, careful not to take his eyes off Mikey. "Look, I don't know what you want from me, but I'm not—"

"Shut up." He said it quietly, more weary than angry. "I know this isn't your fault, but... Well, maybe it is"

Eric wasn't sure how to take that. So much of what he'd seen and heard over the past few days was unexplainable. He wondered if any of it was real. Maybe he was back home in bed and this was all a bizarre dream. Or maybe he was twelve years old, stuck in this room, and everything that had happened since was the dream.

Though he knew it was too much to ask to understand all of it at once, he figured maybe he could start small. "How'd you know I was out there?"

Mikey looked at him blankly. "What?"

"You called to me when I was outside. How'd you know I was there?"

Mikey regarded him for a long moment. He was short and a bit pudgy. Piercing blue eyes stared out of a round face. Despite his weight, his tee shirt and shorts hung off him, at least a size too large. "I don't know, man. When I'm like that, things just come to me. I knew you were out there, and you needed to come inside."

Becky marched back into the room, her cellphone in her hand. "Caleb's only a few blocks away." She was taller than her brother and her thick dark hair hung down past her shoulders. She wore her simple tee shirt and jeans well. Even in his current state, Eric couldn't help but feel a spark of attraction to her.

Something clicked in Eric's brain. Their names. Becky. Mike. Caleb. He'd seen those names before. What she had said about the class reunion suddenly made sense.

"I know who you are," he said. The words came out without any thought. He'd seen the names written on the piece of paper Mrs. Crawford had given him. "You're the other ones who were kidnapped. You were taken, just like me."

Becky crossed her arms and let out a sharp laugh. "Is that what you think?"

"Becky, let him be," Mikey said, but there was no force behind his voice.

She ignored her brother, crouching down so she was at eye-level with Eric. "You think you're like us? Why? Because they took you and gave you a three-week vacation? Threw a little scare into you before they gave you back to your family?"

"It was hardly a vacation," Eric said quietly.

"I'm sure it was real tough for you." The disdain was thick in her voice now. "Maybe you even cried yourself to sleep back in your own bed when it was all over."

Eric had to admit, she had a point. From her perspective, he'd gotten off easy. "I'm sorry about what happened to you. I'm sorry they didn't let you go."

She laughed again, a joyless sound that was nearly a snort. "Oh, you're sorry? You hear that, Mikey? He's sorry."

"Becky, calm down," Mikey said.

Becky glared at Eric. "You don't know shit about sorry. Not yet. But you will. You're going to learn all about sorry real soon."

Mikey leaned forward and put a hand on Becky's shoulder. "Please. Wait until Caleb gets here."

That seemed to calm her a little. "Yeah, okay."

They didn't have long to wait. A few moments later the front door slammed, and heavy work boots clomped up the stairs. A tall man with blond hair and an unruly, reddish-blond beard hurried into the room. His eyes were wild.

"Is he here?" Then his gaze settled on Eric, and his panicked expression resolved into an easy smile. "My God, it really is you."

"It's really me," Eric agreed. He felt a growing sense of dread. Becky and Mikey were certainly odd, but something about this newcomer struck him as dangerous.

The man held out a hand. "Caleb Bloom."

"Eric Partin," he answered as he shook the man's hand.

"No kidding." He turned to Becky. "You said you saw the FBI guy too, right?"

"Yeah," Becky said. "I swiped his wallet outside the Shell station."

"Okay," Caleb said slowly, like he was addressing a dense child. "Then what are we waiting for?"

Mikey gave him a weary look. Eric got the impression Mikey wasn't the biggest Caleb fan. "We were waiting for you."

Caleb stood up and stretched out his arms. "Here I am. Wait no longer. Can we go now?"

"Where are we going?" Eric asked. This man was making him nervous. He knew there was an FBI agent with Eric but didn't have any questions as to why. And now they wanted to take him somewhere?

Caleb shot Eric a smile that had probably been charming the ladies of Wakefield since his early teens. "It's a surprise. One long overdue, if you ask me. Now get up."

Eric didn't move. "I'm not going anywhere with you."

Caleb's smile never wavered. "Well, I could knock you out and carry you, but that sounds like a pain in the ass for both of us."

"We could drug him," Mikey offered. "I think Merle left some stuff in the closet. It's old but it might still work."

Panic fluttered in Eric's chest at that thought. He remembered the drug-induced haze following his kidnapping, the nauseating funk that his brain couldn't seem to shake for a full day, maybe more.

Caleb noticed the reaction, and his smile widened. "I don't think he likes that idea. What's it going to be, Eric? You going to walk, or do I need to find the syringe?"

Eric had no idea what was going to happen next, but he knew he'd need his wits about him. Slowly, reluctantly, he stood up.

"Good man." Caleb clapped him on the back.

They led him down the stairs and out the backdoor, which was still open. How he wished he'd never come here. He could be sitting in his motel room, watching some dopey movie right now. Instead he was accompanying three psychopaths God knew where. He wasn't wearing a watch so he wasn't sure of the time, but he guessed he'd been gone from the motel about thirty minutes. That meant he wasn't due to meet Baughman for dinner for another twenty. Baughman probably wouldn't get concerned for at least fifteen or twenty minutes after that. Hell, he might assume Eric had fallen asleep and just go to dinner without him. He might not realize Eric was missing until morning.

And how would he find Eric when he did notice? Mrs. Crawford had only given the address to Eric. Baughman had no idea where he'd gone.

To Eric's surprise, they didn't lead him around to the front of the house or to the detached garage off to the side. Instead, they took him to the woods behind the house. To the trail.

Caleb walked in front, strolling along like he was taking a relaxed jaunt through the woods rather than escorting a captive. Mikey and Becky walked behind Eric, Mikey holding the gun pointed at Eric, ready to urge him along if need be.

They didn't need to urge him. Despite his situation, Eric felt a twinge of excitement as they stepped into the forest. For three weeks, he'd looked out that third-story window at this trail and imagined that some form of escape lay beyond those trees. Now he was about to find out.

It was early evening, and the sun still shone. But as they stepped into the woods, everything darkened a few shades. The canopy overhead and the thick vegetation on either side of them created a green tunnel. Eric wondered who maintained this trail. If it wasn't walked regularly, it would have become overgrown. As it was, the trail was almost luxurious in its width and the hard dirt left no ambiguity to its path.

They walked in silence for fifteen minutes. Caleb strode the path confidently, like someone who'd walked it many times before. Mikey and Becky were another story. Eric glanced over his shoulder and saw they'd fallen back a few steps, and their faces were tense. It seemed they were none too eager to reach wherever this trail led.

Eric heard a soft sound in the distance. It took him a while to identify it, but it grew louder as they walked. It was water lapping against a shore. Eric racked his brain, trying to remember if he'd seen a lake or pond on the map he'd ripped out of the phone book. He'd been so focused on finding Barker Street that he couldn't remember any of the town's other features.

He almost laughed out loud at the absurdity of it all. Here he was, investigating his thirty-year-old kidnapping, and he'd somehow managed to get himself kidnapped again.

Up ahead, the trail widened. The path led through a grassy clearing, and Eric glimpsed some sort of structure ahead. As they emerged from the woods, he got a better look. A small cabin stood near the edge of a lake. It was a squat, simple log home, and an inlet between them and the cabin almost made it seem to float over the gray waters. Light shone through the single window, and Eric could see the silhouette of a figure inside the house.

Caleb stopped and turned to face Eric. He'd lost a bit of his swagger, and there was a hint of nervousness in his eyes. "Okay, here's what happens next. I'm going up to the cabin. You wait here, and don't make so much as a grunt until I get back. Understand?"

Eric glanced back at the window. "Who's in the house?"

"Let's hope you don't have to find out." With that, he turned, hitched up his pants, and shuffled toward the cabin.

Eric spoke softly, his eyes still on Caleb. "I don't know what's going on here, but you don't have to listen to Caleb."

"We're not," Becky answered. "This wasn't even his idea."

"Okay, but whatever it is, I can help you. You know Agent Baughman's here with me. He can help with whatever you're mixed up with."

Mikey chuckled. "He can't help with this." He pressed the barrel of the pistol into Eric's back. "How about we listen to Caleb on that not even a grunt thing, huh?"

Eric pressed his lips together and decided to wait. He glanced at Becky and saw she was biting her lip, staring at the cabin.

It was only a few moments before the cabin door opened and Caleb emerged. He trudged back over to them.

"Is he coming out?" Mikey asked.

Caleb shook his head. "He wants us to do it. He thinks he might taint the results or something. It's gotta be us."

"How'd he seem?" Becky asked.

Caleb shot her an impatient scowl. "How the hell do you think he seemed? Not great." He sighed and turned to Eric. "Okay, we're going over to that dock now."

"Nah, I don't think so." Eric met Caleb's eyes. He kept his expression devoid of emotion.

There had been some shady characters who'd worked for him at E&J Landscaping over the years. Guys who'd punched previous bosses. Guys who'd been in trouble with the law. Eric didn't shy away from hiring such people. In fact, he sort of leaned into it. Because he knew he could give them a chance at turning their lives around and making a decent living. Donovan had been one such individual. It didn't always turn out as well as it had with Donnie. Sometimes he wound up with his tools missing or a drunk employee. Sometimes it worked and sometimes it didn't, but he never stopped trying.

The look he was giving Caleb now was the same one he used on those guys when he needed them to take him seriously. It was a look that said the topic was not open to debate. He'd seen strong men wither under that look. Guys who would have punched out a boss just for asking them to complete a simple task complied when Eric looked at them that way. And for a moment, it seemed like it was going to work on Caleb too.

"Fair enough," Caleb said. Then he pulled back his fist and drove it into Eric's stomach. The air rushed out of Eric's lungs and he crumpled to his knees. He'd been punched a time or two, but never like that.

Before he could catch his breath, Caleb grabbed him under one arm. "Mikey, get the other."

The balding man did as he was ordered, and the two of them half-walked, half-dragged Eric to the dock. Eric's watering eyes had cleared enough that he could see what lay at the end of the dock as they approached—a piece of board six feet long and two feet wide. Three sets of straps were attached to it. It was the kind of thing a paramedic might use to restrain a badly injured person, except this one had a hefty piece of metal attached to the foot-end.

At the sight of the board, Eric felt a fresh wave of fear. He tried to stand up straight, but Caleb was ready for him. He punched him in the stomach again. When Eric doubled over, Caleb brought his right fist up in a brutal uppercut that slammed into Eric's chin. His jaw snapped shut with a *clank* and Eric tasted blood.

Rough hands grabbed Eric's feet, dragging him onto the board. He struggled, but Caleb grasped his shoulders, forcing them down. Becky and Mikey worked quickly, securing a strap around his ankles, another around his midsection, and a third around his shoulders. And just like that, Eric couldn't move.

His heart was racing now, and his breath was still coming in large gulps as he tried to recover from the two gut punches. What worried him far more was what would happen next.

Caleb stood up and brushed off his hands, a man pleased that a tough job had been done to his satisfaction. He turned to Becky. "You got the guy's card?"

"Huh?"

"The FBI guy. You said you had his card, right? Merle wants to see it."

Becky fished a business card out of her pocket and handed it to him. He slid it into his shirt pocket.

"All right, let's get this show on the road." He crouched down and reached his hand over the side of the dock. He grimaced as his fingers touched the water, as if he were in pain. Then he brought his hand up and flicked his fingers, sending drops of water cascading onto Eric's face.

The moment the water touched his skin, Eric's body spasmed. It was as if he'd been electrocuted. He lost all control of his limbs as he struggled against his restraints. Pain coursed through him in a vicious wave and every nerve in his body screamed in agony.

And just as quickly, it was gone. All that remained was the terrible memory and a few damp spots on his face.

"Jesus," Mikey muttered. "You ever see it like that before?"

A slow smile spread across Caleb's face. "Can't say that I have. I think he'll do just fine."

"He isn't going to end up like Lewis, is he?" Becky asked.

Caleb's smile disappeared. "Of course not. Why would you say that?"

Somehow, Eric managed to find his voice. "Please, we can work this out. Tell me what you want from me."

"What we want is for you to shut up," Caleb said, raising his boot menacingly over Eric's face.

Eric couldn't move. They wouldn't allow him to speak. He was completely at their mercy. He'd never felt so terrified.

"All right," Caleb said. "Let's put him in the water."

Every hair on Eric's body stood up at those words. He hadn't known what they intended, but he'd never expected it to be that. He'd experienced the worst pain of his life from only a few drops of the water from this lake, and now they were going to put him in? It was the worst thing he could imagine.

As they grabbed the sides of the board, he risked speaking one more time. "Why are you doing this?"

"Well," Caleb said, his voice straining with the effort of lifting the board, "I'll bet you've been wondering why you were kidnapped all those years ago. You're about to find out."

Then they dropped Eric into the water.

13

Eric managed to pull in a large breath just before he plunged under water. They dropped him feet first, and the minute the water saturated his pant legs and touched his skin, he let out a cry of pain. The water seemed electrified, and it sent a sharp bolt of agony coursing through his body. The small part of his mind that wasn't reeling from the pain was glad it wasn't any worse than the drops of water had been. It only felt like he was being torn apart nerve by nerve.

He sank fast, his torso and head quickly following his feet into the water. He squeezed his eyes shut as he fought the pain. To his surprise, it slowly began to fade. The sharp agony became a dull ache that thrummed in his core, sending waves of discomfort through him.

With the retreating pain came another harsh reality—he was strapped to a board and sinking feet first toward the bottom of a lake. He couldn't move his arms or his legs. He couldn't even look up at the surface with the way they'd restrained him. He was going to die at the bottom of some lake in Wakefield, Tennessee, and he didn't even understand why.

Caleb had said he'd soon know why he'd been kidnapped all those years ago, but if some great revelation was coming, it had better come fast. His lungs were already craving oxygen. The need for breath was a gentle thing now—a soft reminder from his central operating system that air was required for its continued existence—but he knew the need would soon grow much more urgent. How long could he hold his breath? Two minutes? Three? He had no idea. He'd never timed himself, not since he was a kid. Hell, it had been a few years since he'd even set foot in a swimming pool. Once upon a time, he'd loved his family trips up north to a rented cabin on a lake. He'd loved riding on a tube behind a speedboat as his dad turned lazy circles, sending him whipping around in the boat's wake. He'd loved jumping off docks and fishing.

But all that was a long time ago. E&J Landscaping had taken up all his time for the last twenty summers. Trips to a lake up north weren't on the agenda.

His lungs were screaming at him now, demanding oxygen. He knew he could only fight the need for so long. Eventually, he'd open his mouth and breathe in the chilly water, and that would be the end of Eric Partin. His body was starting to panic, and he struggled harder against the straps.

For the first time since he'd gone under, Eric opened his eyes.

Though he couldn't look up, from the amount of light piercing through the water, he imagined he couldn't be down too deep. The water was probably only a foot or two above his head. He didn't know if it was better or worse to drown in shallow water. He supposed it would increase the chances of his body being found. That was something.

The sunlight cast the water in a rich, bluish hue. Eric

was surprised by its clarity. He could see a good distance. And as he looked, he saw something dark in the water.

His first thought was that it was some sort of fish. But it couldn't be. Granted, he couldn't get a firm read on its size or distance, but the shape was all wrong. The dark shape was a perfect circle. Something in the back of his mind perked up at the sight of it. He'd seen this thing before—or something very much like it—though he knew not where.

As he watched, it pulsed, expanding ever-so-slowly, and then quickly contracting like a giant black heart. With each pulse, it grew a bit bigger.

Then it hit him. He knew where he'd seen that shape before. Back when he was kidnapped. He'd seen the speck of darkness in the thin man's eye. Now that darkness had somehow come to life and it was here in the water with him.

He stared at the shape as it expanded and contracted, and he had a terrible realization. The throbs of pain he'd been feeling since he entered the water were synced to the pulsing of the shape. His body was reacting to its movement.

And then he had one more realization—the darkness wasn't growing larger and smaller; it was moving closer and farther away.

Eric remembered staring at the thin man's eye and having the terrible fear that when the speck of darkness grew large enough, something would emerge from the hole. But he'd been frightened of the wrong thing. The danger wasn't hiding in the darkness; the danger was the darkness itself.

Though his body was screaming for air, he was almost able to ignore that in the face of the primal fear he felt at the approaching darkness. If he went too long without air, he would die. It was a known fact. Not one he wanted but one he understood. If the darkness touched him, he had no idea what would happen.

The darkness was huge now, as large as his torso. He squirmed against his restraints, pressing his body harder against the board in an effort to get even a few millimeters farther away from the darkness.

It paused for a moment, and the pulsing stopped. Then, all at once, it rushed toward him. It was enormous, eight feet across at least. As it touched Eric, pressing itself against his body, an icy blast of force shot through him. He couldn't see anything; the light was blotted out by the strange being pressing against him.

Then suddenly, the pain was gone.

For a moment, Eric thought he might be dead. Then the darkness started to retreat.

He felt nothing. Even his need for air seemed to have lessened. The darkness was pulsing again, but it was retreating much more quickly than it had come. After just a few seconds, it disappeared into the distance.

And then Eric started to move. Someone was pulling him up.

His head broke the surface and he gasped, drinking greedily at the air. They hauled him up onto the deck and laid him on his back as he coughed and panted. Caleb crouched down next to him and patted him on the chest.

"You can relax now. The worst is over." He paused a moment. "Well, that's not exactly true, but the worst is over for now."

"Wha-...wha-..." Everything had felt so unreal, so otherworldly underwater, that he felt the urgent need to speak, if only to prove to himself that he still could. "How... how long was I down there?"

"A minute forty by my watch. I'll bet it felt longer. The

water does that when you..." He trailed off, suddenly looking at something behind him.

Footsteps thumped slowly on the deck, and after a moment someone stepped into Eric's line of sight. His hair was almost gone and he bore thirty years' worth of wrinkles now, but Eric instantly recognized him. The thin man with the speck in his eye.

The man stared down at Eric, a gentle smile on his face. "Hello, Eric. You did very well."

He bent down and grabbed both sides of Eric's head.

"I'm Merle. We've met, though you may not remember."

"I remember you—" That was all Eric managed to get out before a coughing fit overtook him.

The man stared into his eyes for a long moment. Eric once again saw that speck, and he wanted to vomit.

"I once told you that you didn't belong yet," Merle said. "You do now. But first you need rest. Get some sleep. Tomorrow we'll start our work together." Then he got to his feet and turned to Caleb. "He's all set. Make the call."

Baughman had been driving the streets of Wakefield for nearly twenty minutes when an unknown number appeared on his cellphone. He considered ignoring it, but then he remembered that Eric's phone had been stolen. This could be Eric calling from a local bar or something. He grabbed the phone out of his cupholder and pressed the green icon to answer the call.

"Baughman," he said.

There was a long pause, and he almost hung up. But then a man's voice came on the line. "125 Barker Street."

Baughman blinked hard, trying to understand. "Okay. Is that supposed to mean something to me?"

"You want to help Mr. Partin? Don't talk. Just listen."

Baughman shifted the phone to his other ear, his heart suddenly racing. Before, the possibility that Eric might be in danger had been just that—a possibility. He could just as easily have been exploring the town. He may have even found a bar and ordered a beer and some chicken wings. But now, at the sound of that voice, Eric being in danger went from being a possibility to a near certainty.

He gritted his teeth and tried not to let out a curse. He never should have brought Eric back into this. If something happened to him, Baughman would never forgive himself.

The man continued in his raspy voice. "Go to 125 Barker Street. Walk around the back of the house, and you'll see a trail leading through the woods. Follow the trail a mile through the woods, and you'll come out at Stano Lake. You'll find Eric on the dock near the cabin." The man paused. "And do hurry."

After the phone clicked off, Baughman kept it to his ear another moment, too surprised to move.

You'll find Eric on the dock near the cabin.

He didn't like the sound of that. Not one bit.

Baughman quickly pulled up his maps app and located 125 Barker Street. Thankfully, it was only a three-minute drive. He made it in one and a half. The house at the end of the street looked like it might be abandoned, but the address matched. He parked in front of it, jumped out of the car, and ran around the side of the house. A trail ran through the center of the woods behind the house, just as advertised.

He made it nearly a quarter mile before he had to slow. Not bad for a man in his sixties who hadn't laced up a pair of running shoes in more than a decade. His labored breathing forced him to trade in his jog for a fast walk. Still, he pressed on, swinging his arms and moving down the trail as fast as he could.

One image kept popping into his mind, propelling him onward—Eric's cold body lying on the dock, his throat cut, blood draining through the slats and into the lake.

You'll find Eric on the dock near the cabin.

When he finally exited the woods, he immediately spotted the dock. Four figures were sitting on it. One was clearly Eric, but Baughman didn't recognize the others.

Baughman plodded over, getting a better look as he approached. Eric sat with his knees to his chest. He was soaking wet and his eyes were distant. A man sat on either side of him; a pudgy, balding guy to his left and a rugged dude with a reddish-blond beard to his right. And next to the balding guy sat the woman who'd stolen their things at the gas station.

Baughman tried to suppress his confusion. His jacket was unbuttoned, giving him easy access to his shoulder holster if needed.

The bearded man stood up as he approached. "Agent Baughman?"

Baughman stepped onto the dock. "That's me. Who are you?"

The bearded man grinned and gestured toward the others. "You've been looking for us for thirty years, and you don't recognize us? We're the five missing kids. Well, three of them anyway."

Baughman blinked hard. Was it possible? There was something familiar in the bearded man's face. He recognized a glimmer of the child who'd once been Matt Soule. What name did he go by now? Oh yeah, Caleb Bloom.

"So what happens next?" Caleb asked. "Call the law? Call the media? What's the move?"

Baughman glanced at the woman with the dark hair. Both she and the balding man looked uncomfortable. It was so obvious who she was. He almost couldn't believe he hadn't recognized her outside the gas station. "First, we call her father."

He looked at Eric and saw his eyes were on the water, and he was shivering hard.

"Eric, you okay?"

He didn't react immediately, but then he looked up, as if noticing Baughman was there for the first time. "Yeah. I think so. They put me in the lake."

Baughman took a step closer. "They did what?"

"Don't worry about it." He was starting to sound more like himself now. He stood up and took a step toward Baughman. "I'm not going to press charges or anything. I just want to go home."

Press charges?

Baughman swallowed hard. If these really were the kids he'd been searching out for so long, things were about to get very crazy. There would be some tough questions he'd have to answer. He needed to come clean with Eric before that happened.

He figured he'd better start by telling Eric he wasn't really an FBI agent.

He opened his mouth to speak, but something about Eric's face gave him pause. A dark speck.

"You sure you're all right, Eric?" he said. "You've got something in your eye."

PART II

SOMETHING IN YOUR EYE

14

CALEB WASN'T one for sentimentality.

He had waited his whole life to meet Eric Partin, the only one of them who'd managed to break free from Wakefield. The one Lewis referred to as "Six." He'd waited his whole life to get Eric Partin alone and show him exactly what he thought of his privileged little existence. While Eric had gone back to his life in suburban Wisconsin, the rest of them had been raised by parents they didn't know. They'd been confronted with bizarre realities their old families wouldn't have believed possible. And they'd been forced to do the awful and necessary work of living in Wakefield, Tennessee, under the shadow of the Fade.

Still, when the time came, Caleb had behaved professionally toward Eric. He'd struck him twice, but only to keep him under control and not much harder than was absolutely necessary.

He'd carried out Merle's instructions to the letter. They'd strapped Partin down, held him under for less than two minutes, and brought him back up. Then, when the task was over and there was no more need for aggression, they'd called his FBI buddy to come pick him up.

Getting dipped in the lake—seeing the Fade up close and personal—was no picnic. Caleb had never been subject to it himself, thank Christ, but Lewis had explained the experience to him in haunting detail. Still, Caleb's fantasy of meeting Eric Partin had always involved him taking a baseball bat to the guy's head, so this encounter left him feeling hollow.

After Eric and the FBI man were gone, Becky turned to Caleb. "What happens now?"

Caleb had no idea. Why should he? Why were Becky and Mikey always looking to him for answers? It pissed him off, especially on a day like today when the future was so uncertain for all of them.

He took a step toward her and flashed his most menacing grin. "What happens is you and your mentally incompetent brother go back to that house you don't own and await further instructions. And when they come? You follow them. Is that going to be a problem?"

Becky flinched, taken aback by his sudden aggression. "Geez, chill man. No, it's not going to be a problem. By the way, you're welcome for calling you when Eric showed up. Made things a bit easier, didn't it?"

Caleb couldn't argue with that. If Becky hadn't called, he would have had to find Eric himself, which would have been a real pain.

"Thank you," he said. Then, because he couldn't help it, added, "Happy?"

"Utterly delighted."

"Great. Then get gone. Merle has enough to deal with without you two moping around."

Without another word, Becky grabbed Mikey's arm and

led him off the dock. Mikey looked a little dazed from the whole experience, but he went along willingly and without complaint.

Caleb watched them go, wondering for about the millionth time what slight he'd made to God to be strapped to those two for life. Them and Lewis.

When they'd disappeared up the trail and into the woods, Caleb sighed and headed for the cabin. The same question Becky had asked hovered in his mind, and it was time to get some answers.

When he reached the cabin, he grabbed for the doorknob, then hesitated. Thinking better of it, he rapped his knuckles on the door.

"Come," a voice answered almost immediately.

Caleb stepped inside. As expected, Merle was sitting behind the massive oak desk that dominated the cabin, bent over some paperwork.

"The FBI man just left with Partin. Becky and Mikey headed home."

"Good," Merle answered without looking up.

Caleb stood there silently for a moment, waiting for further explanation, but none came. So he decided to ask his question, and he didn't have a better way to phrase it than Becky had. "What happens now?"

Merle finished scribbling for a moment, then set down his pen. He folded his hands and looked up at Caleb. "In what regard?"

Caleb gulped. It seemed he'd spent most of his life trying to get Merle's attention and not knowing what to do once he had it. Merle was a difficult man to please. And yet, he'd held the keys to the kingdom for as long as Caleb had been in Wakefield. Any path to power ran directly through him. "Well, the FBI man took our names. He knows who we are. That we were the kids taken back in the eighties."

"Correct. He's not an idiot."

"So what happens now?" Caleb repeated dumbly. "Do the press come to town? Are we going to have our old families showing up looking for us? Can we even continue our work?"

"No, probably not, and most definitely." Merle gave Caleb a thin, amused smile. "You think I wasn't planning for this? You think my fingerprints aren't on the levers that made this all happen?"

Caleb was so surprised he couldn't speak for a moment. Surprised, and also hurt. He was supposed to be Merle's protégé. Merle was supposed to be teaching him, training him to take over for him here at the lake one day. And he'd kept something this big a secret? "But the FBI man—"

"Is retired," Merle interrupted. "He's working for a private individual, not the Bureau. If his boss tells him to keep quiet about this, he will. He has no other choice. The press will not be informed. Your former families will never know. And, yes, we will be able to continue our work."

"And Eric Partin?"

"We'll find out his true character now, won't we? Maybe he shows up tomorrow and we put him to work. Or perhaps he leaves and heads home, none the wiser. If he goes that route, we'll have to decide how to respond. Maybe we let him carry his portion of the Fade for the next few years until it finally devours him. Most likely, he'll never even understand what's happening to him."

Caleb nodded, suddenly feeling a bit more chipper. Imagining Eric Partin dying alone and afraid in the slowest and worst possible way put a little spring in his step.

"Speaking of our work," Merle said, "I need you to go see Lewis. I have his next assignment."

The joy drained from Caleb as suddenly as it had come.

He left Merle's cabin and meandered down the trail through the woods, past Becky and Mikey's squat, taking his sweet time about it. Despite his pace, it wasn't long before he made it to his car, and only three minutes before he was parked at the Wakefield Motor Inn. He parked around back, figuring this was likely where Partin and the FBI man were staying. He'd prefer to avoid another awkward encounter with those two. Deciding he couldn't put it off any longer, he walked up and knocked on the door of room 114.

Despite having been a resident of Wakefield, Tennessee, since age twelve, Lewis Keller kept a room at the Wakefield Motor Inn. While it was true that he was often traveling the country on business for Merle, Caleb knew that Lewis fancied himself a rambling man. Not owning a home was his way of telling himself he hadn't put down roots. Though it would be hard for anyone to be more rooted to one place than he, Caleb, Becky and Mikey were to Wakefield.

Lewis opened the door, wearing his signature crooked smile, an expression that bordered on a smirk and annoyed Caleb to no end. His nose still bore the crook Caleb had put in it when he'd beat the shit out of him for smirking at him like that. They'd both been fourteen, and the main thing Caleb remembered about the incident was how he'd really gone for it, just pounded the kid, and how the smile had never left Lewis's face. His eyes had been filled with glee even when his face was a bloody mess, as if he were somehow getting one over on Caleb by convincing the boy to beat him senseless.

Lewis had been a weird kid, even before they'd

submerged him in the lake and put him face-to-face with the Fade.

"Hey," Caleb said gruffly. "Can I come in?"

Lewis glanced at the legal envelope tucked under Caleb's arm. Then he gestured him inside.

Caleb took a seat at the table by the window. The room was spotless, as it always was. Old Eddie at the front desk could have rented this room without the housekeeper so much as running the vacuum. Caleb doubted the other beds in this establishment were made with such precision.

Lewis sat down in the other chair and leaned toward Caleb, resting his hands on his knees. "Bossman's got a job for me?"

"Seems that way."

Caleb was about to hand the envelope over, but then he noticed the way Lewis was looking at it. It was the way a starving man might ogle a loaf of bread. Or—maybe more accurately—the way an addict might stare at a plump baggie of crystal meth. Lewis wanted the envelope, and he wanted it badly. That gave Caleb power over him. A rare thing.

As if noticing the shifting dynamic, Lewis leaned back in his seat. "Seems that way? I guess that means you don't know."

Caleb said nothing.

"Which seems a little odd from my perspective. I'd heard that old Merle was grooming you to take the throne. Teaching you the family trade, as it were. Yet here you are, passing along a sealed envelope to the black sheep himself, and you don't even know what's inside."

"I think I've got a fair idea."

"Fair idea's not the same as knowing." Lewis leaned

forward again. "So which is it, Caleb? Are you the crown prince or a delivery boy?"

"I'm the guy who's going to beat your ass if you don't put a little more respect in your voice."

Lewis gave him an appraising look up and down. "Nah. I don't think you will. Living so close to the lake has made you soft, man. Hand over the envelope."

Caleb waited another moment, then did as Lewis asked.

Lewis grabbed it and eagerly tore it open. He pulled a single, folded piece of paper out of the envelope. Unfolding it, he stared at it for nearly thirty seconds. Then he spoke a single word. "Huh."

He folded the paper and slipped it back into the envelope.

Caleb wasn't surprised that Lewis didn't share the information, but it still annoyed him.

"Thanks for the delivery. You can tell Merle I'm on it."

Lewis stood up, but Caleb didn't move. Much of what Lewis did for Merle was secret, but today, Caleb had information Lewis didn't, and he wanted to make that fact known.

"You'll never guess who I saw today."

Lewis ambled to the door and pulled it open. "You're right. Mostly because of my total lack of caring who you saw today. Now if you don't mind—"

"Eric Partin."

Lewis's eyebrows shot up in surprise at that, much to Caleb's delight. "Really? Number Six himself? Here in Wakefield?"

Caleb nodded. Now that Lewis actually wanted the information, he was less inclined to give it.

"Is this a problem for us?" Lewis asked.

"No. We handled it. Strapped him down and dipped him in the lake."

Lewis's confidence was definitely shaken now. "Did he... How'd he do?"

"Better than you," Caleb said. He stood up and moseyed to the half-open door.

"So two of us have seen the Fade up close." Lewis clapped Caleb on the arm. "Don't worry, big guy, your time will come."

"I don't need to see it. I feel it every day."

Lewis's smirk was back now, strong as ever. "Sure you do. Thanks for the delivery."

As Caleb walked back to his car, a memory of his teen years came back to him, and he remembered why he was terrified of Lewis Keller.

15

The waitress led Baughman and Eric to a booth near the back of the diner. The place was nothing fancy, but it was clean. Wakefield didn't offer a plethora of dining choices.

"Get you boys something to drink?" she asked.

Baughman ordered a Blue Moon and Eric went with a Dunkel from Yee Haw, a local brewery the waitress recommended.

When she went to fetch their drinks, Eric leaned forward and spoke softly, though he made no attempt to hide the anger on his face. "So you gonna tell me what's going on?"

Baughman looked at him for a long moment before answering. "First, let me say I'm sorry you got pulled into this."

"Me too." Eric let that hang in the air. Truth was, he was pissed, and he wasn't about to let Baughman off easy. He'd nearly died, and of all the ways he'd ever thought he might go out, being tied to a board and drowned by angry townies wasn't one of them.

Baughman stared at Eric for a long moment, his eyes

searching for some kind of absolution, but Eric gave him none.

"Okay. First thing you gotta know is I retired from the FBI a little over ten years ago. I don't want to say I was forced out, but I'd put in my time. It was made clear to me that I should be making room for the next generation."

"I'm sorry to hear that," Eric said, his voice void of emotion. "Doesn't explain why you lied to me about it. Baughman, I want the truth. Tell it to me plain, and then book me a flight out of this hellhole."

Baughman stared at him for a long moment before responding. "You sure that's what you want?"

"Am I sure I want to get away from the people who tried to drown me and told me to come back tomorrow? Yes, I'm pretty sure."

Baughman shifted in his seat. "Eric, the answers you've been waiting for your whole life are here. If you just stay a little longer, we can find them together. Besides, what do you have to go back to?"

Eric leaned forward, his teeth gritted in anger. "I have a home. Friends. That's not nothing."

There was more to it, things he wasn't ready to say to Baughman or anyone else. He'd experienced the unexplainable that day, and he was pretty sure a few more days of poking around with Baughman weren't going to get to the bottom of whatever the hell he'd seen in that lake.

The waitress reappeared and set their beers in front of them. Eric took a healthy sip of his and liked what he tasted. Baughman just stared into his glass.

"I did lie to you. I apologize for that. But one thing I never lied about was how much I cared about your case. It haunted me for years. I'd look into it in my off hours. On the weekends. Something about the situation stuck in my mind like a kernel of popcorn sticks in your teeth. But all I hit was dead end after dead end. All the way up until I retired."

Eric didn't want to ask the question, didn't want to give Baughman the satisfaction. But he couldn't help himself. "What happened then?"

"I got a phone call one day from a man named Albert Wilson. I was aware of him but we'd never spoken. His daughter was taken the same day you were. I wasn't assigned to his daughter's case, but I knew the guy who was. I got the impression Mr. Wilson was a real pain in the ass. But there was one other thing that set Wilson apart from the other parents. He had money, and lots of it."

"Let me guess. He wanted to give some of that money to you."

Baughman nodded. "He wanted to hire me. Said he liked the way I'd handled my part of the investigation and how I'd never given up, unlike his guy. How he knew this about me, I did not know. Truth was, I didn't much care. He was offering me good money, but more importantly, he was offering a chance to keep working on the case. He funded me. All I had to do was give him weekly reports."

Eric stared at the other man. For the last ten years, Baughman had privately been looking into his case. What did that mean, exactly? Had he been watching Eric? Digging into his past? For some reason, that infuriated Eric as much as the lying did. Eric held firmly to the opinion that obsessing over the past was rarely healthy. Too many people spent their lives thinking about it, talking about it, blaming it for every problem or crediting it with every success. It was better to move on. To live in the present.

And here Baughman was, digging into a thirty-year-old incident because some old man was paying him to.

"And Mrs. Crawford?" Eric asked. "I take it she never really called the FBI?"

"No. We had a tip line and offered a reward. I had strong suspicions you were held somewhere in this part of the country, based on where you were found, so we publicized it pretty heavily down here. Lots of crank calls and con artists looking to cash in, but I knew right away Mrs. Crawford was different."

Eric thought back to the conversation at Mrs. Crawford's house. Baughman had carefully guided it like the professional he was. Neither he nor Mrs. Crawford had ever mentioned the FBI. Come to think of it, that may have been part of the reason Baughman had been so nervous about letting Eric talk with her alone.

"The rest of what I told you was true," Baughman continued. "She said she could supply us the names the kidnapped children were living under now. And she said she would only give it to you. That's why I got you involved."

"That's not exactly true now, is it?" Eric asked. "I've been involved from the beginning."

Baughman's face darkened a little at that. "There's something I have to tell you, Eric. Something I've known for a long time. Ever since you were taken, in fact. I wasn't allowed to tell you when you were a kid, but now... I think I owe you this much."

Eric felt the flutter of panic rise up within him. He'd been through so much over the past few days. He'd seen things—impossible things—that had shaken him to his core. The flickering man at his window. Mikey in the bed, fading, then disappearing while his sister counted to seven. The ball of darkness in the water. Taken alone, any of these might have been explainable. Perhaps he'd been half asleep when the man appeared at his window. Perhaps the stress of being back at the house where he'd been held as a child made him see things that weren't there. Maybe the lack of oxygen had caused a hallucination in the water.

But all together?

He couldn't dismiss these things. Something impossible was happening in Wakefield, and he was part of it, whether he wanted to be or not.

Baughman's words on the dock came back to him. *You've got something in your eye.*

The first thing he'd done when he got back to Baughman's car was look in the mirror. He'd seen nothing out of the ordinary. Whatever Baughman had spotted was now gone.

He'd had just about enough trauma for one day. And now Baughman was about to add to it. Eric didn't want to know, but he found himself powerless to speak. Maybe part of him really wanted to hear it.

Baughman leaned forward and spoke in a soft voice. "Eric, you're adopted. You and all the kids that were taken that day. The way I understand it, your parents tried to go through an agency, but they were deemed too old to adopt. So they did it privately."

Eric said nothing. He wasn't sure he would be able to speak if he tried.

"The private party they went through, well, their papers were fakes. As soon as I started looking into them, I hit a dead end. Turned out that it was the same with everyone taken that day. All the parents had their own reasons for adopting privately, but all roads ended with the same dead end."

Eric took a big swallow of his beer. "So my parents... they lied to me. All my life, they lied."

Baughman wore a pained expression, like he'd been

dreading this conversation for a long time and it was going just as badly as he'd imagined it would. "They loved you, Eric. In all the conversations and interviews I had with them, that much was clear. I think they felt guilty about the way you were taken. They felt like suckers for adopting from somebody with a fake identity and ulterior motives. That's why they never told you."

There was something else here, something Baughman wasn't saying. "What do you mean by ulterior motives?"

"Eric, I have a theory. I don't think the kidnappers were taking you away. They were taking you back."

After dinner, Eric used Baughman's phone to check for flights. He was annoyed to find the first one out wasn't leaving until morning. It looked like he'd be spending another night in Wakefield.

They didn't talk much on the short drive back to the motel. Eric stared out the window, watching the town roll by. Baughman's revelations should have turned his world upside down. In fact, Eric was a bit disturbed by his own reaction, which had been little more than numbness. His parents—the ones who'd raised him since he was a baby—were dead and gone. Eric had stood by his father's side as the man took his last breath. His mother had died in a car accident, but Eric had rushed to the hospital the moment he'd gotten the call, only to arrive after she'd already passed.

What did it matter if those people weren't his flesh and blood? They were his family in every way that mattered.

Baughman had again offered to let Eric stay in Wakefield for a while, even offered to pay for his stay out of his own pocket. He believed he could help Eric find his birth parents.

Eric had only considered the offer for a moment before rejecting it. This town and everything it represented had nothing to do with him. It was just something bad that had happened to him when he was a kid. He wanted to get back to his old life as quickly as possible. He'd keep his plane ticket for tomorrow morning, head back to Wisconsin, and put this bizarre chapter behind him. Maybe he'd think about it every few months over a late-night glass of bourbon, but nothing more than that.

When he reached his motel room door, he found Becky waiting there, sitting on the ground, her back to the brick wall.

She stood up when she spotted him, carefully smoothing her jeans.

"You come to finish the job?" he asked as he approached.

She blinked hard, as if she didn't understand the question. "What? No, I... I forgot to give you this."

She held out his phone.

"Thanks." The word came out automatically as he took the phone, his Midwestern upbringing rearing its overly-polite head. He hated himself just a little for thanking the woman who'd almost murdered him for returning his stolen property.

"Look, about earlier. I should explain."

He crossed his arms, an amused smile on his face. "I would like that very much."

"Ever since we were kids—after we were taken, I mean —we always heard about you. I guess we saw you as the one who got away. We were jealous, like maybe if you hadn't left, things would have been different for all of us."

"That's not much of an explanation for why you nearly drowned me."

"No, I guess it isn't." She hesitated, then gestured to his phone. "You should really put a passcode on that thing."

"Thanks for the tip," he said dryly.

"That woman in the picture, the one on the mower, is that your wife?"

Eric paused before answering. Was the woman who'd tried to drown him now hitting on him? "No. Ex-wife."

"Nice that you're still on good enough terms to keep her picture on your phone."

He waited, saying nothing.

"What are you going to do now?" Becky asked.

"I'm going home."

She paused, looking him up and down in a way that wasn't so much checking him out as appraising him, as if she was trying to determine if he was up for some challenge that lay before him. "That's not a good idea."

"Oh? Why not?"

"Well, for one thing, Merle told you to come back tomorrow. You don't show, he's not going to be happy."

"Then I guess he won't be happy."

"You don't understand. There are things... things Merle should explain. Stay a few more days. Hear him out."

"I went thirty years not knowing who kidnapped me or why. I've learned to live without answers. I find getting on with your life tends to solve more problems than dwelling on the past does." He looked into her dark eyes and saw what appeared to be genuine concern there. On the other hand, this was the woman who'd stolen his phone a few hours earlier. "Two questions, and please answer honestly. You owe me that much."

She nodded. Not exactly a promise, but it would have to do.

"Am I in danger in Wakefield?"

Her answer was immediate. "Very much so."

He hadn't expected that much honesty, even though he'd asked for it. The second question would be more difficult. He wasn't sure exactly how to phrase it. "When I was down in that lake, I saw something. A presence. It wasn't natural. If I stay in Wakefield, is there anything I can do to help the people here? To stop that thing in the lake?"

"Absolutely not."

He sighed. "Thanks for your honesty. I'm going home."

Becky reach up and touched his arm, stopping him from walking away. "He won't let you leave."

"Let him try and stop me."

She stood her head. "Don't say I didn't warn you."

He started to turn, but she held onto his arm.

"One more thing. If it doesn't go how I expect and you make it home, you might have questions. Things you want to talk about. Whatever. I put my number in your phone. Just in case."

He let out a sharp laugh. "You stole my phone just to give me your number?"

Her cheeks reddened. "No, it's not like that. I'm not looking for a date. There aren't many people like us. You might want to talk."

"People like us? That's a really weird thing to say."

"Yeah, I guess it is." She gave him one last look. "It was nice to meet you, Eric. I'm sorry for how things went down. Stay safe."

With that, she turned and walked away.

Eric watched her go, then unlocked his room and stepped inside.

A sudden, powerful urge to be rid of this town and everything to do with it washed over him. Its weird, sick presence seemed to cling to him as strongly as the smell of the lake water. He hurried to the shower and turned it as hot as it would go.

When he finally stepped out of the shower ten minutes later, he picked up his phone, opened his contacts, and deleted Becky's number.

16

Baughman dropped Eric off an hour and a half before his flight. In the small regional airport, this was plenty of time. He was through security and sitting at his gate in less than ten minutes. He didn't stop looking over his shoulder for Merle or one of his goons until he was safely on the plane.

The flight to Atlanta was uneventful, and he slept fitfully on the half-full plane, his dreams filled with turbulent visions of lake monsters. The flight from Atlanta to Milwaukee was completely full. He had an aisle seat toward the back of the plane.

He'd just settled in and was closing his eyes, anticipating another round of low-quality sleep, when the man next to him spoke.

"Headed home? Or leaving home behind?"

Eric glanced at the man. He had lively blue eyes and brown hair cropped close on the sides but piled high and carefully styled on the top. "Headed home. You?"

"Leaving home," the man replied. "My childhood home, anyway."

"Visiting family?" Eric wasn't sure why he asked the

question. Normally, he avoided talking to others on flights. The rare conversation he did have was short and to the point. It wasn't that he was against meeting new people in principle. It was more that he didn't like flying. He considered the experience something to be endured. That attitude didn't lead to the friendliest of conversations.

"No. My family's all dead and gone."

"Sorry to hear it."

The man gave him a crooked, half-smile. "Obviously you didn't know my family." He chuckled at his own joke. "In truth, there's nothing for me back there. I still like to stop by from time to time. The place seems to have seeped into my bones."

Eric let that hang in the air without a response. As the plane taxied down the runway, he got his paperback out of his bag. The book was a thriller with an unlikely mistaken identity premise. The story did its job, and Eric found himself turning pages for the next hour.

He was mid-chapter when a thought struck him, hard and fast like a punch to the solar plexus. Wakefield, Tennessee was his hometown. Something about the way the idea settled in his mind made it seem much more real than it had when Baughman had conveyed the same thought to him the previous day. Eric had a family he'd never met. His birth parents might still be alive. He might have siblings. Cousins. Aunts and uncles. A whole alternative life he'd never known.

And who were these parents?

One obvious candidate leapt to his mind—Marsha Crawford. She'd demanded to meet him in exchange for handing over the list of names. Her cover story, that she'd wanted to meet the man her husband had kidnapped, suddenly seemed less likely than the alternative. Maybe she wanted to meet her son.

With that realization came another. His birth parents had given him up not once, but twice. They'd allowed him to be adopted by the Partin family. Then they'd given him back to the Partins a second time after his kidnapping.

Why?

Why had Eric been returned when the other children were not? Was there something wrong with him? Something they'd seen that they didn't like? He thought back to that day in the room on the third floor. The thin man and the ghostly presence. He felt in his guts that the decision to let him go back had something to do with that day. But what?

The maddening thing was that the answers were all possibly within his grasp. He could ask these questions to Marsha Crawford or to Becky or to any number of people in Wakefield. And yet, here he was, flying away from Tennessee as fast as this airplane could carry him. For the first time, he wondered if leaving had been the right decision.

He pushed the thoughts away. Of course it had been the right decision. What did any of that have to do with the person he was? It was all in the past. Like an asbestos-filled attic, it was best to not go jumping around kicking up dust in there.

Eric set his book on his lap, his concentration broken. He knew he wouldn't be able to get back into the story. No sooner had he set the book down then he felt a sudden, shooting pain in his right eye.

It started near the front of his eye and shot back all the way into his brain. It was a stabbing sensation so intense that his hand went instinctively to his face, and he let out a grunt of pain.

"You all right, buddy?" the man in the seat next to him asked.

The pain continued, growing into a burning sensation now. It was as if a column of fire had been inserted through his eye all the way to the back of his head. He touched his face again, sure his hand would come away bloody, but it didn't.

Was this some sort of migraine? He'd never experienced one before, but perhaps the stress of the last few days had brought one on.

The pain spread, the column of fire in his brain growing wider and wider. He wanted to scream. Instead, he unbuckled his seatbelt and struggled to his feet. The bathroom was only a few rows away, and he staggered his way there, holding onto the backs of seats as he went, doing his best not to bump the people sitting in them but not entirely successful in the effort.

When he reached the bathroom, he was relieved to find it unoccupied. He slid the door open and stumbled inside. The moment the bathroom door latched he felt a tiny bit better. The pain was like a living thing in his head now, and he wanted to be alone with it.

After a moment, he realized why he'd come to the bathroom. Slowly, he raised his head and looked into the mirror.

His body went cold when he saw his reflection.

There was a dark spot on his eye. To call it a speck, as Baughman had, hardly seemed accurate now. It was nearly the size of his pupil, off-center and a little lower. And it was pulsating, same as the thin man's had so many years before.

Same as the thing under the water yesterday.

Each pulse sent a wave of electricity burning into his

brain. His hands were shaking now, and he gripped the tiny sink to try to stop them. The pain was bad. Not as bad as it had been in the lake, but bad enough that part of him wondered if he was having an aneurysm or something.

A terrible thought struck him. He saw an image in his mind. Mikey lying in the bed and flickering out of existence. When he disappeared, the blanket had fallen to the mattress, and he'd reappeared on top of it.

If whatever was happening to Eric was the same thing that had happened to Mike, if he was going to flicker out of existence as Mikey had, he was in a world of trouble. He was on an airplane, thirty thousand feet off the ground. If he disappeared and reappeared a few seconds later in the same location, the plane would be gone. He'd reappear in the empty sky. And then he'd fall.

In the mirror, Eric saw his brow was damp with sweat and his shirt was clinging to his wet chest. "Get it together, man. Get it together."

He glanced again at the pulsating dark circle in his eye. It seemed to have a hypnotic effect, like snowflakes falling on a highway, and he dared not stare at it for too long. Maybe the hypnosis would cause him to flicker out of existence. Or maybe he'd just temporarily lose his mind the way Mikey had seemed to do.

A knock on the bathroom door interrupted his thoughts. "Sir, are you all right in there?" a female voice asked.

For a moment, he was confused. Then he realized he was speaking.

No, not speaking. *Shouting.* "Get it together! Get it together! Get it together!"

His mouth snapped shut, cutting off the mantra. He took a deep breath, in through the nose and out through the mouth.

"I'm fine. Thanks. I'm fine." The lie rang hollow in his ears as he splashed water on his face and forced himself to go back to his seat.

When he sat down, he put his head in his hands. Maybe he could sleep for the rest of the flight. Or at least pretend to sleep. The light hurt his eyes. Wasn't that a sign of a migraine? Even if it was, he was fairly certain that a pulsating black dot on the eyeball and a potentially slipping grasp on reality were not.

They'd be landing soon. Then at least he wouldn't have to worry about flickering out of the plane. One less thing.

"Feel better?" his neighbor asked.

Eric gritted his teeth. The last thing he wanted was conversation. He was barely holding it together as it was. "A little. Thanks. Just a headache."

"That'll happen," the man said. "Especially now. You'll get headaches, Six. Headaches like you won't believe."

Six?

Eric suddenly realized there was something about that voice. Something familiar. Like a half-remembered dream.

No, not a dream. Something he'd woken to at his window. He pried his hands away from his face and turned to look at his neighbor.

The man wore a guilty smile, like he'd been caught somewhere he wasn't supposed to be. He looked quite different. Instead of a ratty old tee shirt, he wore a stylish button down. His hair was combed and styled, and he looked completely sane. Very different from the way he'd looked standing outside Eric's window at three in the morning.

17

"I wish I could tell you some secret to make it easier, Six. But everyone has to find their own path. Caleb stays close to the water. Becky's good at suppressing it, but when an attack happens, hoo boy, people get hurt. Mikey's straight-up bad at dealing with it. Poor guy spends half his life lying in bed wriggling in pain. Let's hope you don't go that route."

Eric stared wide-eyed, his mouth half open, trying to comprehend what this man was talking about.

"Me?" the man continued. "I'm a cutter. As you saw the other night. Probably not the healthiest way of dealing with things, but the pain does bring a kind of clarity. It allows me to roam a bit. I can't stand being cooped up in Wakefield like the others. I guess I've got a wanderlust spirit. That's what Merle says, anyway. I apologize for the way I acted last time you saw me. I'd never been away from Wakefield that long. I started getting a little squirrely in the head."

In his mind, Eric ran through the list of names Marsha Crawford had given him. "You're Lewis."

Lewis chuckled and nodded. "And you're lucky number six. The one who got away."

Eric felt a twinge of annoyance. It wasn't like he'd enacted some great plan to escape his kidnappers. They'd just decided to let him go. He didn't know why and might never. But the way Becky had talked to him, and now the way this man did, it was like they blamed him. Like they were angry at him for leaving them behind. It was like some twisted, reverse version of survivor's guilt. Victim's anger.

And so what if they were angry? What difference did it make to him? All he wanted was to go home, resume his normal life, and put this bizarre incident behind him.

And now, for the next twenty minutes or so, he was stuck sitting next to one of his fellow kidnapping victims. What was it Baughman had called them? The Wakefield Five.

As much as he wanted to put this all behind him, he'd never get another chance to talk openly and honestly with someone who knew more about this situation than he did.

Lewis was his captive audience.

"What the hell were you doing outside my window that night?" he asked.

There was a long pause, so long that Eric wasn't sure Lewis would answer. But then he did. "I guess you could say I was putting the first domino in place. Making sure that when Baughman showed up and asked you to come to Wakefield, he had something to bump up against. I'm an agent of change, you see."

Lewis said it with such earnestness that Eric almost laughed. "And why did you care if I came to Wakefield?"

Lewis shrugged. "I guess I felt like it was time for you to carry your share of the load. Besides, my boss cared, so I was sort of obligated to go with it."

Another bizarre statement. Eric squirmed, trying to figure out what to ask next.

Lewis beat him to the punch. "I guess you're wondering

why they put you through that whole submersion exercise. Tied you up, dropped you in the water. All that."

"The question had crossed my mind."

Lewis chuckled. "I'll bet. Probably crossed your mind when your head was three feet underwater. When you were half-drowned and a living sphere of darkness was swimming at your face. I've been there, man. Not a fun experience."

Eric suddenly remembered something Becky had said on the dock just before they put him in the water. *He isn't going to end up like Lewis, is he?*

"The others are big on secrets," Lewis continued. "Everything's gotta be this complicated ordeal. You show up at old Merle's cabin, I'll bet he'd make you sign a blood oath before he'd even point you toward the pisser. Me? I don't believe in all that."

"Okay." Eric's voice sounded thick in his ears. The headache was as bad as ever, but he was able to ignore it now. He wanted to hear what Lewis had to say. "Tell me."

"Well, some of it I guess you already know. Other parts, you might have figured out. But there's something wrong with Wakefield, Tennessee. Something wrong with some of the people born there. The old joke is there's something in the water. As you saw for yourself, that's mighty accurate."

"What do you mean by *something wrong*?"

"They're infected, Six. The ones that are don't live that long. Life expectancy is maybe fifteen, if they're lucky."

Eric frowned. That couldn't be right. "And yet here we sit."

Lewis grinned and spread out his hands. "Here we sit. And we've got old Merle to thank for that. See, he came up with a plan."

The pieces were coming together in Eric's mind. "Send us away. Have us adopted."

"You're not as dumb as they say, Six. See, Merle knew it was that weird thing in the water that was causing the trouble. It doesn't affect everyone, and it never affects people who move to town later in life, like your pal Marsha Crawford. Seems to be passed on in certain families. The kids are born infected, but Merle theorized that prolonged exposure at a young age caused it to worsen. If they sent us away when we were young, maybe we'd have a chance of living longer."

Eric considered that. Putting it that way gave him a new perspective. His birth parents hadn't been trying to get rid of him; they'd been trying to save him. "The people who stay... What happens to them? How do they die?"

"They call it the Fade. It affects everyone a bit differently. But the end result is the same. The darkness in the water feeds the infection inside of them, making it grow. The flicker gets worse. It's usually a heart attack that gets them. The old ticker can't handle the stress of the nearly constant fading in and out of existence." He shot Eric a grin. "As you might imagine, most of us would prefer to avoid that fate."

Eric blinked hard, trying to understand what Lewis was telling him. No, that wasn't quite right. He understood what was said on an intellectual level. The struggle was more about believing it. "That doesn't explain why they kidnapped us back. I get why they'd send us away, but why bring us back to the source of the trouble?"

"The Fade stays dormant until the kids are nine or ten, then it becomes active. They get a little speck in their eye. It's small at first, not like the one you've got now. Most never even notice it. So they brought us all back from our cozy little families to give us a test. Most of us failed the test. You did not."

A memory flashed in Eric's mind: the thin man in the chair saying, *Keep your eyes focused on me.*

"The Fade was active in us, but not in you. You got lucky."

"That's why they hate me." Eric now understood why Mikey, Becky, and especially Caleb, disliked him so intensely.

"Don't take it personal. They're just jealous."

"I still don't understand. So you had the Fade. So what? Why keep you in Wakefield?"

"Because once the disease is active, you've got a real Catch-22 situation on your hands. You stay away from Wakefield, the Fade grows weak and dies, taking you with it. But if you stay in Wakefield, the Fade grows stronger and eventually kills you. It gets you either way, but you get a longer life staying close to the source in Wakefield, so that's how most people play it." He took a sip of Coke out of his plastic cup and then wedged it back between his knees.

Looking past Lewis out the window, Eric saw they were nearly on the ground now. He could clearly identify the cars and trucks rolling down the highway.

"There's no easy answer. Merle tried a number of solutions, but most of them didn't end well. Sending us away until the Fade became active helped. Here we are on the far side of forty and all still walking the earth and contributing to society in our own little ways. It was an experiment worth repeating." He reached into his jacket pocket and pulled out a small notebook. He began to flip the pages. "All I can tell you, Six, is find your own way to cope with it. I'd suggest going back to Wakefield and living the rest of your miserable existence there, but your call."

"Wait, you said the Fade isn't active in me."

"I said it *wasn't* back then. It certainly is now. I can practically smell it coming off you."

Eric suddenly wanted to punch Lewis, irritated with his smug way of talking around things rather than saying them right out. And yet, he was giving Eric more information than he'd gotten from anyone else. "That doesn't explain why they dunked me."

"The way I figure it, Merle knew you must have a strong resistance, seeing as you managed to remain uninfected until now. So they decided to give you a concentrated dose, right at the source to see if you could withstand it." He gave Eric a wink. "Guess you couldn't."

"Lucky me," Eric said glumly. "They said something about having done the same to you."

Lewis's face darkened. "Yes. I have a strong resistance too. Not as strong as you, apparently, but I can go farther from Wakefield than the others. So they gave me the dip. It wasn't my finest day. I screamed for hours afterwards. I guess you could say I went a little bit insane." He shot Eric a grin. "Some might argue I stayed that way."

"So is there any way to get rid of it? What do we do?"

"The best we can, Six. The best we can. But it's not all bad. Some of us have learned to control it a little. Hell, Merle's pushing sixty-five and he's still kicking. No one can use the Fade as well as him."

Eric felt a shiver at that. "When I was a kid, when they were holding me in Wakefield, Merle came to see me. He did something... I saw two of him. A ghostly version and the real thing. Is that... was that the Fade?"

"Don't know. I expect it must have been, though I've never seen anything like that."

Eric felt a jolt as the plane touched down and began to slow.

Lewis flipped to another page of his notebook. "Say, you ever heard of a place called North Prairie?"

"Sure. It's not far from here. Why?"

"I've got business there. Merle sends me on these little retrieval missions now."

The chill came again, stronger now. Eric suddenly understood something Lewis had said. *An experiment worth repeating.*

"Lewis... what are you doing in North Prairie?"

"I'm doing my job. Can't say that I mind. It's challenging work, but I'm good at it, if you'll forgive the lack of modesty. Thanks to my skill with the Fade, what used to take three men now only takes one. Sometimes the parents have to die, but many times they don't. Either way, Merle gets his kid, and I get the satisfaction of a job well done." Lewis's finger grazed the paper as he tried to find the spot. "This time I'm retrieving a young lady named Tonya Barrington."

Eric's heart was racing and he felt a thick lump in his throat. "Retrieving. They did it again? They gave up more kids for adoption and now they're going to take them back?"

Lewis smiled up at him. The plane was taxiing slowly down the runway now. It wouldn't be long before they reached the gate. "Six, you don't know the half of it. They've got so many kids out there now; it's going to take me years to bring them all home." He let out a soft chuckle. "Guess I'd better get to it."

And suddenly, his seat was empty. Lewis was gone.

Eric drew a sharp breath and tried to stave off his growing panic. He looked up the aisle and back behind him, but there was no sign of Lewis.

Then something outside the window caught his eye. A man casually strolling down the runway away from the plane.

It may have been a trick of the light, but Eric was almost certain he saw the man flicker.

18

Eric watched the man go, unable to move. He'd hoped he was leaving all this weird shit behind him. The headache, whose source he knew was the dreadful dot in his eye, was terrifying, but he could power through it; and maybe he'd figured out a way to survive. But this? A man with supernatural abilities threatening to kidnap a child? This was something Eric could not ignore.

The option that immediately leapt to mind was to simply wait. After all, he knew where Lewis was taking Tonya Barrington. He could have the cops or the FBI—the real one this time—waiting for Lewis in Wakefield when he arrived with the stolen child.

He didn't consider that option long. For one thing, Lewis had mentioned the possibility of killing the parents. But almost as importantly, being stolen from her home would leave a lasting scar for Tonya. Eric knew that for a fact.

There was no way he was letting another kid experience what he'd gone through. No way.

He turned back to the window and saw Lewis was gone. Had he ducked behind something or faded from existence?

Eric cursed himself through gritted teeth. He should have called the flight attendant over the moment he'd spotted Lewis walking the tarmac. No, he couldn't convince her that the man teleported to the pavement, but he could have pointed Lewis out. He'd bet that in this day of enhanced security and three-ounce travel liquid limits, an unauthorized man on the runway would have caused alarm. Maybe they'd have thrown Lewis in jail and maybe not. But either way, it would have slowed him down a little.

Eric sighed. No use thinking about what he should have or could have done. He needed to take action now. And the best way to do that was probably to find this Tonya Barrington before Lewis did.

Opening the Chrome app on his phone, he searched 'Tonya Barrington, North Prairie, Wisconsin.' He quickly scanned the results but didn't see anything promising. There was a Barrington Construction in North Prairie. Possibly owned by Tonya's parents or grandparents? He made note of it for later.

The fact that he found absolutely nothing about Tonya worried Eric. What if Lewis had been lying? What if Tonya Barrington was a name he'd made up to throw Eric off his trail? Weren't all kids online these days, posting about every aspect of their lives? Eric had no idea, but that was the impression he'd gotten from some of his grumpy employees.

But why would Lewis bring up the kidnapping if he was going to lie about it? He hadn't sounded like a man who was lying. He'd sounded like a man issuing a challenge. It was as if he wanted Eric to try to stop him.

Eric cleared the word 'Tonya' from his search bar, leaving only 'Barrington, North Prairie, Wisconsin.' Then he hit search again. This time, the results were much more promising. Along with the construction company, he found three names. Sarah Barrington, and Glen and Tammy Barrington.

He quickly navigated to WhitePages.net and searched for Glen and Tammy Barrington. An address and phone number appeared. His index figure hovered over the phone number for a moment. Then he tapped it, placing the call.

The phone rang twice before a male voice answered. "Hello?"

"Hi, is Tonya there?" Eric spoke quickly, acting on instinct. It didn't strike him until after he'd spoke that an adult man calling for a young girl might seem odd.

"No Tonya here. Think you've got the wrong number, pal."

The line clicked, disconnecting the call before Eric could speak again. He flipped back to WhitePages.net and searched for Sarah Barrington. No results.

"Damn it," he muttered out loud.

On a whim, he opened his Facebook app and searched for Sarah Barrington there. A long list of women with that name appeared on his screen. He had to click to the third page before he found the one from North Prairie. But there she was, a pretty brunette in her late forties. And her profile was public, complete with phone number.

He was about to click the phone number when he thought of something—if his name appeared on Sarah Barrington's caller id, she'd have a record of him. Instead of clicking the number, he copied it and flipped over to his phone keypad. He dialed *67. As a boss whose work-ethically challenged employees sometimes ducked his calls, he knew all about blocking his number. He knew it wasn't perfect—surely the police or the phone company could still retrieve the number —but at least his name wouldn't pop up on her phone.

He pasted Sarah Barrington's number and clicked the call button. A woman answered mid-way through the third ring.

"Hello?"

"Hi, is Tonya there?"

There was a long pause. "Who is this?"

Eric's mind went blank. Why the hell hadn't he anticipated that question? He said the first thing that came to mind. "This is Tonya's teacher."

The woman's voice was cold when she spoke again. "No, it isn't. I know my daughter's teachers."

Eric considered hanging up. After all, he'd confirmed that Sarah Barrington was Tonya's mother. That's what he'd needed to know, right? Tonya Barrington existed and she lived in North Prairie. But the woman's next words gave him pause.

"Who are you, really? Talk now or I'm calling the police."

Eric knew what he had to do. He looked around, making sure the people near him on the plane weren't paying attention. They were all occupied on their own phones.

He lowered his voice, both in volume and pitch. "You're right to be concerned, Sarah. I'm not Tonya's teacher. In fact, she doesn't even know me. But she will soon. I'm coming for her."

"What?" Sarah's voice had a fragile, panicked quality that almost broke Eric's heart.

"That's right. See, I know everything about you and Tonya. I've been watching. I know where you live. The car you drive. Your schedule. You think you keep her safe, but you don't. Why, just last week, I walked by you two and my fingers brushed up against her hair as I passed." He swallowed hard before continuing. "I can take her any time. And

I'm going to. Say your goodbyes. And tell Tonya I'll see her soon."

He ended the call. Hunched over in his seat, he wanted to vomit. His hands were shaking as he put his phone in his pocket, and a thin layer of sweat covered his forehead. What he'd done had been good. It had been for a purpose. Yet, he still felt like the scum of the earth. The sound in that woman's voice when he'd threatened her daughter—that strange combination of primal fear, disbelief, and rising anger—Eric knew he'd never forget it.

It must have been how his own mother had sounded after he'd been taken to Wakefield. Now he was inflicting her pain on someone else.

No, not inflicting, he reminded himself. Protecting. A little fear and pain now would stop the much bigger pain she'd feel if Lewis actually got to her daughter. Still, this knowledge was head-level. His body was physically revolted at what he'd done.

The worst part was that he wasn't finished yet. Yes, Sarah Barrington had sounded upset. And she might be the type to be prompted into action by a single phone call. She might contact the police. Change her routine. Keep a more careful watch over Tonya. On the other hand, she might not. As the minutes and hours passed, the reality of the threat might fade for her. She might explain it away as a cruel prank. After all, she'd never experienced anything like that, had she? Wouldn't it be easier to believe that some teenager with a deep voice was playing a trick on her rather than believing someone was actually after Tonya?

Eric didn't know which response was more likely, and he couldn't take the chance. But when he took the next step, he wanted to be somewhere quiet. Somewhere alone where he could play the role more effectively.

He waited impatiently in his seat as the plane sat at the gate for what felt like an hour. Then the cabin door opened, and there was yet another long wait as the passengers in front of him got their bags from the overhead compartments and made their way out the door. His headache was back, stronger than before, but he tried to ignore it. This wasn't the kind of situation where he could call in sick. Young Tonya Barrington needed his help.

As he waited, he fired off a quick text to Donnie: *Hey, I don't need a ride after all. I'm going to hang in Milwaukee for a couple days.*

The reply was almost immediate. *Milwaukee? You meet a chick on the plane or something?*

I'll explain later.

The response took a bit longer this time, and it was brief when it arrived. *K. Talk soon.*

Eric sighed as he slipped the phone back into his pocket. He hated lying to Donnie, but the last thing he wanted was to pull him into this.

When it was his turn to deplane, he stood up and slid into the aisle. The woman across from him took one look at him and smiled sympathetically. "Nervous flyer?"

Eric did his best imitation of an aw-shucks grin. "Is it that obvious?"

"You're just a little pale, is all."

He nodded politely but didn't continue with the conversation. He'd have to improve his poker face if he wanted to make it very far in this challenge Lewis had set up for him.

When he stepped into the terminal, he made a beeline for the car rental desk. He picked a Toyota Corolla. In his mind, it was about the least conspicuous car in existence. For a moment, he considered asking the man at the rental counter if he could use his phone. The idea of placing this next call from an airport phone was mighty appealing. In the end, he didn't do it. His performance was important, and he couldn't say what he needed to say with this Alamo guy staring at him and listening to every word.

When he reached his Corolla, he drove to the cellphone lot. Then he parked and searched for the North Prairie police station's non-emergency number. He dialed *67—knowing it would probably be useless—and called the station.

"North Prairie Police." The voice was male, gruff, and seemed a bit on the older side.

Eric took a deep breath and let it out in a big blast of air, doing his best to sound panicked. "Yes, I... I need to report a crime. One that's going to happen, I mean."

There was a pause. "Okay. I can help you with that. What's your name, sir?"

"No names!" Eric nearly shouted. He wanted to sound like a man on the edge. A man who might hang up at any moment.

"Okay, no names. I got you." The officer's voice was a bit softer now, like a man trying to calm a wild animal. "What would you like to tell me?"

"I can't... I can't say how I know. I just do. There's a man, a very bad man named Lewis Keller. He's about five eight. Forty-two years old. Brown hair. He's coming to North Prairie, and he's going to kidnap a little girl named Tonya Barrington."

Another pause. "Tonya Barrington. Got it. What else can you tell me?"

"Isn't that enough? A girl's in danger!"

"I understand. Maybe if you could come in and we could talk face-to-face—"

"No!" Eric shouted. "She's in danger. He's going to kill her mother and take her. You have to protect them!"

Eric tapped the End button and stared at the black screen. He wasn't shaking as he had after the call with Sarah. On the contrary, he was exhilarated. He half expected they'd trace the number and call him back. If so, he'd just ignore the call. Things were underway now. No use worrying about what might happen. He needed to move.

Pulling out of the cell phone lot, he angled the Corolla onto the road and started toward North Prairie.

19

After Baughman dropped Eric off at the airport, he had an hour to kill. He decided to go to Rook Mountain, a slightly larger town that was east of the airport, rather than north like Wakefield. He'd worked a case in Rook Mountain a few years back, a weird thing involving a cult leader, some mass delusions, and more than a few things the FBI, Homeland Security, and a dozen other agencies hadn't been able to explain in their reports.

Most of his memories of the experience weren't pleasant, but there was one aspect of Rook Mountain he looked back on with great fondness: the pizza.

He made it to Leon's Pizza at 11:04, and though the sign said it opened at eleven a.m., the door was still locked and the place was dark. A young woman unlocked the door a few minutes later and ushered him inside. As she poured him a glass of water, he spotted a tattoo on the inside of her wrist. A broken clock. This woman had been one of the Zedheads, Baughman realized, a member of the cult that had held this town hostage. Still, that was a long time ago, and he believed everyone deserved a second chance. Plus, he was very hungry.

He made it halfway through his 'Trail Man' pizza—mushroom, peppers, and about eight meats—before he glanced at his watch and saw he needed to head out. The pizza had been just as good as he'd remembered, but he'd definitely feel it later. His stomach didn't let him enjoy such things without consequences these days.

Mr. Wilson was waiting on the sidewalk when Baughman pulled up. He had his arms crossed, his roller bag next to him, and he did not look happy.

Baughman pulled up beside him, threw it in park and hopped out.

"Hey, welcome to Tennessee. Good flight?"

Wilson nodded briskly. "It was fine." He placed his bag in the open trunk and climbed into the passenger seat without further comment.

Neither of them spoke again until they were back on the road and headed toward Wakefield. Then Wilson said, "Any updates since last night?"

Baughman thought a moment. He still hadn't decided exactly how much to tell Mr. Wilson about Eric and what the others had done to him at the lake. On the one hand, he was out here on Mr. Wilson's dime, so he owed him transparency in any matters related to the case. On the other, he owed something to Eric, too. Maybe something deeper than what he owed Wilson.

At the same time, there were some things he *had* to reveal.

"I saw your daughter last night."

Wilson looked over sharply. "You spoke to her? How?"

"Well, Eric went for a walk and ran into Mikey—that's

Colin James. I guess he called the others, and they all met out at the lake. Had a little chat."

"How nice for them," Wilson said. "And Rachel? How did she seem?"

Baughman adjusted his hands on the wheel, considering how to answer that question. He figured he'd leave out the part where she'd stolen his wallet and wristwatch. At least for now. "She seemed good. I don't know, she seemed like a normal woman in her early forties."

There was a long silence. Then Wilson asked, "Did she seem happy?"

Baughman let that hang in the air a moment. "Honestly, Mr. Wilson, I saw your daughter for all of three minutes. I didn't get to probe deeply into her psyche. But yeah, I guess she came off as happy enough."

"She'd have to be, wouldn't she?" His voice was quieter now, and he stared absently out the window. It was almost as if he'd forgotten Baughman was there. "She'd have to be to live her entire life here and never even try to get in touch. Not even a note to let us know she was alive. When I think of all the stress she could have saved us. Her mother in particular. You know, that woman never had a decent night's sleep after the kidnapping. Not a single one. She was always waiting for the phone to ring or a knock at the door. Always expecting her daughter to come home."

Baughman swallowed hard. He'd met more than his share of parents of kidnapped children. They all had their own ways of reacting, their own little quirks for handling the agony. But one thing was consistent—they were all screwed up in a very major way.

Wilson turned and looked at Baughman. "Who does that? Who doesn't let their parents know they're alive? We kept the same phone number for thirty years, just hoping she'd call it. Why didn't she?"

"We don't know the things she's been through. They might have brainwashed her. Maybe convinced her something bad would happen to you and Mrs. Wilson if she ever reached out." He shrugged. "It's just a guess, based on nothing. There's only one person who can answer that question for certain. So why don't we go ask her?"

Mr. Wilson perked up a bit at that. He was quiet the rest of the car ride. Contemplative, but not sullen. Baughman let him sit in silence as they entered the little town of Wakefield. He hadn't been hired to give Mr. Wilson therapy; he'd been hired to find his daughter. And on that front, he'd succeeded.

BECKY ALMOST DIDN'T ANSWER when the doorbell rang. She was on the third floor, sitting in Mikey's room—the one with three locks on the door—reading a book and waiting for him to come home. She wanted to put the weirdness of the past few days behind her.

The sound startled her. She and Mikey didn't get many visitors, and the few that they did get—Caleb and Merle for example—weren't big on doorbells. They were more the let-themselves-in types. In the end, her curiosity got the better of her. She set her book down and padded down the stairs to see who had rung the bell.

She eased the door open and spotted the FBI man first, which made her instantly regret the decision to answer. She figured he was probably there for his wallet and watch, and she'd have no choice but to hand them over. Then she saw the other man, and she immediately forgot about Baughman.

He was thirty pounds heavier than she remembered, and his hair was mostly gone now, but that face was unmistakable. She'd sat on his lap, staring up at that face as he read her bedtime stories every night. He'd been her hero and her best friend, and she'd been absolutely certain she'd never see him again. Now he was standing at her front door.

"Dad?" Her voice came out weak and choked with emotion.

Through the screen door, she saw tears spring to his eyes.

"Rachel." He pulled the door open and moved toward her so quickly it was almost alarming. He threw his arms around her and pulled her close in a fierce hug. "I spent so long looking for you, girl. So long. And here you are!"

Her first instinct was to recoil. No one had hugged her like that in a very long time. But then the smell of his aftershave hit her, and the memories came back even stronger and more viscerally than before. Tears filled her eyes, too. "Dad, what did you... how'd you find me."

He released her, and took a step back, smiling as he looked into her face, drinking in her features. "Mr. Baughman works for me. He helped find you." He wiped at his eyes with the back of one hand. "Can I come in and talk?"

"Of course."

"I'll let you two catch up," Baughman said. He tossed the key to the other man. "I think I'll walk back to the motel. Nice day for it."

"Thank you, Baughman," Wilson said, his voice thick with emotion.

Becky led her father into the sparse living room. She

took a seat in the room's only chair, leaving the couch for him.

"Rachel," he said. "Before we get any further, I have to tell you something. About your mother."

"I heard." Becky had a Google alert set up on both her parents, and she'd received an email when the obituary appeared online. The news had hit her hard, especially the optimistic line, *She is survived by her husband Albert, 68, and her daughter Rachel, 39.* They had no proof she was alive, and yet they'd believed strongly enough to put it in the obituary. "I was very sorry to hear it. Are you doing okay?"

Wilson shrugged. "It was difficult. I only wish we'd found you while your mother was still alive." He paused. "Are you all right, Rachel? Healthy, I mean?"

A bit of reality came rushing back at that question. Because she wasn't healthy. In fact, she was pretty far from healthy. The Fade ran through every cell of her being. And while she was better at suppressing it than Mikey was, she knew it would be just as deadly for her as it was for him. The headaches had been growing recently, and she knew its presence was taking its toll on her body.

But she couldn't tell her father any of that.

"I'm fine. And I go by Becky now. Not Rachel."

"Ah." He tried to hide it, but she could see that hit him hard. She was rejecting the name he'd given her. "Becky, then. Listen, I don't mean to come in here and jump right into... but I have to ask. If you knew about your mother, you must have been paying attention to our lives, at least online. You didn't forget we existed."

"Of course not. How could I?"

His eyes met hers, and she saw a sadness in them that stretched back decades. "Then why didn't you ever reach out? You could have called. Or sent a letter."

She blinked hard. "Dad—"

"I'm not accusing," he said quickly, holding up his hands. "I'm sure you had your reasons. I just need to know. Why?"

She had no idea how to answer that question. She wasn't even entirely sure of the answer herself. Part of it was that life in Wakefield was so troubled, so bizarre. She had to take care of Mikey, and she had to deal with Caleb and Merle and their damned mission. It was all she could do to get through the days.

Her pre-Wakefield childhood had been beautiful. Idyllic, even. Its memory gave her strength, and she didn't want to taint it by mixing that life with her messed up Wakefield existence.

That wasn't the only reason, but it was part of it.

When she didn't answer, her father said, "Baughman thought maybe there was some sort of brainwashing. Like maybe you blamed us for what happened."

"No," she said quickly. "That's not it at all. I never blamed you for a moment."

But was that true? Somewhere in the back her mind, did she blame her father for not being able to protect her?

He nodded, the relief clear on his face. "Good. I'm glad."

"It's tough to explain, Dad. I have a whole life here. I have a brother. A biological one. Michael is his name. Mikey. He's sick a lot of the time, and I have to take care of him.

"Oh? I'd like to meet him."

Becky felt a chill at that. This was exactly the type of mixing of her two lives that she'd wanted to avoid. If her dad met Mikey, he might also end up meeting Merle. And meeting Merle was dangerous, especially for outsiders.

Her headache was raging now to the point where she

wasn't sure if she could control it much longer. The Fade threatened to overtake her, and it was all too much.

"Dad? I'm sorry to do this, but I need a little time. I think that's enough for today."

His eyes widened in surprise, the hurt clear on his face. He'd waited thirty years for this, and now his daughter was pushing him away after only five minutes. "All right."

"Thanks for understanding."

She walked him to the door, and he paused before walking through.

"I'm staying at the Wakefield Motor Inn. I plan to stay for a while, but I won't push. When you're ready to talk, give me a call."

"I will. It's good to see you, Dad."

He walked to the car, suddenly stooped over and looking ten years older than when she'd first seen him. After he'd driven away, she went back to the living room and sat in alone in the quiet, wondering what she was going to do next.

20

Eric's headache came back with a vengeance as he drove into North Prairie. It had never left completely, not since it started on the plane earlier that morning. For most of the day, it had been a dull throb. Something he couldn't quite ignore, but that didn't demand his full attention. It was like a radio station playing a pain medley at a low volume in the back of his mind. But now someone had grabbed the volume knob and spun it hard.

He did his best to ignore the pain and keep driving. The life of a little girl was hanging in the balance. He hoped that his phone calls to her mother and the police would stop Lewis from carrying out his grim mission, but he somehow doubted it. The man didn't seem like the type to let a little thing like law enforcement get in his way, and that wasn't even taking into account his supernatural powers.

After multiple searches on his phone at stoplights, Eric had found Tonya Barrington's home address. He had even stumbled on a Facebook post that revealed where Tonya attended school. Douglas Miller Elementary. He had found their website and seen that school let out at ten minutes before three. It was almost two-thirty now, so time was running short. He figured his best bet was to be at Douglas Miller when school let out just in case Lewis made an appearance.

But now this damned headache.

Eric powered through for another thirty seconds, but when the world started getting blurry around the edges of his vision, he knew it was time to pull over. He wouldn't be able to help Tonya Barrington much if he wrapped his rental car around a telephone pole. He spotted a Walgreens off to his right and pulled into the parking lot.

Once he was parked, he left the car running, turning up the air conditioner to full blast. He gripped the steering wheel and squeezed his eyes shut, willing the pain away. After another minute or so, the pain wasn't better, but he found it bearable. He slowly opened his eyes and adjusted the rearview mirror, dreading what he might see.

The dark spot in his eye was as big as his pupil.

He remembered his childhood fear upon seeing the thin man—Merle, he now knew. He'd thought something might crawl out of that dark hole. The thought came back to him with all the terror he'd experienced as a child.

He had no idea what was happening to him, and he needed to understand. Maybe if he could put a name to it, the pain would stop its relentless assault on his senses. Or at least let up a little. He picked up his phone and fumbled his way to the contact list before remembering he'd deleted Becky's number.

Her words suddenly made sense now. *There aren't many people like us. You might want to talk.* And wow, did he ever. She couldn't have been a bit clearer about what she meant? He was damn sick of riddles and mysteries. It was time for people to start saying what they meant.

The pain was a fire in his mind now, and it threatened to consume him. It overtook his thoughts, his feelings, his sense of who he was. Glancing up at the mirror, he saw the spot was bigger than his pupil now. In fact, it seemed to have swallowed his pupil along with his iris. It wouldn't be long until his entire eye was black.

Then, just when he felt like he couldn't take it anymore, the pain swallowed his very will to fight it. For a split-second, there was peace. And then the world changed.

For a beautiful moment, he reveled in the fact that the pain was gone. But then he realized not only was the pain gone; *he* was gone.

He could still see the world around him. The car. The rearview mirror. The neon-red sign of the Walgreens. But he couldn't see his own body. He tried to raise a hand and found he couldn't move. And then he realized why—he couldn't move because he had no body.

He couldn't breathe. His heart wasn't beating. He tried to scream, but no sound came out. There was nowhere for it to come out of.

The world around him looked different. The colors were muted, and the cars seemed to be moving at half speed. He wondered why that was. Perhaps because he wasn't seeing with human eyes? Then how was he seeing?

A profound sense of panic gripped him, and yet it didn't have the attributes that normally accompanied such feelings. No racing heart or catching breath. And the lack of these caused even greater panic. It was a self-feeding cycle of fear, a feedback loop of terror. He wasn't alive. He wasn't dead. Trapped somewhere in between, he had no idea how to get back to himself.

Maybe that was what Becky had wanted to explain to him. Maybe that was why she'd given him her number. But he'd been an idiot, and now he was trapped in this hellish limbo. Maybe forever!

This wasn't helping. He needed to get hold of himself. But how? He couldn't take a deep breath. He couldn't close his eyes. He couldn't even blink!

He was—what?—some kind of ghost? But in the movies, ghosts could move and float and bang windows. He was something less than a ghost, then. A disembodied presence.

Eric forced himself to concentrate. If he wanted to get out of this, he needed to stop panicking. And there *was* a way out. He'd seen Lewis flickering in and out of existence outside his window. And he'd seen Mikey disappear and reappear. Mikey had even been able to control how long he was gone. Seven seconds, just like Becky had dictated.

There'd been such terror in Mikey's face when Becky had said he needed to be gone for seven seconds. It hadn't been pain Mikey had feared; it had been this cold, empty feeling of nothing at all. Eric understood. The headache had been bad, but this was oh so much worse.

He was getting off track again. Time to focus. Bottom line, if Lewis and Mikey could do it, so could he.

But how?

Panic wasn't the answer. He knew that much. He'd never been big into meditation, but Jennifer had. She'd taught him a thing or two about how it focuses the mind. If ever he'd needed a focused mind, it was now.

Remembering what she'd told him, he let the panicked thoughts wash past him. He didn't try to stop them, but he didn't dwell on them either. Whenever he found himself holding a thought, he let it go. After a few minutes, he felt much calmer.

But still disembodied.

Another idea came to him. Out of the bottom of his field

of vision, he could see the spot where his leg should have been. He imagined it was there. Imagined what it felt like to have a leg. The feel of the denim of his jeans against his knee. An itch between his toes. He pictured all of it as clearly as he could.

Nothing happened.

You can do this, Eric, he thought. *Work the problem backwards. What were you doing when you disappeared?*

That question was easy to answer. He'd been fighting the pain and staring at the black hole in his eye.

He tried to put himself back there now. He took the memory of pain and tried to make it reality. He tried to see that black dot in his eye. He let that black dot and the pain fill his mind.

And then he was back. The reality of his existence hit him all at once, like a punch to the stomach.

Opening his mouth, he made a sound like a grunt, just to assure himself he could. Tears sprang to his eyes, and the grunt turned into a laugh. He was alive. He was back. As the laugher subsided, he let out a shout that bordered on a scream. Then he looked in the mirror. The black dot was still there, but it was tiny. The size of a pinprick.

And then he noticed something else: the pain was gone. Completely gone.

A pleasant, contented glow washed over him, humming over every inch on his skin.

Eric's mind went back to Mikey on the bed. Becky had told him he needed to stay faded for seven seconds because the pain was so bad. And she'd indicated that the pain wouldn't come back for a while if he stayed faded for that long.

How long had Eric been faded? Three minutes? Five? He should have looked at the clock. But it had been a hell of a lot longer than seven seconds. Hopefully, that meant he wouldn't have to deal with this again for a while.

Eric considered himself a principled person. He believed in justice. Tolerance. He helped elderly Mrs. Perkins next door with her yard work free of charge, and he donated to the local foodbank. But in that moment, he would have pushed Mrs. Perkins in front of a truck and burnt the foodbank to the ground if it meant he could go an extra hour before the next Fade.

The dip in the lake in Wakefield had been awful, but this was so much worse. Being conscious but unable to breathe, move, look around, not sure if he was alive or dead. It was by far the worst thing he'd ever experienced. And, based on what he'd heard of Becky and Mikey's conversation, it was going to come back. It was only a question of when.

And yet, there was still a little girl at Douglas Miller Elementary getting off school in less than ten minutes, and there was someone who wanted to hurt her. Eric couldn't abide that. He doubted he had much of a shot against Lewis Keller, a man who could apparently Fade at will, but he had to try.

He gripped the steering wheel hard until his hands stopped shaking. Then he started the car and drove into North Prairie.

21

Lewis Keller didn't believe in luck; he believed in momentum. If you're moving fast enough, you tend to roll right over life's little obstacles. That was his philosophy, anyway. Sometimes it felt like you might fall, but that was all part of the excitement. For a man like Lewis, a smooth road was a boring road. He loved feeling like he might lose control of everything at any moment.

Thankfully, today's road contained a few significant obstacles. The first being the surprising police presence at Douglas Miller Elementary.

As a veteran of the child retrieval game, Lewis had staked out his fair share of elementary schools, and there was always some sort of law enforcement. But when you looked a little deeper, you saw most of it was no real threat. Many of those you might assume were police officers were actually crossing guards or security personnel. Granted, many of these were retired cops themselves, so they weren't to be ignored. But they weren't the world's biggest problems. They were looking for school shooters or violent assailants or creeps who stared at kids. As long as Lewis was smart and kept moving, he didn't draw their attention.

But this was different. There were manned police vehicles near every parking lot entrance. And they weren't sleeping in their vehicles either. Lewis couldn't tell for sure, but he'd be willing to bet these cops were writing down license plate numbers. Which meant there'd been a credible threat against the school or one of its students. Lewis had a pretty good idea which student.

He couldn't help but smile as he rolled on past the school, not even slowing down, not risking a long look at the building where Tonya Barrington was probably waiting for her mother to pick her up. Eric Partin—trusty number Six—wasn't letting him down so far. He was making sure this road would have plenty of bumps.

Caleb would have berated Lewis for risking the mission by telling Eric about his target, just like he'd be pissed if he knew it was Lewis who'd set the wheels in motion to bring Eric back to Wakefield in the first place. Merle would have just given Lewis a disappointed, withering glare.

Both Merle and Caleb were skilled with the Fade—Merle far more skilled than Lewis—but neither of them truly understood it. Not the way Lewis did. Sure, it had its downside. Not even Lewis could deny the agonizing terror of being trapped in the Fade, cut off from his own body. But there was another side to it, too. If used properly, the Fade could be fun. That's what Caleb and Merle didn't get. They took the whole thing so damn seriously that they forgot the simple joy of doing what other humans could not.

Sometimes Lewis thought the Fade was wasted on them.

That was part of the reason Lewis didn't stay in Wakefield all the time. He was afraid he'd get caught up in their bureaucratic bullshit and start taking himself too seriously.

Besides, he liked the work. He liked strategizing and testing his mettle against a society that thought itself safe. A society that thought it had inoculated itself from viruses like Lewis Keller. But it hadn't. Not even close. There were still so many cracks for him to slip through.

Lewis enjoyed planning on the fly. Like he'd have to do now.

Not that he was ever planning to reclaim young Tonya at her school. Even if there hadn't been law enforcement, there would still have been far too many eyes for him to make a clean grab. He just liked watching his targets go about their daily routines. It was part of his process.

The best place to grab them was usually their homes. He was quite good at finding his way into a home undetected at night. With the Fade on his side, locked doors weren't a problem. And children slept so deeply, especially after he'd delivered his little injection. If all went smoothly, he'd be halfway back to Wakefield before the kid's parents found little Johnny or Suzie's bed empty in the morning. By the time they called the authorities, he'd be well beyond their grasp.

Still, he had the interesting problem of Six to consider now. Eric had alerted the authorities, and if they were camping out at Tonya's school, there was a good chance they'd be camping around her house too.

Lewis was left with two options. Proceed with a very risky grab, or wait until the police stopped watching the house. The second option would give Eric time to plan his next move. Lewis wondered if he should have just killed number Six. It would have been easy to do it on the plane. He could have made it look like Eric was asleep.

That might have been wiser, but this was far more interesting.

Lewis turned his rental car onto Violet Lane. He spotted the three police cars immediately. The marked car was parked in the Barrington's driveway, and the two unmarked ones were a couple houses down on either side. Once again, Lewis cruised by, not slowing or even glancing at the house. He circled the block and found exactly what he'd expected—there were no police cars on the street behind the Barrington's house. All Lewis would have to do was park on that street, sneak through a couple yards and approach the Barrington's house from behind. It would mean having to lug the unconscious child further, but it was doable. A little risky, but not in the realm of reckless.

With that tentative plan in mind, Lewis felt a bit lighter. He whistled softly as he drove back toward the highway. By the time he reached the Courtyard Inn, he was borderline giddy. He booked a room for two nights, though he doubted he'd be staying that long.

He headed up to his room and spent a few hours reading about North Prairie, studying maps of the city, and digging up information on the North Prairie Police Department's responses to serious situations in the past. There hadn't been many. He plotted out three separate escape routes from the Barrington residence to State Highway 67, the road that he planned to take out of North Prairie. After he'd inspected each route on Google Maps, using their street view feature to see the important intersections, he memorized the routes. Then he visualized them in his mind. It was long, tedious work, but he never shortcutted this part of the process. It could mean the difference between a clean getaway and an unfortunate confrontation with the police. On a couple of occasions, it had.

When he was certain he had all three escape routes down cold, he planned the retrieval itself. Despite his initial thoughts, he eventually decided against sneaking through the back neighbor's yard and approaching the house from behind. It would mean too much time on foot. And when he was carrying the child, his options with the Fade would be limited. He could blink himself out of existence if needed, but that would mean leaving Tonya behind, and *that* was not going to happen.

Which left only one alternative. He was going to have to kill some cops.

The task itself didn't bother him, but it would mean this case would get more media attention than his usual jobs. He didn't love that, and neither would Merle. Lewis didn't see what other option he had with the way Eric had escalated things. He supposed he could wait the cops out—they wouldn't guard the Barrington's house forever. But that would mean hanging around this crummy Wisconsin town for another week, and he'd rather kill a few cops than let that happen.

Once it was decided, he lay on the bed, on top of the covers, hands folded over his stomach, and he went to sleep. He didn't bother setting an alarm. He simply planned to wake up in three hours.

Sure enough, when he opened his eyes, it was eleven p.m. on the dot. He felt a twinge of pride knowing his internal alarm clock had worked again. He went to the bathroom and gargled some mouthwash before setting his backpack on the bed and unpacking it, making sure he had everything he needed.

Syringe. Zip ties. Small burlap sack. And, of course, his trusty pocket knife. The knife was of the folding variety, small enough that it didn't seem odd a man might carry it in his pocket, but large enough to do real damage. And Lewis kept the blade razor sharp. He'd used that knife to slice tendons, open jugulars, and pierce eyeballs. It had never let him down. Other folks could have their automatic weapons and their silenced pistols. Lewis preferred the simple pleasure of sliding a sharp knife through skin, muscle, and tissue. He found it far more intimate than pulling a trigger.

Once the items were stowed in the backpack—except for the knife, which he slipped into his pocket—he sat at the room's small desk and prepared for the least pleasant part of any job. He took out his phone and called Merle.

Though it was one hour later in Wakefield, Merle answered on the second ring. The man never seemed to sleep.

"Are you in place?" Merle asked by way of greeting.

"I'm in place. Checked in at the Courtyard Inn by the highway. About to go get the girl now."

"Good. Do you foresee any trouble?"

Lewis grimaced. He'd really been hoping Merle wouldn't ask that. He was fine lying to the old man by omission, but he couldn't avoid answering a direct question truthfully. In spite of everything, he respected Merle too much. "Yeah, there's going to be a couple dead cops by the time I'm done."

"That's so?" Merle's voice was calm and even, but there was something like menace creeping in around the edges.

Lewis told him about Eric. How he'd sat next to him on the plane and let the name Tonya Barrington slip.

"It will be quite interesting to see what he does," Merle said.

Lewis couldn't disagree. "You want me to wait on Tonya?"

"No." The answer was immediate. "Get the job done. Tonya's been in the wild long enough. It's time for her to come home. Just be careful. And don't kill anyone you don't have to."

"I'll do my best. See you tomorrow afternoon."

"Good luck, Lewis."

Lewis ended the call, and a feeling of relief swept over him. He'd checked in with the boss and gotten the green light. Now it was time for the fun part.

He made his way down to the lobby, whistling again. As he passed the tired-looking clerk at the front desk, he threw her a playful wink. She flushed a little and gave him a close-lipped smile.

It took him a minute to locate his rental car. It looked different in the dark. Smaller than he remembered. He finally spotted it near the back of the lot and trotted over to it. He threw his backpack onto the passenger seat, set his cellphone in the cup holder, and started the vehicle.

He didn't see the Toyota Corolla rushing toward him as he pulled out of the parking spot. Not until it was too late. He looked up at the last second and saw the car, Eric Partin behind the wheel, his lips pulled back in a snarl.

Lewis only had time for an involuntary gasp before the Corolla slammed into him.

22

Eric never went to Tonya's school after the Fade passed. Instead, he headed to her home address. It was an upper-middle-class neighborhood on the north side of North Prairie. The houses were nice, and they all had a bit of personality unlike some of the cookie-cutter subdivisions in Eric's neck of the woods. It was the type of neighborhood Jennifer would have seen as a potential target for E&J Landscaping's marketing efforts.

He turned onto Tonya's street and spotted a squad car in her driveway. There was another vehicle he thought might be an unmarked cop car a few houses down. He felt an unexpected burst of pride at that. Eric didn't know if the police would be able to stop Lewis, but at least he'd done something to make Tonya a tiny bit safer.

On his way out of the neighborhood, he noticed something interesting—there was only one road in and out of the subdivision. That meant anyone who wanted to get to Tonya's house would have to drive past that spot. Including Sarah and Tonya. And Lewis.

Eric found a spot under a shady tree just inside the

subdivision. Whenever anyone slowed to turn into the neighborhood, Eric got a nice long look at their faces. He'd been sitting there for less than ten minutes when a black coupe pulled up. Eric spotted Lewis behind the wheel. He immediately sank down in his seat, hoping Lewis hadn't seen him. Apparently he hadn't, because he rolled past Eric and turned down Tonya's street.

The question became what to do next. Call the police again? Eric decided against it. He thought it likely that Lewis was just scouting out the neighborhood, same as he was. The theory was confirmed a few minutes later when Lewis passed him again, this time on his way out of the neighborhood.

Eric let him get half a block ahead and then followed him out of the subdivision, across town, and finally to the Courtyard Inn near the highway. He parked where he could see Lewis's car and waited.

During the hours-long wait, Eric had plenty of time to think. He considered slashing Lewis's tires. He considered phoning in an anonymous tip to the police again. But in the end, he decided he needed to handle this himself. The police wouldn't understand what they were dealing with and Lewis would slip through their fingers, perhaps literally.

Eric wasn't sure he had a much better chance against Lewis, but he wanted to try. In the long hours of waiting, he decided his best chance was catching Lewis off guard. All of this was so far beyond the pale of what he would have considered possible even a few days ago. Earlier that day, he'd called a mother and threatened to kidnap her child, and now he was planning a vehicular assault. What a difference a few days could make.

It was a muggy evening, and Eric had to occasionally

turn on the car and run the air conditioning to keep from getting too hot, even with the windows down. But as uncomfortable as he was, Eric promised himself he wouldn't leave no matter how long it took. He was well aware Lewis might not leave the hotel again until morning, but he was willing to wait. Ever since the Fade, he'd felt not only pain-free but energized. It was like he was buzzing with electricity. He felt like he could sit in that car, not sleeping, watching for Lewis for three days if that was what it took.

It didn't take three days, just until 11:30 p.m. He spotted Lewis walking out the hotel's front door, a backpack slung over his shoulder, and he eased his Corolla out of its parking spot, the headlights off. He drove to the end of the row where Lewis was parked and let his car idle. When Lewis's car started forward, Eric gritted his teeth and stomped the gas.

He caught one deeply satisfying glimpse of Lewis's surprised expression, and then his car slammed into Lewis's.

Eric had hoped to ram into Lewis's driver's side door, going for maximum injury, but his timing was just a little off. He hit the front of the car, the right side of his bumper colliding just above Lewis's front tire. He couldn't have been going more than thirty miles per hour, but the impact rattled his teeth. Lewis's car slid to the right, slamming into the car next to it.

When both cars came to a stop, Eric looked himself up and down and was pleased to find no obvious injuries. But he couldn't stop now. The element of surprise was still on his side, but it wouldn't be for much longer. He threw the car door open and stepped out, the tire iron he'd retrieved from the trunk earlier clutched in his right hand.

Lewis was still behind the wheel of his car. He stared straight ahead, a dazed expression on his face. He slowly turned his head. When he spotted Eric stalking toward him, he smiled.

Eric slowed a little at that, but he didn't stop. Lewis's door was crumpled and Eric doubted he'd be able to open it. That meant he'd either have to go out the passenger door or—

Lewis blinked out of existence, and Eric froze. He raised the tire iron and looked around, his heart thudding in his ears as he waited for the man to reappear. And then, Lewis was standing in front of him. There was a cut above his left eye and a wide grin on his face.

"Guess I should have been wearing my seatbelt," Lewis said.

Eric knew he should be attacking. Lewis had power, sure, but Eric hadn't seen anything to indicate he was immune to a hard hit upside the head with a piece of iron. Instead, Eric remained frozen. He was so unnerved by Lewis's nonchalant reaction that he couldn't move.

Lewis glanced at the tire iron. "So that's the plan? Beat me to death?" He shook his head. "Honestly, I didn't know you had it in you, Six. And from the way you're just standing there, maybe you don't." He took a step toward Eric. "You know, I've been thinking, maybe we got off on the wrong foot. There's really quite a bit I could—"

Eric sprinted forward, closing the gap in a second. He brought the tire iron down hard, swinging across his body and aiming for Lewis's head. He connected with nothing but air, and the force of his swing made him stumble. He managed to keep his feet under him, but just barely. Once again, Lewis had disappeared.

"You're new to this whole thing. I get that." Lewis's voice was coming from behind him now.

He spun and saw Lewis standing five feet away. He

raised the tire iron, ready to try again. But before he could, something in his brain seemed to explode.

"I'm not going to kill you, Six, but that doesn't mean I'm going to go easy on you."

The headache—what he was beginning to think of as the Fade headache—was back, stronger than ever. It was all Eric could do to remain standing as the pain rocked him.

"What are you doing to me?" The words came out like a groan.

"What am I doing?" Lewis grinned at him. "I'm just getting started. Now watch this."

Eric felt a sudden blunt force hit him in the center of the forehead. Lewis hadn't moved, but it felt like he'd smacked Eric with a baseball bat. And then suddenly, Eric was floating ten feet in the air, looking down on his own body. He couldn't move. Couldn't breathe.

He was back in the Fade, but this time, his body hadn't vanished. It lay prone on the asphalt, limp and empty.

Lewis reached in his pocket and pulled out a small object. It took Eric a moment to recognize it through the panic and disorientation, but when he did, he tried to scream. It was a knife. The same one Lewis had used to cut himself outside Eric's window.

"You might not know it to look at me now," Lewis said, "but I used to be kind of a weirdo. I had trouble connecting to other kids socially. Those first few years in Wakefield were tough." He slowly opened the knife and took a step forward. "Caleb used to beat me up fairly regularly. He was confused, just like me, and I was a convenient way for him to take out his frustration. And part of it was Becky. She was always nice to me, friendly, and he had a thing for her. She wasn't much interested in either of us, truth be told. She only had eyes for this older boy, Glen. But that's another story. Point is, Caleb didn't like me, and he wasn't afraid to show it."

He crouched down next to Eric's body and pried the right eyelid open. In the iridescent glow of the parking lot lights, Eric could see his eye had turned completely black. He tried to force himself back to his body. He desperately imagined a rope between him and his unmoving form, and he imagined pulling on that rope, hauling himself to his body. Nothing happened.

"The thing Caleb failed to recognize was that I was taking to the Fade faster than he was. Merle was teaching all of us, but I was the star pupil. Course, that only served to make Caleb hate me more. But he didn't understand the full implications. He didn't understand it gave me power."

Lewis cupped Eric's face almost lovingly in his hand. Then he drew the knife across Eric's cheek, leaving a red line in its wake. Blood seeped from the wound and ran down Eric's face.

Eric felt no pain—he felt nothing—but that almost made it worse. His body was being injured in front of him, and he couldn't even scream. He desperately tried to remember how he'd gotten out of the Fade the last time. He'd imagined the pain, right? Maybe he just had to do that again. He remembered the pain, let it fill his mind. Nothing happened.

"One day, when we were seventeen, Caleb cornered me in the woods. I ran as usual, but he was faster. He tackled me and was about to give me the standard-issue beating when I did to him what I just did to you. I used the Fade, but I didn't send him into it completely. I trapped him halfway between here and the Fade. Just far enough that his body didn't ghost out. Then I got my knife and went to work. You should ask him to see the scars."

Lewis turned Eric's head and dragged the knife across his other cheek. Now there were twin bloody wounds on either side of Eric's face.

Eric tried again, remembering the pain, letting the image of the dark spot in his eye fill his mind. Nothing.

"After I'd had my fun, I left him there, half in the Fade. I wasn't sure what would happen, but once I got far enough away, he came back to his body. Thing is, he didn't react like I'd expected. I thought he'd leave me alone after that. Instead, he came for revenge. That's when things got serious."

Lewis grabbed the collar of Eric's t-shirt and pulled it downward, stretching it. Then he made a long cut across Eric's chest, just under the collarbone.

"I faded him out of his body again, and this time I cut him in more...let's say *discreet* areas. I'm guessing he won't show you those scars, even if you ask nicely. After that, Caleb stayed away from me. Even now, he doesn't talk to me unless it's absolutely necessary."

He let go of Lewis's shirt. The blood made a dark line across the cotton as it seeped through.

"So, Six, my question is, are you going to be a Caleb, or are you going to be smart? Because if I have to do this again, it'll be more than a few shallow cuts." He wiped his knife on Eric's shirt and stood up. "Now if you don't mind, I'm going to borrow your car. It's in a bit better condition than mine."

With that, he stood up and moseyed to Eric's Corolla. He climbed in and drove away.

Eric could still see the Corolla in the distance when he came back to his body. The headache was gone now, but the cuts stung his face and chest. For almost a minute, he didn't move. He lay shaking on the pavement, wondering how things had gotten so messed up so quickly. He thought about how his home in Mequon was a forty-minute drive away. He could be showered and in his own bed an hour from now.

Then he thought of Tonya Barrington, and he got up and walked to Lewis's car.

23

THE CUTS on Eric's face weren't overly painful, though the feeling of blood seeping down both sides of his face wasn't pleasant. The cut on his chest stung. It seemed every step he took made the cut open a bit wider; he felt the wound stretching and contracting with the movement of his body.

But that didn't matter. The fact that he had no idea how to stop Lewis also didn't matter. All that mattered was getting to Tonya Barrington's house and standing between Lewis and that child. That was his job now, and he needed to remain focused on it. To think beyond that would overwhelm him.

He picked up the tire iron off the pavement and walked to Lewis's car on shaky legs. The driver's side door was crumpled and Eric knew there was no way he was getting it open. The passenger's side was dented from colliding with the next car over, but thankfully the collision had knocked that car a few feet away and there was room for Eric to squeeze in between them. Eric pulled the door open and slid inside.

The first thing he noticed after squirming his way into the driver's seat was that the keys were still in the ignition. Good. The second thing he noticed was a cellphone in the cup holder. Very good.

He picked it up and unlocked the phone, smiling when he saw there was no passcode on it. Lewis might be a genius when it came to the Fade, but he'd apparently flunked data-security as badly as Eric had.

He was about to set the phone down when an idea struck him. He opened Lewis's contacts, scrolled to the Bs, and tapped the first number.

Becky picked up on the third ring. "What the hell, Lewis? It's the middle of the night."

"It's Eric." His voice came out thick and scratchy.

Phone wedged between his shoulder and his ear, Eric started the car and eased it forward. He didn't like the whining sound it made, but it seemed to be functional.

"Eric?"

"Eric Partin."

"Yeah, I know. I just..." She sounded like she was slowly fighting her way out of a deep sleep. "What are you doing with Lewis's phone?"

Eric considered how to answer that question. He and Becky hadn't gotten off to the best start. Besides stealing his phone, she'd held him at gun point, called Caleb, and helped put him in the lake with that awful dark presence. So why was it that when he picked up Lewis's phone she was the first person he'd thought to call for help?

He wasn't positive, but he thought it might be that she'd returned his phone and programmed her number into it. He'd seen the conflicted look in her eyes. This whole kidnapping thing Merle and his crew had going on, she wasn't completely down with it. Now it was up to him to convince her to come down on the side of the good guys.

"Lewis and I had a bit of an...altercation." He didn't think he'd ever used the word *altercation* before, but it was the only one that seemed to fit now. "He stole my car, but he accidentally left his phone behind."

Eric pulled out onto the road and headed toward the Barrington residence. If he remembered correctly, the house was only a five-minute drive from the hotel. He opened the Maps app on his own phone for directions. The address was still saved in his recent places.

"Okay." She spoke slowly, carefully, as if she knew she was heading into dangerous territory. "And you're calling me why?"

He took a deep breath. "You offered me help once. You said I could call you if I needed to talk to someone about what was happening. I'm taking you up on that offer."

There was a long pause. "I meant if you needed help with the Fade. Understanding how to deal with it. I didn't mean help with Lewis. He's..." she broke off again. "Lewis is like a force of nature. The best thing you can do is stay out of his way."

"Yeah, well, that's not an option. He did something to me, Becky. He used the Fade. Knocked me out of my body. Then he took off."

"Like I said, stay out of his way."

Frustration crept up in Eric's belly. "You're not listening to me. Staying out of his way isn't an option. He's going after a kid. A little girl. I have to stop him."

"No, *you're* not listening." Becky's voice was sharp now, her own frustration coming through. "I get why you're freaked out about this. It's all new to you. You were lucky enough to not grow up around it like I did."

The bitterness came through when she said that, and her tone stuck in Eric's craw. He was getting really sick of people being pissed at him because his kidnappers let him go. "This girl, Tonya Barrington, she's twelve years old. You want her to go through what you went through? You want her to be ripped away from her family?"

"Of course I don't. But I also don't want her to die confused and in agony when the Fade takes her."

"There's another way," Eric said. "There's gotta be. One that doesn't involve traumatizing this kid for life."

Becky let out a bone-deep sigh. "We all get traumatized, Eric. We've got no say in that."

"I didn't call for a debate on the ethics of kidnapping," he said. "I called to find out what I can do against Lewis when he pulls that Fade trick on me again. How do I stop him from knocking me out of my own body?"

"You don't. You can't. Listen, the five of us were raised with the Fade from the time we got to Wakefield. We were taught how to deal with it. Merle worked with us in these weekly lessons. He called them 'lessons for the rest of your life' and we were expected to take them very seriously."

That phrase—*lessons for the rest of your life*—brought back the horror of his own kidnapping. Merle had said those words to him once, too. "I got one of those lessons. Only one. Guess I didn't do very well."

But was that true? Or had he done *too* well? Had he somehow demonstrated a resistance to the Fade that let Merle and his people feel comfortable letting him go home?

"The point is we were trained," Becky said. "And Lewis? He was the best of us. Mikey never really got the hang of it. Caleb and I got halfway decent. Carrie was occasionally brilliant. But Lewis blew us all out of the water. Thing is, he's a little bit crazy. Always has been. I don't think he cares if he lives or dies. And that lets him go farther with the Fade than the rest of us. It's why you'll never beat him."

"Well, I'm going to try. If you don't have any advice for me, then I'm sorry I bothered you."

"I gave you my advice, Eric. I know it's difficult to wrap your mind around, but Lewis is doing a good thing here. He's not a good person, but he's doing a good thing. Bringing these kids home is going to save their lives."

Eric gritted his teeth. He was sick of this. Sick of people telling him impossible things were real. Sick of people telling him things he knew to be vile and evil were actually good. "That girl's not dying this week. If what Lewis told me is true, she has years. We can figure out another solution."

The laugh that came through the phone was full of bitterness. "Oh, that's it? You're going to find a solution? Be the big hero who comes in and solves all our problems?"

"It's not like that, Becky. I don't know the answer, but it's not this. Look, if stopping a kidnapping isn't enough for you, how about saving a life? Lewis doesn't seem like he'd be all that averse to killing, and there's at least one police officer waiting outside that girl's house."

Becky's voice was cold when she spoke again. "And whose fault is that? You called the cops, didn't you? You stuck your nose in and started meddling in things you didn't understand. If anything happens to a police officer, it's on you."

Eric was so surprised by that answer that it took him a moment to respond. "I don't understand. Why are you being like this? How can you defend what Lewis is doing as right?"

"Because it's my only shot at getting my son back." She sounded utterly weary now. "I had to send him away when he was a baby. Adopt him out to some family, Merle wouldn't even tell me where. I have to wait three more years, and then Lewis is going to bring him back to me. I understand that it sounds crazy to you, but this is the way it has to be. I gave up spending my son's childhood with him in order to keep him safe. But there's no way in hell I'm giving up the rest of my life."

Eric let the silence hang in the air. This woman was not his ally. She was just as delusional as the rest of them. There was no denying something supernatural was going on in Wakefield. But to resort to this? Moving children around like trading cards? Adopting them out and stealing them back? It made no sense. Merle had them brainwashed. That was the only explanation Eric could muster.

"I shouldn't have called," he said. "Good night, Becky."

He was about to hang up when he heard her speak again.

"Eric, wait. I know I can't talk you out of this, but please hear me. Most of us, we put up with the kidnappings as a necessary evil. The men who took us from our homes when we were kids hated what they were doing. But Lewis isn't like that. He enjoys hurting people. He'll enjoy hurting you. Don't give him an excuse to do any more damage, understand?"

Eric thought of the gleeful look on Lewis's face when he'd cut Eric's empty body. He'd actually been excited when Eric rammed into his car.

"Yeah, I got a little taste of that."

"So you'll leave him be?"

"No. Not unless he leaves that kid alone." Eric's phone beeped, indicating the turn into Tonya Barrington's neighborhood. "I've got to go, Becky."

He disconnected the call without waiting for a response.

When he turned onto Violet Lane, he pulled over and parked on the side of the road. The car was making too much noise, and he didn't want to let Lewis know he'd arrived. He got out of the car, grabbed his tire iron, and started walking toward Tonya Barrington's home.

24

After Becky hung up with Eric, she lay in bed staring up at the ceiling for ten minutes.

It had been one gut-punch of a forty-eight hours. She'd met the mysterious sixth member of their reclamation class. She remembered the long hours she and the others had spent speculating about Eric Partin and why he'd been released while they had not. Of course, Merle could have avoided that by simply not telling them Eric Partin existed, but he hadn't gone that route. Instead, he'd brought Eric up in great detail during nearly every one of their lessons. It was almost as if he wanted them to hate Eric.

She was still reeling from that when the even bigger shock had happened—her adoptive father had shown up on her doorstep. In the years after she was brought to Wakefield and reunited with her biological parents, she'd missed the people she still thought of as her real parents. She'd cried for them. She'd dreamed of reuniting with them. After a couple years of feeling a tangled knot of raw emotions, she'd learned not to think of them at all.

And then he'd shown up. He'd never given up looking

for her, not in thirty years. Thinking about it now was like touching a raw wound. She instinctively flinched away, pushing it out of her mind. There would be time for that, but the time was not now. Because something was happing in the town of North Prairie, Wisconsin. Something potentially very bad, and she needed to decide what to do about it.

Finally, she picked up her phone. She stared at Merle's name on her contact list for a long while, trying to work up the nerve to touch it. He needed to know what was happening in North Prairie, and it was her duty to tell him.

After thirty seconds of staring at the screen, she reached into her purse and pulled out a business card. Then she began to dial.

The former FBI agent's voice was husky with sleep when he answered. There was a hint of panic in it too, a natural reaction to receiving a phone call in the middle of the night. "Hello?"

"Hi, Mr. Baughman. It's Becky Talbot."

"Oh. Hi, what... what can I do for you?"

She swallowed hard. "Something's happened. Things have changed, and Wakefield isn't going to be safe for you much longer. You and my..." She paused, having to force the word out. "You and my dad need to leave town. Now."

"I don't understand. Why?"

"Please, Mr. Baughman. I can't explain. I'll contact you later with more information, but you have to leave."

There was a long pause. "Okay. But you owe me an explanation."

"And you'll get it. But not tonight. Call me when you've left town. I need to know that he's safe."

"Okay, Becky. I can do that."

Becky ended the call and sat on the edge of her bed,

hugging herself to stop the shaking. The room was chilly, but she knew that wasn't the cause. She needed to make the other call, the one to Merle, but she wouldn't be able to until she knew her father was safely out of Wakefield.

Things were changing fast. If Eric was right, Lewis would probably kill a few cops before the night was over. He'd probably kill Eric too. That would bring media attention. Merle already knew that Albert Wilson was in town and had contacted Becky. For some reason, he'd allowed it. But Merle was a cautious man. With the news reporting a multiple homicide related to a kidnapping, and one of the victims being Eric Partin, her dad might put the pieces together. He might realize the kidnappings had never stopped. And then he'd go to the real FBI. Or the media.

Merle wouldn't allow that type of exposure. Becky had seen him deal with such things before, and he did so decisively. That's why she had to make sure her father was long gone before Merle learned about what was happening in North Prairie.

She only had to wait two minutes before her phone rang again.

"Hello?"

"He said no." Baughman sounded much more alert now.

"Excuse me? What do you mean he said no?"

"He said he's waited thirty years to see you, and he's not leaving town because of some second-hand message passed along in the middle of the night."

Becky felt a pit of fear growing in her stomach. "You have to convince him. Mr. Baughman, if he doesn't leave—"

"He wants to see you first. We'll swing by the house, let him say goodbye, and then we'll go. That's the only way this is happening."

"No!" The word came out louder than she intended, but

the panic she felt couldn't be contained in a whisper. There was no way her father could come to the house. It was much too close to Merle. "I'll come to you."

"Are you sure?"

She stood up and grabbed her purse off the table. "Yes, just make sure he's ready to leave. I'll say goodbye and see you on your way. I'll be there in five minutes."

"All right. See you then."

Becky hung up and hustled up the stairs to her brother's room. She knocked, then opened the door without waiting for a response. "Mikey, wake up."

He woke with a start, jolting from sleep to an alert state in less than a second. "What is it?"

"We've got trouble. Eric somehow found out what Lewis is doing, and he's trying to stop him."

It took Mikey a moment, but then he got it. "Oh, Jesus. Lewis is going to kill him."

"Exactly. And Merle's going to lose it if Eric dies. He's got his hopes pinned to that guy."

Mikey sat up and rubbed his eyes. "What do we do?"

"Well, first we get my dad, Albert, out of town. If Eric's dead, Merle will want to be damn sure nothing that goes on in this town leaks, and that probably means killing Agent Baughman and Albert."

Mikey nodded slowly. "Okay. But we have to tell Merle what we know, right?"

"Of course, but not until Albert is safe. I'm going over to the motel now to make sure he leaves. I need you to stay here. I doubt Merle or Caleb will show up, but if they do, I need you to run interference."

"Of course."

"Thanks." She leaned down and kissed him on the head. "I'll see you soon."

BAUGHMAN HAD his bag packed and loaded into the car five minutes after Becky called. He didn't understand why Wakefield was suddenly unsafe, but he'd heard the desperate, frightened tone in the woman's voice. And he'd seen enough weirdness in Wakefield to know it wasn't smart to take her fear lightly. He'd strapped on his shoulder holster and prepared to leave town.

Albert Wilson was proving a bit harder to convince. He was moving now, carefully packing his suitcase, but he did it without any urgency. He'd told Baughman he was only willing to leave if he saw his daughter first, but Baughman doubted he'd go even then.

Wilson had contacted Baughman a few years after his retirement from the Bureau. Wilson had done his homework, and he knew more about both Baughman and the case than was publicly available. Wilson had money, and he was willing to put that money to use to find his daughter. After his wife's death, finding his daughter gave him purpose. For Baughman, it was an opportunity to continue an investigation that had always haunted him and at a salary much higher than the one he'd made at the FBI. He'd spent years turning over every stone. While his investigation hadn't led him directly to Wakefield, he'd gotten close enough that he'd attracted the attention of a few people connected to the kidnappings, including Marsha Crawford. Of course, he'd been delighted when she called and offered to tell him the new names of the five missing children, but some small part of him had been annoyed he hadn't figured it out himself. He'd been close. In a couple of months, he would have cracked it. Or so he told himself.

Baughman leaned over and peeked out the window.

Headlights painted the pavement as a car pulled up in front of Wilson's ground-level room.

"Looks like she's here," Baughman said.

Wilson set down the pants he'd been carefully folding and nodded. "Okay then."

Baughman couldn't help but feel sorry for his employer. He'd worked so long and hard for this, and the reunion hadn't gone at all how he'd planned. And now his rediscovered daughter was telling him to hit the road, using outlandish stories of danger to get him to go away. It must have all seemed like a bad dream to Wilson.

There was a soft knock. Wilson stared blankly at the closed door as if unsure what the noise meant. Baughman pushed himself to his feet and walked over to it.

No sooner had Baughman opened the door than Becky pushed her way inside. She didn't even give Baughman a glance. Her eyes went straight to her father.

"You ready to go?" she said.

"Hi, Becky." Wilson took a deep breath. Calling her by a name other than the one he'd given her clearly took effort. "Yes, we'll go shortly. I thought we might sit and chat for a while first."

Becky's face scrunched up in confusion. "Maybe you don't understand. People are coming here. Serious people. You know about the reclamations. Things have changed, and they won't want you to leave."

"The reclamations?" Baughman asked.

Becky scowled. "That's what they call the kidnappings. Reclamations. Because they're taking back their own."

Wilson's face darkened. Baughman had seen the man annoyed, and he'd seen him upset plenty of times. But this was the closest Baughman had ever seen him to angry. "That's... it's insane. They have no right! No right to tear apart people's lives. It's not like they loaned you out to us! It's a forever thing!"

"Calm down, Dad." Becky held up a hand. "You're shouting."

"You're damn right I am. These people stole my daughter. They stole you away from me!" Tears filled his eyes now. "And now that I've found you, they want to bully me into leaving town?"

"Albert," Baughman said, "maybe we should—"

"Maybe we should what? Run like frightened rabbits? Leave my daughter behind again?" Wilson grabbed the top of his suitcase and slammed it shut. "I don't think so. If these men really are coming, I think I might wait for them here. I'd like to look them in the eyes and let them explain themselves. Let them try to justify tearing our family apart."

Becky drew a deep breath. When she spoke again, her voice was calm but heavy with authority. "Dad, they're not going to explain themselves. They're not going to chat about the ethics of what they've done or let you have your big moment of telling them how they destroyed your life. They are going to kill you."

Baughman thought it likely Becky was overstating the case, but he didn't want to find out either way. He wanted to be gone before Merle arrived.

"I don't care if they kill me." Wilson spit out the words through clenched teeth.

"I do." Becky took a step forward and put a hand on his shoulder. "Dad, please. I don't want you to die."

Baughman glanced at the window, and once again saw headlights. He swallowed, pushing down the lump in his throat. "Guys?"

The others turned and saw it too. Wilson's face remained

locked in an angry expression of defiance, but Becky went pale.

"That's impossible," she muttered. "How could they be here already? They don't know about Eric."

The car pulled into the spot next to Becky's car, and three men got out.

Baughman turned to Becky. "What do we do here?"

She shook her head. "I don't know."

A few beads of sweat stood on Wilson's forehead. "Look, if they're really that dangerous, we'll just lock the door and phone the police."

"Trust me, it won't help. The door won't stop them, and the police let Merle do anything he wants."

Wilson frowned. "What do you mean the door won't stop them?"

Before Becky could answer, there was a soft knock.

Baughman touched the butt of his gun and waited, hoping he wouldn't have to use it. There was so much about this situation that he still didn't understand.

"Maybe I can talk to him. Maybe he'll listen to me." Becky walked to the door and opened it. When she had it halfway open, she froze.

Caleb and Mikey stood outside, their expressions grim. An older, thin man stood between them. It was clear the old guy was in charge.

"Mikey?" Becky said, the disbelief thick in her voice. "You told them?"

Mikey couldn't meet her eyes. "I had to."

The older guy stepped through the door and the others followed. Caleb had a backpack slung over his shoulder, and he set it on the table.

"Gentleman," the older man said. "I'm Merle. I'm sorry

to visit you at this time of night, but we have a bit of a situation."

Wilson clenched his fists and glared at the man. "You. You're one of the ones who took my daughter, aren't you?"

Merle stared at him for a long moment before answering. "In a manner of speaking. I didn't physically retrieve her, but the whole thing was my idea." He nodded to Caleb, and Caleb shut the door. "Mr. Wilson, would you like to see why I took your daughter?"

As Baughman and Wilson stared in disbelief, Merle began to flicker.

25

THE FIRST THING that gave Eric pause was the police car still parked in the Barrington's driveway. He wondered how best to proceed. If he alerted the cop, the officer would have plenty of questions for Eric, which might give Lewis time to escape out the back. At the same time, trying to sneak around the officer would look much worse if he were caught.

In the end, he decided subtlety wasn't his friend in this situation. He needed to sound every alarm he could. He walked up the driveway, making no attempt to hide himself.

"Excuse me. Officer?" He stopped three feet away from the vehicle and waited for a response. When there was none, he tried again a little louder. "Officer? I need help."

He waited ten seconds but still no response. Either the police officer was sleeping or he was dead.

Eric stepped up to the car and gently rapped on the window. Through the darkness, he saw the officer's head lulled back, his vacant eyes staring up at the roof of the car. Eric didn't know exactly how Lewis had killed him, but it was clear he was dead.

Eric turned and stared at the house for a moment. The windows were dark and there was no sign of movement. He pulled out Lewis's phone and dialed 911. When the woman answered, he simply said, "There's a dead police officer at 1630 Violet Lane. Please. Send help."

Then he hung up and let the phone fall from his fingers onto the pavement.

He crept to the front porch, more conscious of trying not to be seen now. When he reached the door, he gently tried the knob. As he'd expected, it was locked. Why would Lewis bother trying to break or pick the lock when he could simply pass through a closed door? Eric peeked through the door's small window and into the darkness, considering his next move. He could ring the doorbell, hoping to wake Sarah. But that might get the woman hurt. He could wait for the police to arrive; he assumed his call about a dead officer would have them double-timing it to Violet Lane. But they still might not arrive before Lewis left with the girl.

He was still trying to decide when a dark shape entered his field of vision. He had to stifle a gasp at what he saw. Lewis walked through the dark living room, a small body in his arms.

Eric took an involuntary step back. He suddenly understood what he needed to do. He crouched down and readied his tire iron.

He waited silently, willing himself not to move, doing his best to breathe as shallowly as possible. He didn't know a lot about the Fade—the way Lewis had knocked him out of his body proved that—but it seemed to revolve around manipulating your own existence. He thought there was a very good chance Lewis would have to open the door to get Tonya through with him.

As if in response to his thoughts, the door knob began to turn ever-so-slowly.

He leaned forward on the balls of his feet, gripping the tire iron. He'd only get one shot at this.

The door slowly opened, and a pair of dangling legs poked out. Lewis stepped through, and as he reached back to pull the door shut, Eric exploded forward. He swung the tire iron over his head and brought it down hard. With Tonya's unconscious body between him and Lewis, the angle was awkward, and he only managed a glancing blow to the side of Lewis's head.

Still, it was hard enough to knock him off his feet. He stumbled backward into the doorway, and Tonya slipped from his hands.

Eric couldn't stop now. He'd struck a blow, but Tonya wouldn't be free until Lewis was dead. He stepped over the fallen girl and made his way to Lewis, who was sprawled backward, a hand to his head as he squirmed on the floor. He blinked up at the approaching Eric, squinting to see him better.

Eric raised the tire iron again and brought it down even harder this time, intending to end things with this blow. He felt the tire iron hit, but then it suddenly crashed against the hardwood floor. Lewis had Faded mid-strike.

He heard a groan from behind him and turned. Lewis stood in the middle of the yard, hands on his knees. Eric leapt over Tonya and sprinted toward him. He'd gotten Lewis a little with that last blow, and Lewis was still reeling. If he could get to him again before he recovered, he might have a shot.

Behind him, he heard a woman scream, but he tried to ignore it. Still, the noise made him hesitate, losing a step or two. Lewis looked up, a crazed look in his eyes. There was anger in those eyes, and pain, but there was something else too. It was glee. Lewis was loving this.

Just before Eric reached him, Lewis disappeared again. Eric skidded to a stop and whirled around, looking for him. Frustration threatened to overwhelm him. He was trying to fight a man who could blink out of existence, who could disappear and reappear somewhere else at will.

Then he remembered the screaming woman.

Sarah Barrington crouched in the doorway, her eyes wide with terror. Her hands were on her daughter, but her eyes were on Eric. "What did you do to her? What did you do?"

"Mrs. Barrington, it's not safe here. We have to—"

"No kidding, it's not safe," she said, spitting out the words like venom. "What did you do to my daughter?"

And then, Tonya began to stir. She rolled over onto her side and looked up at her mother, her eyes half open. "Mom? I'm cold."

Sarah pulled her daughter close and wrapped her arms around her. "It's going to be okay, honey."

"It's really not." Lewis reappeared on the porch and casually strolled toward the two females in the doorway. "She probably didn't understand what you said anyway. The drug I used puts her in sort of a twilight state. She's going to be pretty out of it for the next six hours or so."

Eric ran toward Lewis. It seemed futile to keep attacking him again in exactly the same way, but what choice did he have? He had to do something. He had to fight the only way he knew how.

Sarah looked from Lewis to Eric and back to Lewis, confusion and fear in her eyes. "Stay away from us!"

"No can do," Lewis said. Then he turned to Eric. "And you? I'm pretty sure I told you what would happen if you followed me. Not to be a jerk, but I gotta stick to my guns on that one."

Eric let out an involuntary shout as his mind exploded with pain. He was only eight feet from Lewis, but he couldn't take another step. He couldn't even remain upright.

"Don't feel bad, Six," Lewis said. "You made a stand for your principles, right? That's something. You gave it a swing. So what if you whiffed big time. You were going up against forces you could never hope to understand, and you did better than anyone could have expected. You don't have anything left to prove."

Eric felt himself slipping. Lewis was doing it again. In just a moment, he'd be pushed out of his own body, and he felt certain that Lewis wouldn't simply do a little cutting to teach him a lesson this time. Lewis was going to kill him.

There had to be a way out of this. A way to fight against the Fade. If only he had a few more seconds to think. But the pain was so bad that it was almost impossible to hold onto his thoughts. It was as if the pain was pushing everything else out. The blinding agony was taking up all the space in his brain and...

Then a realization struck him. The pain wasn't just pain; it was fuel. Fuel for the Fade. Lewis couldn't just push him out of his own body instantly. He had to let the pain build first. And in his car, when he'd entered the Fade for the first time, the pain had been at a crescendo and had been gone when he'd returned. But it was the memory of Mikey and Becky that confirmed his suspicion. Mikey had been suffering, barely coherent, and Becky had told him he needed to stay in the Fade for seven seconds so he'd feel better. The longer you were in the Fade, the more of the fuel that was used.

And Eric's head was screaming with fuel.

That was the answer. He had to use it before Lewis did.

Eric drew a breath to calm himself, and then he stopped fighting the pain. Instead, he embraced it. He tried to pull it deeper into himself.

And then he was gone. In the Fade.

Lewis flinched as if he'd just been slapped in the face. His eyes scanned the yard. When he didn't see Eric, he stepped forward and put his hands on the porch's railing.

"Gotta say, Six, I'm impressed. Wasn't expecting you to learn the Fade so quickly. Usually takes a lot longer. Hell, Mikey can still barely do it." His eyes scanned the yard again.

Sarah was standing now, her daughter in her arms. She glanced from the police car in the driveway to the house, trying to decide where to run.

Eric felt the now-familiar panic at being unmoored from his body. He'd successfully entered the Fade, but now what? If his only goal was to stay safe, he might as well not have come. He needed to find a way to act.

"I could tell you it's not always this easy," Lewis said. "Sometimes the Fade pushes back and threatens to swallow you. You have to find a way to remain grounded, like I did by cutting myself outside your window, but you're not going to be around much longer, so what's the point?"

Eric fought the panic, once again trying to think. If the pain was fuel for the Fade, it had to still be there even though he couldn't feel it. If only he could find a way to access it, maybe he could use it. Lewis moved from place to place in the Fade, right? But how?

Lewis reached back and pulled something out of his waistband—a pistol. "I'm not really a gun guy, but it's hard to grow up in Wakefield and not get a little experience. So when I killed that cop and I saw his gun sitting there, I thought, why not?" He leveled the gun, pointing it at Sarah. "What's it going to be, Eric, you or her?"

"Stay away from us!" Sarah growled.

"Nah, I'm having too much fun." Lewis grabbed her by arm. "Last chance, Eric."

In the distance, Eric heard sirens.

Eric couldn't feel anything, but he thought he could *sense* something. A tiny ball of energy in his core. The pain. He tried to embrace that feeling and concentrated on where he wanted it to go.

And then he was standing on the porch, six feet from Lewis.

"Ah, there you are." Lewis smiled and pulled the trigger.

The bullet hit Sarah Barrington in the temple and passed straight through her skull exploding out the other side of her head. The bullet hit the doorframe along with a splatter of bone and brain matter. Her daughter slipped from her arms and landed with a thud.

On the ground, Tonya whimpered in confusion. "Mom?"

"I'll get to you in a second dear." Lewis turned to Eric. "Now if we—"

Eric was already in motion, charging Lewis. Fury had overtaken rational thought. He was going to kill Lewis.

He slammed into him, grabbing the gun with one hand and drawing back his other to punch, when—

Lewis once again disappeared.

The gun was still clutched in Eric's hand.

Why had the gun stayed when the rest of him had Faded? After all, his clothes Faded along with him, so it was clear he was able to take inanimate objects into the Fade. Maybe it was because it had happened so fast. The Fade had almost been a reflex to avoid the charging man. Maybe it was because Eric had been gripping the gun so tightly.

It didn't matter now. What mattered was the girl. Eric squatted down next to her.

"Mom?" Tonya whispered again in a distant, dreamy voice.

"It's okay," Eric said, echoing Sarah's words to her daughter. Sarah hadn't been right about that, and Eric suspected he wasn't either, but what else could he say to a scared girl whose mother had just been murdered?

He crouched over Tonya, protecting her with his body as he waited for Lewis to reappear. His eyes darted from the yard to the police car to the porch. Nothing.

And then he remembered the open door behind him. If Lewis wanted to get the jump on him, that's where he would reappear. He twisted his body around just in time to see Lewis blink into existence two feet behind him. Lewis stretched out his arms to grab Eric, but Eric was ready. He squeezed the trigger three times, sending a trio of rounds into Lewis's chest.

Lewis fell backward onto the floor. He let out a tremendous wheezing groan, and then his body went slack.

Eric scurried over to him. Lewis's eyes were open and empty, but Eric checked for a pulse anyway. There was none.

He turned his gaze from Lewis to Sarah. And then he turned to Tonya. The twelve-year-old girl lay whimpering on the porch, afraid, confused, and drugged half out of her mind.

Eric stood up. The sirens were close now. If he wanted to have any chance of getting out of this neighborhood with its single exit point, he had to go. But there was something he had to check first.

He reached through the open door and fumbled around until his fingers found the switch that turned on the porchlight. In the light's yellow glow, he bent over and looked at Tonya's wide, frightened eyes. A chill ran through Eric. There was a black speck in Tonya's right eye.

Eric's mind went numb as he shifted into survival mode. He reached into Lewis's pocket and found the car key. Then he ran to the rented Corolla parked across the street, leaving Tonya alone with the bodies of her attempted kidnapper and her mother.

Maybe he should have stayed with her. Maybe he should have tried to explain to the police what was happening. But he didn't think that was the right move. As he drove the rental car out of the neighborhood, headlights off, turning the opposite direction of the flashing lights in the distance, there was only one thought in Eric's mind.

Lewis had said there was nothing left for Eric to prove. That was incorrect. For this to be over, he had to do one more thing.

Eric drove to the highway and started south toward Wakefield.

PART III

SOMETHING LEFT TO PROVE

26

Mikey sat on the bed in silence, a knot of worry twisting in his stomach as Merle explained the Fade to his sister's adoptive father. Back at the house, this had all seemed so straightforward. Becky was behaving rashly, trying to save her dad and not thinking about the consequences. Not thinking about what the decision might mean for her son.

He didn't blame her. He probably would have done the same for his adoptive parents if they were still alive. His dad had died ten years ago, and his mom eight, so he'd never get the chance to find out. Still, if the situations were reversed and he was the one acting out of some nostalgic memory of childhood love or some instinct to protect his family, he hoped that Becky would do the same as he had done. Their Wakefield mission couldn't be exposed. Becky was risking everything—including her son—and Mikey had to stop her.

That's the way everything had seemed when he was lying in bed back at the house, anyway. Now, looking in the face of the confused old man who'd just wanted to reunite with his daughter, things didn't seem so clear.

The man had to be in his late seventies. That was no

surprise, really. Merle selected his adoptive parents from a pool of those who'd tried to adopt from traditional agencies and been rejected. One of the most common reasons for the rejection was the age of parents, especially back in the seventies and eighties when a parent in their forties with a baby seemed outside the norm. Mikey's own adoptive parents had been nearly fifty when they'd taken him into their home.

Mr. Wilson blinked, his face pale with bafflement. "So you're telling me my daughter has some sort of disease."

"I suppose that's one way to look at it, yes," Merle said. "The Fade has infected her. Not your fault. Not anyone's. She was born with it. And now she needs to be near the source."

Mikey glanced at Becky and saw she was watching the interaction between Merle and Wilson with rapt attention and something like terror. He supposed this was the ultimate in her two worlds colliding. Merle was the symbol of everything weird, frightening, and—yes—exciting about Wakefield. Those with the Fade were treated differently in Wakefield, and that was all because of Merle. He'd found a way to prolong their strange lives. And Wilson was the man she probably still thought of as her father. If she was anything like Mikey, she still dreamed about those innocent days with her adoptive family.

And here they were, two of the most important men in her life, staring each other in the face.

"If she's infected, she needs doctors, not whatever this is," Wilson said. "Does the Center for Disease Control know about this? It needs to be studied if it's going to be solved."

Mikey sighed. Wilson had just seen Merle flicker in and out of existence before his eyes, and he was talking about the Center for Disease Control.

At Wilson's words, something in Merle's face changed, and a chill ran through Mikey. He'd seen that expression on Merle's face only once before. The night he'd sent Nancy away. Though that had been five years ago, he still relived it frequently in his nightmares, and there wasn't a day he didn't wake up thinking about it. He'd lost the love of his life, all because she'd let the wrong words slip out of her mouth.

From Merle's expression, Mikey knew that Wilson was dead.

Still, Merle forced a soft smile onto his face. "See, Mr. Wilson, that's where we have a problem. When you start talking about bringing government agencies into Wakefield, I get a little nervous."

Mr. Wilson reflected Merle's smile in a way that made Mikey think maybe he'd underestimated the man's intelligence. "What's wrong, Merle? You think they'd frown on all the kidnappings? Or this strange illness you've been hiding for however many decades?"

Merle met Wilson's eyes. "I'm a reasonable man. I don't like hurting people, especially people who may not understand what they've stepped into. But when you talk about endangering me and mine, I tend to get less civil. Makes me think you shouldn't be walking out of this room."

"Please, I never believed I was going to be walking out of this room." Wilson's voice was strong, but it dripped with sadness.

Baughman took a step toward them. His hand was on the butt of his gun. "Now let's all take a deep breath and think about things. I believe there's a way we can all get what we want."

Merle kept his gaze on Mr. Wilson. "Caleb?"

Caleb darted forward, dashing with surprising quickness for a man of his size. His right fist slammed into Baughman's face, sending the man sprawling onto his back on the bed. Caleb pounced, rolling him over, pinning his arms behind his back. In a moment, he had a zip-tie secured around Baughman's wrists. He slipped the gun out of the shoulder holster and stuck it in the back of his pants.

"What the hell!" Baughman shouted. "Do you have any idea what you're doing?"

Caleb marched across the room and got a roll of duct tape out of his backpack. He ripped off a nice big piece and taped Baughman's mouth, wrapping the tape around his head twice.

"Where were we?" Merle asked. "Oh yeah." He reached out, his hand stretching toward Wilson. The hand seemed to flicker. Then it disappeared into Wilson's chest.

Wilson looked down at the arm sticking out of his chest, and his face grew suddenly pale. He tried to take a step back, but he couldn't move. Something was holding him there. He spoke in a weak voice. "What are you doing?"

"I'm grabbing your heart," Merle said. "And now I'm squeezing."

Wilson let out a grunt. His eyes bulged and a vein on his forehead stuck out so far Mikey thought it might pop.

"No," Becky whispered. She sounded like a scared little girl.

Caleb shot her a look. "Stay cool, Becky. Don't make me put you on the bed with the FBI man."

It wasn't clear if Becky even heard, but she didn't move.

Baughman grunted through the duct tape, squirming on the bed to free himself. The fury was clear in his eyes, but Caleb had done his work well.

Wilson let out a series of groans before the life finally

went out of him. When he went limp, Merle pulled back his hand. It was slick with blood.

Wilson collapsed to the floor. His shirt was intact and there was no blood seeping through. Somehow, Merle had managed to destroy the man's heart without so much as leaving a mark on the outside of his body.

Mikey had seen a lot during his time in Wakefield, but he'd never seen anything like that. He looked up at Becky and saw she was still frozen in place, but her face was streaked with tears now.

Merle disappeared into the bathroom and the water turned on. He remerged a few moments later, drying his hands with a towel.

"Want me to stay here and clean up?" Caleb asked.

Merle shook his head. "I need you to help me take Baughman to the cabin. I'd like to have a little chat with him. I'll call someone to handle this."

Caleb grabbed Baughman's arm. "You heard the man."

For a moment, Baughman didn't move. Then his eyes flickered toward the dead man on the floor, and he got to his feet.

Merle turned to Becky. "I'm sorry you had to see that, dear. I wish it hadn't played out like that." Then he put a hand on Mikey's shoulders. "You did good, son."

Mikey's heart was in his throat as Caleb led the FBI man out of the motel room.

Merle paused at the doorway. "You two go home and get some sleep. We'll talk tomorrow. There's work to be done."

Then he walked out, pulling the door shut behind him, leaving Becky and Mikey alone with the body.

27

The drive from North Prairie, Wisconsin, to Wakefield, Tennessee, took Eric nearly twelve hours. He waited until he hit Racine before stopping at an ATM. He withdrew five hundred dollars from his bank account and took a five hundred dollar cash advance on his credit card. A thousand dollars might be overkill, but he didn't plan on using his cards again.

He also reset his cellphone to factory settings and shoved it down into a trashcan, under an old McDonald's bag. Again, he wasn't sure the move was strictly necessary. Could authorities track him by his cellphone even when his phone was off? He had no idea, and he wasn't eager to find out.

The bigger question was whether the police were after him. They would be eventually; he was certain of that. They would eventually uncover that the blocked calls to the police station and Sarah Barrington had come from his phone. And if they found him, the fact that the dead officer's gun was currently in Eric's glovebox probably wouldn't help matters.

In the end, he figured better safe than arrested. He needed to get to Wakefield. When he was done there, the police could have him.

He was going on thirty hours without sleep by the time he crossed the state line into Tennessee, not counting twenty minutes of fitful rest on the plane the previous morning, but he didn't feel tired. Through the entire drive, his anger never faded. He remembered his ex-wife's words from a few days before. *I hope whatever you do next, it helps you find it again... The passion. The thing that made you a force of nature.*

Is that what had happened? Had he found his passion again?

He wasn't sure, but he did know he had never felt anything as strong as the anger he felt now. He'd left a drugged little girl on her front porch next to her mother's dead body. And that little girl's troubles weren't over. If Lewis was to be believed, the Fade would come for her soon, if it hadn't already.

Had Eric done the wrong thing? He didn't think so. He'd fought to keep the girl out of the hands of Merle's insane cycle of kidnappings.

As for Lewis, Eric felt nothing. He could shoot him again a hundred times and not feel a lick of guilt. How many kids had Lewis taken from their parents? A dozen? More? Whatever the outcome for Tonya, Eric was pleased he'd taken Lewis Keller out of the world.

Sleepiness began to creep in during the last three hours of the drive. He blasted the stereo, thankful for the rental car's satellite radio, and he kept the windows down. The assault of music on his ears and wind on his face kept him alert.

He made it to Wakefield at a little after two in the afternoon. As he passed the Wakefield Motor Inn, he considered stopping. It might have been good to discuss some of the theories running through his head with Baughman. But time was already against him, and he didn't know how to even start explaining the things he'd seen. Instead, he drove straight to Barker Street.

The house was draped in late-afternoon shadows when Eric pulled up. He parked in front of the house, grabbed the gun out of the glovebox, and walked to the front door.

He tried the door and found it unlocked. Not too surprising when he thought about it, and not because of some small-town lifestyle. When your enemies could walk through doors, what was the point of a lock?

After not finding anyone in the kitchen or living room, he trudged up to the second floor and went to a door he'd only glimpsed the previous day. He knocked with the side of his hand, good and loud.

The voice that answered was groggy with sleep. "Mikey?"

Eric opened the door and stepped inside. "Definitely not Mikey."

Becky sat up. Her eyes went to Eric's face, to the gun held at his side, and back to his face. "Lewis didn't kill you, I see."

"No, he did not."

"I'm glad." She paused. "You come for a little payback?"

Eric shook his head. "I came for answers." He sighed. "The last twenty-four hours, I've seen some things, and I need someone to explain them to me, straight out. No more riddles or mysteries or half-answers. I just want the truth laid plain."

The room was silent for a moment. Eric still wasn't sure why he'd chosen Becky to ask his questions of. After all, she hadn't exactly proven herself trustworthy. He could have gone to Marsha Crawford for more answers, but his gut told him it should be Becky. Maybe he felt a connection to her because of their shared experience of having been kidnapped. Or maybe he was just a sucker for a pretty face.

After a moment, she threw back the covers and stood up. "Okay. Truth I can do. After last night... talking it out with someone doesn't sound half bad."

"Wait, what happened last night?"

Becky stared at the floor. She looked dazed, like a woman trying to wake up from a dream. "Merle killed my dad." She looked up, meeting Eric's eyes. "And he took Baughman."

"Oh my God. Is Baughman... is he alive?"

"I don't know," Becky said, her voice distant. "I'll get Mikey. Meet us downstairs."

THE THREE OF them sat around the small kitchen table. Mikey had his arms wrapped around himself, as if trying to get warm. Becky leaned forward, her dark hair dangling over the table. Despite not having slept the previous night, Eric felt very alert indeed. He wanted to hear what Becky and her brother were going to tell him.

Becky and Mikey were avoiding looking at each other, Eric noticed. Something had happened between them.

"They say the glow started in Lake Stano sometime in the mid-sixties," Becky said. "As far as we've been told, there was no clear event that kicked off the glow. No meteor crashing into the water or earthquake that released it from the depths. One day, something in the lake just started glowing. Apparently, people got pretty scared. This was the Cold War era, after all, and folks had all sorts of theories about what could be causing it, most having to do with Russia. Government agencies were called, but by the time they showed up and investigated, the glow had stopped. It only lasted a couple days. But that was all it took."

"Who told you all this?" Eric asked. "Is it something people in town talk about?"

"No," Mikey said quickly. "I think people know better than to talk about it these days. Even those who don't know exactly what's happening understand that was the start of what's wrong with Wakefield."

"Merle gave us these... lessons, I guess you'd say." Becky stared down at the table. "He told us about the glow. Anyway, after the glow was gone, a few people in town started experiencing these unexplained headaches. Doctors couldn't help them much and usually diagnosed them as migraines. But they weren't."

"They were the Fade," Eric said.

Becky nodded. "There were about fifteen families affected. They all lived quite close to Lake Stano. After a few months, the headaches turned into something worse. People in those families developed black spots in their eyes that came and went, and not long after that, they began to have strange out-of-body experiences."

"And what did the medical community have to say about that?" Eric asked.

"Delusions," Mikey said. "Mental healthcare being what it was back then, people stopped reporting it after a while."

Becky nodded. "It was less than a year before the older folks with the Fade started dying. And within a couple years, they'd realized that their children, even those conceived after the glow was gone, they had it too. Seemed to be hereditary. And even in cases where one of the parents had the Fade, it was passed on to the child."

Eric leaned back in his chair and crossed his arms. "I'm

thinking that if it were me, my first step would be to get out of Wakefield. I'd assume Lake Stano had some radioactive element that was causing the problems, and I'd want to get as far away as possible."

"You wouldn't be alone," Becky said. "People moved away. But the headaches got much worse, and the Fade progressed even faster. It seems the disease craves whatever residual energy is in Wakefield. Most of those who left came back relatively quickly. Those who didn't come back died within a year."

Eric considered that a moment. Lewis had touched on this topic, but he wanted more details. "How did they die? How does the Fade kill you? I mean, seeing as I've got it now, it would be nice to know how I'm going to go out."

Mikey and Becky exchanged a glance. Then Mikey spoke.

"There are two possibilities, neither of them very pleasant. For those who stay away from Wakefield too long, the Fade weakens, and so do they. People waste away, getting thinner and weaker. They're little more than skin and bones by the end. They generally die of heart failure."

Then why didn't that happen to me? Eric wondered. But he didn't ask the question aloud.

"The other option is to stay in Wakefield. The Fade gets stronger, allowing the infected a longer, more pleasant life. At least for a while. But eventually, the Fades get more frequent and last longer. Ironically, most of us die of heart attacks, too."

"Damn," Eric said. Mikey was right. It didn't sound like the most pleasant way to go. "Okay, so how does this lead to the kidnappings?"

"This is the part where Merle enters our little tale,"

Becky said. "He was ten when Lake Stano started glowing, and by all accounts, he was a weird little kid."

"Shocking," Eric said.

"Instead of being afraid of the glow like everyone else, it seems that he was drawn to it. One night, he snuck out of the house and went for a swim in the glowing waters. He told us it was the best night of his life."

"You weren't lying about the weird kid thing."

"No, I wasn't. He was also the only one who managed to have any control over the Fade. While others were dying, he was thriving. He figured out how to use it to his advantage. And he was also the one who had the idea of sending babies away from Wakefield to see if being raised elsewhere helped them. His theory was sending them away when they were young would help them build up a resistance."

Eric scratched at his chin. Something was bothering him about all this. "Okay, here's what I don't understand. You've got this weird, terrifying disease no one can explain. You have to live near this dumb lake in Tennessee or it gets worse. You know it's hereditary. So why have kids? Why not just embrace birth control?"

Mikey chuckled. "You'd think that would be the way to go, wouldn't you? And some did go that route. From what Merle told us, there were forty-seven kids under eighteen infected by the glow. Many of them died childless. But others?" He shook his head. "I guess the biological imperative to reproduce was too strong for some, even knowing the consequences."

Eric remembered the line from *Jurassic Park*. *Life finds a way*. Maybe that was even true of life infected with the Fade. "The next part I think I know. Merle and the others start finding parents who have been turned down by adoption agencies and offering them the babies."

Becky nodded. "It wasn't exactly legal, but Merle was very good at convincing the adoptive parents it was all legit. They used fake names on the paperwork, of course. They didn't want the law to be able to trace it back to Wakefield once the kidnappings started."

"So when the kids were twelve, they stole them back, brought them to Wakefield, and tested them for the Fade?" Eric asked.

"Yes," Mikey confirmed. "Most of the town didn't know, of course. But there were enough infected families to get the job done. Our year, there were six. The three of us, plus Caleb, Lewis, and Nancy."

"I've been meaning to ask about Nancy," Eric said. "Is she—"

"She's dead," Mikey said quickly.

His tone made it clear it wasn't a topic he was keen on discussing, so Eric let it go. For now.

"Our memories of the time after we were brought here are odd," Becky said. "Mikey and I have compared notes, and we remember it differently. I remember Merle taking us to the lake and us all meeting there for the first time. Mikey remembers it happening in the barn where we had our lessons."

"I suppose that's understandable," Eric interjected. "You'd just been through a significant trauma. It's not surprising that some of the details are fuzzy."

"What's not fuzzy is that he told us about you right from the start," Mikey said. "He told us you'd passed the test and been sent back to your family. We'd failed, and so we had to spend our lives here, with our new families. It was pretty clear he wanted us to hate you right from the start. I think he was using you as a stick for us to measure ourselves against. To push us."

"He taught us to use the Fade," Becky said. "We started our new lives in Wakefield, and the cycle continued. Every year, a few new kids would show up and join our little group. Some of them have died. Others haven't. But Merle always seemed to favor us over any of the others. Caleb became his right-hand man. Lewis became his expert kidnapper. And he gave Mikey and me this house. Said he wanted to keep us close."

Eric rubbed his chin, deep in thought. "How many kids are out there now? The adopted ones who will be brought here eventually?"

"Somewhere in the neighborhood of thirty," Becky answered.

Eric felt a shiver. Thirty children who would be torn from their homes if Eric couldn't stop Merle. And if he could stop Merle, they'd die horrible deaths from the Fade.

"One more question. When you guys were brought to Wakefield, what was the test Merle gave you?"

Mikey's brow furrowed. "Same as the one you got, I'd imagine. He had me stare into his eye. Then the headache started. After a few seconds of pain, I entered the Fade for the first time."

Eric turned to Becky. "Is that how it played out for you, too?"

Becky nodded. "You?"

"Not exactly. He had me stare into his eye, but I didn't get the headache. I saw something. A ghostly version of Merle came up from behind me and grabbed me."

A look of concern crossed Becky's face. "Why would it be different for you?"

"I don't know," Eric said, "but I'm starting to put together a theory. Maybe one we can use against him."

Mikey flashed a thin smile. "Care to share with the class?"

Eric leaned forward. "I don't think Merle sent me away because I was immune to the Fade. I think he sent me away because he was scared of me. He sent me away because I'm like him."

28

Neither Becky nor Mikey spoke for a long moment. Then Becky met Eric's eyes. "Like him how?"

"It took me a while to figure it out," Eric said, "but the way you guys talk about the Fade is different from the way I experience it. At least so far. Lewis talked about it being something that builds up in your head over time. He had to cut himself to keep it at bay. And I saw the way it was for you that day in bed, Mikey."

"I wish you hadn't," Mikey said, his eyes downcast. "When I'm like that, I don't want anyone to see me. Not even Becky."

Becky put a comforting hand on his arm.

"It's okay," Eric said. "I'm glad I saw it. I think it's important that I did. Because the Fade is different for me. There's pain, terrible pain, just like Lewis talked about, but there's something else too. When the Fade comes, how does it feel? Aside from the pain, I mean?"

Becky's face scrunched up in distaste. "It feels... disgusting. Like a foreign presence is invading my mind. I feel soiled when it's over."

Mikey nodded weakly. "That's about it."

"See, that's not what it's like for me. I feel, I don't know, invigorated. The Fade feels right. Like it belongs."

Becky looked at him curiously. It reminded him of the way she'd looked at him up in Mikey's room the day he met her. Like she was revolted by him. She tried to hide it, but it was there in her eyes.

Eric couldn't deny that the look stung, but he had more important things to worry about at the moment than what this woman thought of him.

"If Merle's afraid of you becoming too much like him, why'd he have us put you in the lake?" Mikey asked. "Wouldn't that make you *more* like him?"

"I don't know," Eric said. "I'm still trying to work that out. That's part of why I want to get back there. Maybe I can absorb more of the Fade. Get strong enough to take Merle down."

Becky's eyebrows shot upward in surprise. "Hang on, you want to go back in the lake?"

"I don't know if *want* is the right word. But I feel like I need to. I'm hoping you two can help me. Maybe distract Caleb and Merle while I go for my little swim. That is, if you want to stop him."

Mikey and Becky exchanged a glance.

After a moment, Becky spoke. "I've never been the biggest Merle fan, but I've always been too scared to do anything about it. But after last night? After what he did to my dad? Yeah, I want to take the son of a bitch down."

Eric turned to Mikey.

"I've wanted the old man dead for years," Mikey said.

"Good. Then I say we make our move now. We don't know what he's done to Baughman. Maybe there's still a chance to save him."

"There's something we haven't thought about," Becky said. "Lewis. He's much stronger than Caleb. Not as strong as Merle, but still... He's gotta be on his way back here. I don't know how you survived him the first time, but if he comes back, we don't stand a chance."

Eric's eyes were cold when he answered. "You don't need to worry about Lewis. I already killed him."

Becky's only answer was shocked silence.

BEFORE THEY LEFT for the cabin, Eric excused himself and went to the bathroom. As he made his way through the house, he felt the weariness in his legs. He was still mentally alert, but the long two days of travel, violence, and lack of sleep were taking their toll on his body. But there was no way he could afford to rest. Not now. Not when Merle had Baughman.

Eric didn't know what Merle wanted with the FBI agent, and Becky and Mikey claimed not to know either. For all any of them knew, Baughman was dead already. But Eric suspected he wasn't. If there was even a chance to save him, Eric had to take it.

After relieving himself, Eric washed his hands. Then he stood, staring in the mirror at his haggard face. His hair was a mess, and the stubble on his face was threatening to turn into a beard if he didn't do something about it soon. And then there was the black spot in his eye.

Eric wondered if it would ever go away again, or if it was just a part of him now. He could feel the Fade in the back of his mind, simmering but not quite boiling. Good. That was how it needed to be. The pain humming in his head meant he had the Fade ready if he needed to use it. And if they were going to defeat Merle, he'd almost certainly have to access it.

He hoped that they'd be able to catch Merle by surprise. Hopefully, the old man hadn't heard about Lewis yet. On the drive down, Eric had monitored the news and hadn't heard anything about the events in North Prairie. He had to assume it wouldn't be long before it was national news.

Eric squeezed his eyes shut and splashed a bit of cold water on his face. As the icy water rolled down his cheeks, he felt something like a breath on the back of his neck.

A chill ran through him.

In the past few days, he'd remembered so many things about his time in this house when he was twelve. Things he hadn't thought of in thirty years, at least not consciously. The woods behind the house. The strange test Merle had given him. The smell of the room. And now, he was experiencing the one thing that had remained forgotten until now.

The way he'd felt when he heard the voices in the night.

He heard it now, a strange groan, like air being forced through a disfigured mouth. He wanted to believe it was something natural in the house—the pipes maybe—but he couldn't. The noise sounded like the mouth was mere inches from his ear.

He didn't want to open his eyes. Even after everything else he'd seen in the past few days, he didn't know if he could handle this. But he had to. Because this was another piece of the puzzle. Terrifying as it might be, it was a clue that he needed.

Very slowly, Eric opened his eyes.

He saw nothing but himself in the mirror. Turning around, everything was as it should be. He was alone.

Then the noise came again, close to his left ear now. An inhuman groan.

"What are you?" Eric didn't expect an answer to the whispered question, and he didn't get one, but he felt a breath again, this time on his arm.

The Fade roiled in the back of his mind, breaking his concentration. An idea came to him then. He reached into the pain, drawing on it to dip into the Fade. Not enough to disappear, just enough that he felt like he was on the edge of vanishing.

And then, he saw a woman's face hovering next to him in the mirror. Her eyes were pure black, and her cheeks were drawn. Her mouth opened wider than humanly possible, and a sickly groan escaped her great, gaping maw.

Eric let out a shout of surprise and he stumbled backward, slamming his back into the wall behind him. He pushed the Fade away, hard and fast. Once again, his was the only face in the mirror.

He left the bathroom, tingling with the now-familiar buzz that came when he used the Fade. He clenched his hands into fists to stop them from shaking. His heart felt like it might beat out of his chest.

"You okay?" Becky asked when he rejoined them in the kitchen. "Thought I heard a shout."

"Yeah," Eric said.

"Good. Before we do this, I have to point out that there are other access points to the lake. We could go to one of the houses on the other side of the lake and dip you there."

Eric considered it. Going into the lake far from Merle's cabin did sound appealing, but he didn't think it would work the same way. "The presence in the lake... it hangs out near the cabin, doesn't it?"

"Seems that way," Mikey confirmed.

"Then we have our answer."

"So we're doing this?"

Eric nodded absently. He needed to get his head right. This wasn't the kind of thing you wanted to go into without total concentration. But he also needed to understand what he'd just seen. "Listen, I know this is a weird question, but have either of you ever heard voices in this house?"

Becky tilted her head. "Voices? What do you mean?"

"In the night. Or, I don't know, a breath on your neck when no one else is there."

A surprised grin crossed Mikey's face. "Are you asking if our house is haunted?"

"No. Well, maybe. Have you?"

Mikey shook his head. "No, man. Not even a little."

"Why you asking?" Becky said.

"Something I remembered. From the time I spent here after the kidnapping. Probably just nightmares."

Becky gave him a strange look. "Something you're not telling us, Partin?"

"Nah. Like I said, just a weird memory echoing down through the years." He went to the door and put his hand on the knob. "The sooner we get this over with, the better."

"Couldn't agree more," Mikey said.

The three of them went out the back door and headed for the forest. Eric strode a few steps in front of the others, trying to display a confidence he didn't feel. The trail was just as dark as he remembered, but it felt a few degrees cooler. The trees seemed taller. They leaned over the trail menacingly, warning passersby not to stray from the path. The last time Eric walked this trail, he'd been journeying into the unknown, a gun at his back. This time he knew all too well what lay at the end of the trail. He wasn't sure which situation was worse.

It seemed to Eric they'd only gone about halfway, but then he spotted the clearing up ahead. The immediacy of what they were about to tackle hit him hard and sent his heart racing. He stopped fifty feet from the clearing and waited for Becky and Mikey to catch up.

"Everybody good?" Eric asked when they reached him. It was a ridiculous question. Of course they weren't good.

Mikey shrugged. "Good as I'm going to be."

Becky frowned. "Just so I'm clear, the plan is we head to the cabin, a place we never go, use some bullshit excuse to distract Caleb and Merle, and you go for a swim on the off chance it amps up your Fade abilities."

Eric couldn't help but grin. "Sounds kinda dumb when you say it like that."

"Uh-huh. And what if we do all that, you get in the water and nothing changes?"

Eric's expression grew more serious. "Look, end of the day, I'm going to do what it takes to get Baughman back. That's my first priority."

"If your man Baughman, gets out safe, that's great. But he's a distant third priority after killing Merle and getting me and my brother out safely."

Mikey took a step between them. "Can we just do this? If we're going to die horrible deaths, I'd just as soon get to it."

"No argument here," Eric said.

Becky nodded. "Okay. Mikey and I will go scout it out. If it's all clear, we'll come back and tell you. If we're not back in two minutes, that means someone is out there. Give us an extra minute, and then take your chance."

As Becky and Mikey walked out into the clearing, Eric waited in the shadows, the Fade shimmering in the back of his mind.

THE THIRTY YARDS between the edge of the woods and the lake was an open area with a thin dirt path winding through the long grass. From the woods, the cabin blocked the place where the trail split off in two directions, one that led to the cabin, and another that led to the lake.

As Becky and Mikey rounded the curve, they saw Caleb Bloom standing at the split. His arms were crossed over his chest as he stared out at the water. From what Becky could see of his face in profile, he appeared transfixed.

Becky and Mikey exchanged a worried glance, and then approached.

When they were about ten feet away, Caleb addressed them without turning. "Figured you two would still be sleeping it off."

Becky walked up next to him. "That's our reputation, huh? The ones who sleep all day?"

He shrugged, neither confirming nor denying. Then he turned to face her. "Becky, I'm sorry about what happened to your father. Seeing that, I can't imagine how it felt."

Becky swallowed, pushing down the emotion that threatened to rise up. "It sucked is what it did. I waited so long to see him again, and then that happens?"

Caleb nodded. "He had to die. I understand that. But Merle didn't have to end his life the way he did. That was cruel."

Becky was momentarily taken aback. She didn't think she'd ever heard Caleb say a negative word about Merle. Certainly not since they were teenagers. "No argument there. He was just a guy trying to find his daughter. He didn't deserve to die like that."

Caleb turned back to face the water. His worried expression revealed that he thought maybe he'd said too much on the topic. "What brings you two out here? I mean, you come to the lake twice in three days? That's gotta be some kind of record."

"Same reason both times," Mikey said.

Caleb looked at Mikey, suddenly far more interested. "What's that supposed to mean?"

"Eric Partin," Becky said. "He showed up at our house a few minutes ago."

A shadow passed over Caleb's face. "That so?"

"He was pretty pissed. Waved a gun around and was shouting about the Fade. I think it's fair to say he's not adapting as well as Merle had hoped."

Caleb let out a sad chuckle. "Can't say I'm surprised. You saw what Lewis was like after he was dipped. Guy barely knew his own name for two weeks. Not sure why Merle let Eric go in that condition. Where is he now?"

Becky shrugged. "He took off after a few minutes. Said he needed to talk to Baughman. So maybe he went back to the motel. Obviously, he has no way of knowing Baughman is here with Merle."

Caleb sighed. "Okay, thanks. I'll let Merle know. Call if he shows up again."

"Caleb, there's something else." She paused, letting that hang in the air a moment. "I don't know if it's true, but Eric... he claimed that he killed Lewis last night."

Caleb stood up a bit straighter, suddenly more alert as he realized the gravity of the situation. He scratched at his chin a moment, then turned toward the cabin. "All right. Come with me. Merle might have questions."

ERIC WAITED three minutes and then crept down the trail through the long grass, staying low and doing his best to move silently. When he reached the bend in the trail, he proceeded slowly until the entire area between the cabin and the lake was visible.

He smiled when he saw there was no one there. His two co-conspirators had done their jobs. Of course, Eric had no way of knowing if someone was watching from the cabin window, but he knew this was the best chance he was going to get.

Still crouching, he hurried the rest of the way down the trail. When he reached the dock, he didn't dare glance back at the cabin. He just kept moving, striding across the boards to the end of the dock.

When he reached it, he sat down, letting his legs dangle over the edge. The soles of his shoes just touched the water. He set his phone and his pistol on the dock, squeezed his eyes shut, and said a silent prayer. Then he took a deep breath and slipped into the lake.

29

MERLE'S CABIN was a small structure consisting of only three rooms, but it always felt much bigger to Becky. Maybe it was because she'd been so young and afraid the first time she'd seen it. Merle had brought her there a few weeks after the kidnapping. After she'd passed his little test and first experienced the Fade. It was here she'd met Caleb, Lewis, and Nancy. And it was here where she'd been reunited with her twin brother.

Mikey remembered things differently. He always claimed the meeting had taken place in the barn on the other side of the lake, the same one where they'd had the rest of their lessons. It had been an ongoing debate over the years, both of them completely convinced that they were right. Once, they'd asked Nancy, hoping she'd be the tie-breaking vote. Her response hadn't been what they'd expected. She didn't remember the encounter at all, and she had gotten a little angry when they pushed her on it.

Just another Wakefield mystery, Becky supposed.

The main room of the cabin was dominated by a large

oak desk and a wall of file cabinets. When it came to bookkeeping, Merle was old school. He didn't own a computer as far as Becky knew, and it seemed every time she entered the cabin—which was as rarely as possible—he was writing in one of his big brown ledger books. Today was no exception.

Becky's eyes darted to the filing cabinets. She wondered what they could possibly contain. She knew he had to keep records on his whole temporary adoption scheme, but that many? What other information was stored there? If Becky were to search the cabinets, would she find information on her son?

The thought was maddening. More than likely there was a piece of paper in one of those filing cabinets with her son's new name and address. All that stood between her and reuniting with him was a stack of paperwork.

That and Merle.

The old man looked up as they entered. When he saw the three of them, he gently set his fountain pen down and folded his hands on the desk. His expression was unreadable.

"I didn't expect to see the Talbots this morning. I hope you're not angry about last night."

"I am," Becky said. "But that's not why we're here."

Caleb stepped in front of the other two. "They had a visit from Eric Partin."

Becky felt a twinge of annoyance at the way Caleb took over. It had always been like that. Despite his desire to come off as a rebel, Caleb was always jockeying for position with the rest of them. He wanted to make sure he was the one who got Merle's approval.

Merle raised an eyebrow. "That so? Last I heard, he was in Wisconsin. Must have driven through the night to get down here. Or perhaps he caught an early morning flight. Did he say why he'd come?"

"He wasn't too coherent," Mikey said. "And I was a little more concerned about the gun he was waving around than what he was saying."

"Tell him the other part," Caleb said.

Mikey nodded. "He claimed that he killed Lewis last night."

Merle's expression didn't change in the least, but there was a long pause before he answered. "Is that so?"

"Is it even possible?" Caleb asked. "Eric's been using the Fade all of, what, two days? Lewis should have knocked him into next Tuesday."

"Perhaps." Merle smiled thinly. "But the Fade isn't the only way to kill someone. And Eric is strong."

"So what are we going to do about it?" Becky asked. "He said he was going to the motel to talk to Baughman next. When he finds him gone, it's only a matter of time before he shows up here."

"I hope to God he does," Caleb growled. "He won't be so lucky against me."

"It may not come to that," Merle said. "If Lewis is really gone, that's very unfortunate. But it also means we need Eric even more."

"Need him? I don't think some guy with no training is going to—"

Merle held up a hand, cutting him off. There was a strange, distant expression on his face. His eyes drifted shut. "I believe there's someone in the water."

Lake Stano was warmer than Eric remembered. As he slid into it, his first thought was that he wished he'd remembered to take off his shoes. Even if he got the big infusion of power he was hoping for, he'd squeak his way to the confrontation with Merle on sopping-wet sneakers. Not ideal.

His second thought was a realization—he wasn't feeling the blinding pain he'd experienced the first time he'd entered these waters. He didn't feel much of anything except wet.

He let himself sink until the soles of his feet touched the muddy lake bottom. Looking up, he could see the sun cutting through the water, its image distorted by the wavy surface. The bottom of the lake couldn't have been more than ten feet deep. The murky waters gave Eric pause. There was no ball of darkness in these waters. He felt no power here.

They'd played a big hand to get him into the lake. If he came up empty that would pretty much be it. He'd be left to decide whether to confront Merle with the limited power he had or run away. And if he ran, what then? Go home? Turn himself in to the police and try to explain the situation? He had a feeling that would not go well for him.

His lungs were beginning to gently remind him of his body's need for oxygen. As he was about to head to the surface, he noticed the subtle hum of pain that was always in the back of his brain now. He figured it was worth a try.

Just as he'd done when looking in the bathroom mirror earlier, he gently touched the Fade, tickling its surface with his mind. In an instant, the dark presence appeared in front of him.

He felt it now, the electricity in the water. The vicious sting that made every nerve in his body cry out in pain. But he didn't flee from it. He pressed a little harder on the Fade, and the dark sphere grew larger, moved closer.

When it was as large as his torso, he reached out and touched the darkness.

The pain exploded, and he let out a muffled scream in the water. His brain was on fire as the power of the Fade coursed through him. Every fiber of his being sang its agonizing song. It filled him, threatening to unmake him.

Through the pain, a wide smile broke out on Eric's face. He'd been right. This was why he'd come down here. He'd found the power—so much power! With this sweet darkness, he could take on Caleb. He could crush Merle. There was no one who could stand up to him. No one in the world! With this power, he could move mountains. Boil oceans. There was nothing he couldn't do if he—

And then it was gone.

The darkness hadn't drifted away; it had ceased to exist. It was as if the door between Eric and the Fade had slammed shut.

Even the gentle humming pain in his mind had disappeared. He tried to touch it, but there was nothing to touch.

The Fade was gone.

Merle slowly opened his eyes. "I wasn't expecting that. He came here voluntarily. Dipped himself in the water."

Becky didn't dare move. If she glanced at her brother or turned toward the door, she was positive Merle would see through their little ruse. She kept her mouth shut and hoped against hope.

Caleb shifted his weight to his other foot, his face

betraying his concern. "What's that mean? Aside from the fact that he's a psycho."

Merle's gaze drifted to the window. He stared at the blue sky beyond the glass. "It means he can take in a great deal of power. I had you keep him down there for a minute and a half, but now he can stay as long as he likes. Exposure to that much Fade will either drive him insane or make him the most powerful person on the planet. Possibly both."

Caleb's brow furrowed even more deeply. "That... it doesn't sound like a good combination."

"No, indeed," Merle said with a chuckle. "Fortunately, I noticed in time."

"What did you do?" Mikey asked in a weak voice.

"I blocked him from the Fade. He won't be able to touch it again. Not unless I want him to." He looked at Caleb. "Grab him out of the lake and bring him here, would you? He's bound to be a little surly."

Caleb grinned. "Let's hope so. Otherwise I won't have a reason to get rough with him."

Merle watched in silence while Caleb went outside. When the door shut, he turned back to Becky and Mikey. "Kind of interesting timing, wouldn't you say? Eric showing up at the same moment as you two?"

"Not at all," Becky said. Her heart was beating so loudly she was almost sure Merle could hear it. "He left our house only a couple minutes before we did. Told us he was headed to the motel, but I guess he lied."

Merle leaned back, and his chair let out a squeak. "You don't know how much I'd love to believe you. It would make my life so much easier. I've already got a furious former-FBI agent locked in the other room, a strange man from Wisconsin who apparently means me harm, and a dead employee. The last thing I want to believe is that the two of you turned on me."

"We didn't," Mikey said quickly. "We came here to help. Why would we want to hurt you?"

Merle slammed his palm onto the table and the slap echoed loudly through the cabin. "Enough lies." He drew in a deep breath and let it out slowly. As he did, the anger melted off his face, leaving an expression of sadness. "I've lost Lewis already, if Eric is to be believed. I don't want to lose the two of you. But I can't let this go unpunished."

"Merle, you killed my father right in front of me," Becky said, her voice cold. "You didn't expect me to hit back?"

"You're right. This is my fault. I've been too soft on the two of you. Letting you live in that house. Not making you pull your own weight. It's time you started contributing around here."

AS THE FADE DISAPPEARED, Eric's need to breathe reasserted itself with urgency. For a moment, the shock of what had just happened lessoned. He kicked his way to the surface. When his head broke through the water, he took a long, deep breath.

He stayed there for a moment, treading water, his mind desperately trying to figure out what to do next. Becky and Mikey were inside the cabin, and they were expecting him to come bursting through that door, brimming with power. He was supposed to be the guy who took down Merle. Now he couldn't even make himself flicker.

A sound interrupted his thoughts—footsteps on the dock.

He stayed as still as he could while keeping afloat,

hoping against hope whoever that was wouldn't notice him. After a moment, Caleb reached the end of the deck and crouched down, a wide grin on his face.

"Hi, Eric. Going for a little swim?"

Eric said nothing.

Caleb shifted his gaze to something next to him on the dock. "Huh. Mighty nice of you to leave this for me." He picked up the gun and pointed it at Eric. "I think it's time for you to get out now. Merle wants a word."

Eric gritted his teeth, anger seething in his belly. Without the Fade, the pistol was his only hope. Maybe he could shoot Merle, same as he'd done to Lewis. If he'd surfaced and swum to the dock immediately after the Fade disappeared, he would have beat Caleb to the weapon with time to spare. But he'd forgotten about the gun.

Caleb gestured to the ladder on the side of the dock. "Don't make me ask again."

Eric paddled to the ladder and climbed. Just as he'd predicted, his shoes squeaked as he stepped onto the dock. Caleb gave him a wide berth, keeping the gun trained on him.

"Good. Now let's walk nice and casual-like up to the cabin."

Eric started down the dock. Though he couldn't see Caleb, it seemed he could feel the gun's presence as it pointed at his back. "This is the second time in three days I've had a gun pointed at me. It's starting to get a little annoying."

"I hear you killed my buddy Lewis, so forgive me if I don't shed a tear over what annoys you."

Eric let out a weak laugh. "Your buddy? That's not how he told it. He said you used to beat him up in school. He figured it was on account of your little crush on Becky, and her being nice to him. That sound right to you?"

Caleb said nothing.

Eric stepped off the dock and started down the trail toward the cabin, taking his time. "He also told me you pushed him too far. He knocked you right out of your body and started cutting."

"Shut up," Caleb said softly.

Eric turned, and a few beads of water flew off his hair. When they landed on Caleb's face, he flinched as if he'd been burned. A hand went to the wet spot.

Eric remembered Caleb had never been in the lake. Not only that, but he'd probably spent years terrified of it. If Eric could find a way to get him in that water...

Caleb leveled his weapon at Eric again. "Did I tell you to stop?"

At the sight of the gun, Eric's delusions of heroically tackling Caleb into the lake vanished. He turned back around and started walking, but he couldn't resist getting in one more dig.

"Lewis also told me you're a slow learner. He said he had to knock you out of your body twice. And he said you weren't too fond of where he cut you the second time."

The barrel of the gun pressed up against his back. "Not sure what you're trying to accomplish, but how about we stay quiet for the rest of the walk? Merle wouldn't like it if I killed you, but I'm pretty sure he wouldn't mind if I shot you in the hand."

Eric complied, and they walked to the cabin in silence. Eric sloshed his way inside, his wet shoes leaving a trail of water on the wooden floorboards.

Merle sat behind a desk, Mikey and Becky in front of him.

Merle watched Eric with a careful eye as he approached.

"That's close enough," Caleb said when Eric was five feet from the desk.

Merle looked at him for a long moment. "I'm glad you decided to join us, Eric. It's time for you to join in our great work."

30

"Great work?" Eric said. "Is that what you call taking kids from their families? Locking them up for weeks, terrified? Keeping them trapped in this town for the rest of their lives? Is that your great work?"

Merle smiled. "That's part of it, yes. I'll admit it's not the most pleasant part."

Eric looked around at the others. Becky stared at Merle, the hatred clear on her face. Mikey was a little tougher to read, but Eric thought he'd be on their side when it came down to it.

But so what? It was three against two, sure. But one of those two had a gun pointed at Eric, and the other could play the Fade like Jimi Hendrix played guitar. What were they going to do? Rush Merle? He'd probably knock them right out of their bodies, assuming Caleb didn't shoot them dead first.

"I understand your hesitation to embrace what we're doing here," Merle said. "I hope that you'll keep an open mind for the next few minutes. I think once I explain the situation, you'll be able to look at his more rationally." He glanced at Mikey and Becky. "I hope you all will."

"You've been explaining things to me for the last thirty years," Becky said. "I think I've had about enough of your explaining."

"Too bad. You're going to get a little more. Caleb, will you bring Mr. Baughman out here please?"

Caleb hesitated. It was clear he was reluctant to lower the weapon aimed at Eric.

"It's okay," Merle said. "I can handle him."

Caleb nodded. Then he walked to a door on the far side of the room. When he opened it, Eric caught a glimpse of a dim bedroom. He saw a bed, a dresser, and someone tied to a chair. Baughman.

Caleb bent over the chair, and after a few moments of fussing with the ropes, he helped Baughman to his feet. "If you try anything, you'll regret it."

Baughman didn't respond. He just walked forward woozily. If it hadn't been for Caleb supporting him, he might have toppled over. He put a hand on the doorframe when he reached it, and he stepped into the light.

Eric let out a gasp.

The left side of his face was so badly swollen that only a tiny sliver of his eye was visible. His nose was clearly broken, and dried blood speckled his lips and chin. He paused in the doorway, taking in the room.

"Looks like the gang's all here." His broken nose made the words come out garbled and nasally.

"No talking." Caleb shoved his back, and he staggered forward. He would have fallen, but Eric caught him and helped him regain his balance.

"Baughman, what did they do to you?" Eric asked.

The former FBI man looked up at Eric with weary eyes. "Hell of a situation I got us mixed up in, isn't it?"

"I thought I told you to shut up!" Caleb raised the pistol, ready to bring it down on Baughman's head.

Merle held up a hand. "Caleb, please. I think you've beaten on Mr. Baughman enough for one day. I'd still like to recruit him to our side. You're not exactly helping my case."

Eric glared at Caleb. He distinctly remembered the feeling when Lewis had hit him right between the eyes with the Fade, knocking him out of his own body. He longed to do that to Caleb now. He'd make him relive some of the terror he'd experienced as a teenager when Lewis had cut him. Maybe he'd even give him a little new terror to add to the mix.

Of course, that was all a little difficult with zero access to the Fade.

Baughman's attention had shifted to Merle now. "I told you, I'm not going to help you with your sicko kidnappings. Beat on me all you want. It's not happening."

Merle shrugged. "We'll see if you feel that same way in a few minutes. I think you'll be surprised how quickly circumstances can change."

His eyes scanned the room again, resting a moment on each of them. Something like contentment crossed his face.

"You don't know how long I dreamed of this. All of you together in one place. In some ways, this is the culmination of my life's work." His gaze flickered to Baughman. "Of course, I imagined Lewis here instead of you, but we make do with what we have." He looked down at the desk for a long moment. "I'd pictured it going differently with dear old Nancy, too."

Anger flashed on Mikey's face. "Don't say her name."

The pure emotion in Mikey's voice caught Eric by

surprise. Mikey struck him as a mild man who went with the flow.

"He killed Nancy, didn't he?" Eric said. He turned to Merle. "What? She wouldn't comply with your orders? She wouldn't be a good little soldier like Caleb and Lewis?"

Merle let out a soft chuckle. "She's not dead, Eric. In fact, she's here with us today."

"I don't understand."

Tears filled Mikey's eyes. "He didn't kill her. That would have been too merciful. He left her alive. Forever, maybe. Is that how it works, Merle? Will she live forever now?"

"I honestly don't know," Merle said thoughtfully. "I'll be interested to find out."

Eric and Baughman exchanged a glance. Baughman was just as confused as Eric was. "Somebody's going to have to explain."

Becky's eyes were on the floor when she spoke. "Nancy tried to contact her old family. Her adoptive family. So Merle punished her."

"How?" Eric asked, not sure he wanted to know the answer.

"He knocked her out of her body. Then he shot her in the head. There was no body for her to come back to, so she's out there now. For good."

Eric went cold.

He remembered the helpless feeling of being outside his body. The complete lack of sensation. The utter isolation. To be stuck like that for eternity was just about the worst thing he could imagine.

"It's been an interesting case study," Merle said. "Not the first time I've done it, but each person is a little different. They're all like lost little shadows, never to be found. They gain a small amount of control over time. They can move within a limited area. Their mind seems to conjure some semblance of their old body in the Fade. But I don't believe they regain their ability to feel. I've tried to hurt them. Oh, how I've tried."

Mikey surged forward. He moved with surprising speed, reaching the desk before any of the others had time to react. He lunged, hands stretching out to grab the old man's neck. Just before he reached Merle, his body went limp. He collapsed onto the desk and slid to the floor.

"No!" Becky shouted.

Merle's head whipped around toward her. "You want to join him?"

"Idiot," Caleb muttered. "I guess he's with his precious Nancy now."

Merle leaned back and scratched his chin. "Interesting thought, but I don't think they can see each other."

Eric wanted to scream. He was standing in a cabin in the middle of nowhere in Tennessee, watching an old man turn people into ghosts. How was any of this real?

"Want me to kill his body?" Caleb asked.

"No. Not yet." He glanced at Eric and Becky. "Maybe if everyone can keep their cool for the next few minutes, we can let him come back to it. But that's a big if."

"We'll keep our cool," Becky said quickly. She turned to Eric. "Won't we?"

"Yeah, we're cool." Eric scanned the room with his eyes. Though he couldn't see him, Mikey was here somewhere. Along with Nancy. And maybe others. Eric wondered if they were screaming. A thought struck him, and he looked at Merle. "That was the real test, wasn't it? Back when we were kids. To see if we could sense the ghosts?"

A contented smile crossed Merle's face. "That's good, Eric. Very good."

Caleb's expression darkened. "What's he talking about?"

Merle shook his head. "Maybe it's time I explain."

"I'd say it's way past time," Baughman said.

"When the Fade first made itself known to us, many of those infected were terrified. Rightly so, it turned out. Most of them died within a few years, but not before passing the infection on to their offspring. I was different. I was never afraid. It energized me. Every time I used it, I felt a deep sense of contentment." He looked at Eric. "Sound familiar?"

Eric didn't answer, but he couldn't deny that it did.

"I grew concerned when people started dying. Not for the people themselves, cold as it might sound. This was bigger than them. Children were dying at fifteen years old. Some younger. If they didn't live long enough to procreate, how could the Fade live on? To be the only person left to experience it, well, that was just too sad to consider. The Fade needed to continue. It needed to thrive. So, I came up with the idea of sending children away for the first dozen years or so of their lives."

Caleb's face was knotted with surprise and distress. This clearly wasn't the version he'd heard. His voice was soft when he spoke. "You told us it was to protect the kids."

"It was," Merle said quickly. "At least, that was an important part of it. I didn't lie. You all would have died if you'd stayed here. Once we started adopting the children out and bringing them back, I was shocked at how effective it was. It turned out that growing up away from the Fade not only slowed the process of corrupting your bodies, but it also made you stronger in the Fade once you returned. You could do things other infected people couldn't. Such as disappearing and reappearing at will and knocking people out of their bodies. Before the first group of kids came home, I was the only one who could do those things."

Baughman's confusion was obvious even on his swollen face. Eric realized he must know very little, if anything, about the Fade.

"After my initial success, I had another idea. What if I left one of the kids with their adoptive families? Would they continue to grow stronger if they stayed away from Wakefield into adulthood? But to give this person the best chance at survival, I needed to find someone unusually strong in the Fade." He paused a moment, looking up at Eric with pride in his eyes. "In the first few rounds, I'd noticed a few children able to sense the people I'd removed from their bodies. It was rare, but it was always an indicator of great strength. So, I put you all in houses near the lake, waited a few weeks for your Fade senses to grow keen, and then checked to see if you'd sensed the disembodied. The Faded. Only one of you did."

Becky turned to Eric. "Him."

"Yes. I suspected he would be strong because he didn't have the speck in his eye like the rest of you. He clearly had unusual resistance. But he exceeded my expectations. Not only did he see the Faded, he heard them! He actually touched one! I didn't know such a thing was possible. So I sent him home, let him age away from the overwhelming power of the Fade here in Wakefield. I wasn't sure he'd survive, but I was delighted when he did. Then I decided to test him, to find out what sort of man he'd become. I had Marsha Crawford place a phone call to Mr. Baughman, who I knew was investigating the case for Albert Wilson. I had Lewis pay Eric a visit in the night. After we dipped you in the lake, I allowed you to leave Wakefield, and I sent Lewis to test you again. And just as I hoped, you came home. Thank God, Eric. You came home!"

"Forgive me if I don't share your excitement," Eric said

through gritted teeth. "Every time I try, I just see Tonya Barrington lying on a porch next to her dead mother."

Merle continued as if he hadn't heard. "The way your natural skill combined with your seclusion from the Fade... incredible. See, the Fade is a unique phenomenon. Once the Fade becomes active, you need at least some exposure to survive. But that wasn't the case with you. It went into a dormant state, but it never died. It survived for thirty years, waiting inside you."

"Sounds a little like you're describing a parasite," Eric said, his voice bitter.

Merle shrugged. "A small-minded way to look at things, but not an entirely unfair comparison. The Fade has a corrosive effect. Even Becky and Caleb probably won't last another ten years."

Caleb shifted his weight uncomfortably at that, but he kept his gun on Eric.

"But you? Eric, you're like a pristine engine. Zero wear and tear. You're built for speed, and I have the fuel to run you properly."

"What are you talking about?" Eric asked.

"The final part of my plan. Remember when I said I want the Fade to thrive? With your help, I believe I can finally make that happen. Want to see?"

Eric didn't move.

"I'm going to give you access to the Fade again. But behave, or I'll have Caleb shoot you somewhere painful."

Eric nodded.

"Okay. Here we go."

The wall between Eric and the Fade disappeared, and he felt the power rush back into his mind. Despite Merle's words, he didn't stop, didn't hesitate. This was his chance.

Without even turning, he visualized the spot on the

center of Caleb's forehead, and he pushed as hard as he could with the Fade. He felt something like a pop, then Caleb collapsed.

Becky spun toward him. "What did you do?"

But Eric was already moving on. He felt something in the room. Though he couldn't see him, he knew Mikey was there. An idea struck him. If you could push someone out of their body, could you put them back in?

He visualized the center of Mikey's forehead. This time, instead of pushing, he pulled. It was much more difficult. The pain in his head flared and he felt something resisting him. But after a moment, the resistance disappeared.

Mikey slowly sat up, a dazed look on his face.

Eric turned to Merle. Maybe he could end this. The old man had basically given him the blueprint. Knock the person out of their body. Kill the body. If he could do that, it would be over.

He stared at the center of Merle's forehead, letting the spot fill his mind. Then he pushed as hard as he could with the Fade.

It was like punching a brick wall.

Eric staggered backward, his mind exploding with pain. By the time he'd regained his balance, Mikey and Becky had both gone limp and Caleb was moving again.

"What the hell, man?" Caleb groaned. He scooped the gun off the ground and pointed it at Eric. "You said I could shoot him if he tried anything."

"Change of plans," Merle said. "If he tries anything else, shoot Becky and Mikey instead."

Caleb blinked hard. From the look on his face, it was clear he didn't want to do that. He took a deep breath and glared at Eric. "Just be cool, man. Okay?"

Eric nodded. He wasn't going to risk Becky and Mikey.

He'd taken his shot and missed. It was a hollow feeling, but a definitive one. There was nothing left to do but see what Merle had in store for him.

Merle grinned. "You are strong, Eric. I gotta say, I'm very pleased. The Fade is going to thrive at last!" He nodded toward Baughman. "Grab his head."

Eric hesitated. As much as he wanted to protect Becky and Mikey, he wasn't going to hurt Baughman. That was where he drew the line.

"It's okay," Baughman whispered. "Just do what he wants."

Eric raised a shaky hand and put it on Baughman's head.

"Good," Merle said. "Now brace yourself. This is going to be intense."

31

THE PAIN STARTED behind Eric's eyes and quickly spread. It felt as if he were a balloon into which too much air was being forced. He felt like his brain might explode. But even more powerful than the pain was the strange clarity. The Fade he'd experienced so far had been nothing compared to this. It had been diluted; this was the pure stuff.

It was more than power. More than darkness. It seemed as if this truer version of the Fade was alive. It wanted something. It wanted *him*.

The Fade filled him, threatened to push him out of his own body. It was growing, and there was no room for it inside him. But there was also nowhere else for it to go.

Nowhere except his fingertips, which touched Baughman's head.

Eric didn't will the Fade to go there. Like a liquid seeking equilibrium, it surged there of its own accord. He felt it in his fingers, and then it was gone.

He pulled his hand away from Baughman's head and took a step back. The Fade was manageable now, but its pure essence was still inside him. Everything looked different. Brighter. He looked up and saw a ghostly version of Mikey standing over his fallen body. His mouth was open in a scream. Becky was there too, her eyes wide with horror as she stared down at her body. And there were others. Faded versions of people Eric had never met. Some of them were moving quickly, so it was difficult to keep count, but he tried anyway. He spotted three—no, four—figures moving through the air, swirling high in the rafters. Four others stood throughout the room. These seemed more confused and less angry than their floating counterparts.

These were the Faded, Eric realized. The ones Merle had pushed out of their bodies. And when he'd killed their empty forms, they'd remained this way, trapped in a hellish existence between life and death, maybe forever. Merle could do this to any of them, if the mood struck. Eric had tried to knock him out of his body and hadn't even come close to budging him.

The realization hit Eric like a hammer. He was at Merle's mercy. They all were. And, God help him, Eric would do whatever Merle wanted if it meant he'd be spared the same fate as Nancy and the other Faded.

Baughman stared down at his hands, as if seeing them for the first time. "What... What did you do to me?"

He looked up, and Eric saw a black spot in his right eye.

"Yes!" Merle shouted. "I did it. It's real!"

Eric was shocked to see tears filling Merle's eyes. The man bore an expression of absolute ecstasy.

"Everyone! Come. You have to see."

Becky and Mikey whooshed back into their bodies at Merle's command, and groggily got to their feet.

"Please, no more," Mikey said.

Merle ignored the comment. He slowly stood up from

his chair and walked around the desk. "I was right. Eric was the engine I needed to make this possible."

"What are you talking about?" Eric asked. His voice sounded hoarse. He knew all too well what Merle was talking about, but he didn't want to believe it.

"All these years, so many attempts, I was never able to get the Fade to spread to someone outside the families already infected. But now we've done it."

Baughman was still staring at his hands. "What's happening to me?"

As he finished speaking, he flickered.

"No," Eric said, his voice a choked whisper.

Baughman flickered faster now. He tried to speak, but all that came out was an indecipherable series of half words. "Th...ot...ssi...he...ien...ere...ead."

"Baughman," Eric said. "You have to calm yourself. You can make it stop."

"Actually, he might not be able to," Merle said. "I expect the transition will be harsh for those who weren't born to it. Many of them won't survive. But it will be worth it to spread the Fade."

"Why?" Becky asked. "Why would you do this?"

Merle grinned at her. "Why does any species try to replicate itself? It's a biological imperative. It's why we're here."

Eric retreated another step, and his back thumped against the wall. It was all too much to handle. The disembodied Faded circling around the room faster and faster. Baughman flickering in and out of existence, speaking what sounded like an indecipherable language. The knowledge that he'd done this and that Merle would force him to do it again and again.

Merle turned toward him, and the look he gave Eric was something like love. "We have so much work to do together.

We're going to change so many people. I believe there may even be a way for us to create other Fade sources like Lake Stano." He let out a sharp laugh. "I mean, we're going to have to. All of the Faded we create aren't going to fit in Wakefield. They'll need their own wells of power to draw from. Eric, we're going to change the world."

Something Merle had said clicked in Eric's mind. *Why does any species try to replicate itself?* An idea came to him suddenly. It was just a hunch, but he was almost certain it was correct. He suddenly realized why he hadn't been able to push Merle out of his body. "There's no one there."

Merle tilted his head curiously. "What did you say?"

Eric lunged toward Caleb, wrapping his arms around his chest and slamming him into the wall. The bigger man was completely unprepared for the hit. By the time he reacted, Eric had already snatched the pistol out of his hand.

Merle slowly came around from behind the desk. "Eric, don't do anything stupid."

Eric inched backward until he felt the door. He opened it, keeping his eyes fixed on Merle and Caleb. "It's too much. There's too much here."

Baughman was flickering faster now. His attempts at words blended together in what sounded like a guttural scream.

"I don't want to hurt you," Merle said to Eric. "Every time you get knocked out of your body, it does damage, and I want you pristine."

Eric had the door half open now. "I just... I need a minute. Need to think."

"You'd better consider the consequences for your friends," Merle said.

But Eric had already slipped through the door and was running toward the woods.

IN THE LAST FIVE MINUTES, Becky's world had fallen apart.

She'd known it was a possibility. Or maybe more than a possibility. Coming down here to confront Merle was a giant middle finger to the status quo she'd lived with since her teenage years. She knew that she needed the Fade to survive, and Merle controlled her access to the Fade. Pissing him off was beyond stupid, even before you considered the cruel and unnatural punishments he tended to inflict on those who opposed him.

But now everything was different. Merle had proven that the Fade could be spread. That meant this strange affliction that had affected a few dozen people in her hometown was about to get a whole lot bigger. The Fade was no longer the small, sinister thing she depended on for survival. It was a potentially world-changing threat.

And the key had been Eric Partin. Maybe she and the others had been right to hate him for all those years.

For a long moment after Eric ran out of the cabin, no one moved. Then Caleb took an uncertain step toward the door. Becky could practically see his wheels spinning. As Merle's long-time enforcer, this was likely his responsibility. At the same time, Eric had already proven he could best Caleb when it came to the Fade, and he was now armed with a pistol.

He walked to a wooden cabinet near the door and unlocked it, one eye on Mikey and Becky the entire time. Then he pulled out a shotgun and looked back at Merle. "Want me to go after him?"

Merle grimaced. He was clearly disappointed that his moment of triumph had been tainted. "No. I'd prefer that neither of you gets injured. I'll handle this." He started toward the door, then paused. "I did make Eric a promise, though. I said if he tried anything else, I'd have you shoot Becky and Mikey. I'm a man of my word. Take care of it for me?"

Becky froze. The man who'd been her mentor since the age of twelve had just ordered her death.

Caleb stared blankly at Merle, as if he couldn't believe what he'd just heard.

"Is that a problem?" Merle asked.

"No," Caleb answered quickly. "No problem."

Merle walked out of the cabin without another word.

Baughman's indistinct shouts were growing more sporadic now. He was still flailing around, looking like some bizarre version of a silent movie played at the wrong framerate, but he had stopped shouting.

Caleb looked at Becky. "I'm awfully sorry about this."

Becky and Mikey exchanged a panicked glance. In a fair fight, it was questionable whether they would be able to take Caleb down, and this was not going to be a fair fight. Getting knocked out of your body did a real number on your Fade abilities. It had only happened to Becky twice, and it had taken her days to recover. Still, she felt like she could probably disappear.

But what about Mikey? He'd been knocked out of his body twice, and he was the weakest of them when it came to the Fade. Could she really leave him to his fate just to save herself?

As if in answer to her question, Mikey suddenly disappeared. It was all Becky could do not to smile.

Caleb snarled. "So that's how we're doing this?"

Becky tried to Fade but found she couldn't. Her reserves of power were dry. She was left standing there while Caleb leveled the shotgun at her. "I'll make it quick, Becky. For you and your brother both."

At that moment, Mikey reappeared behind Caleb and immediately charged. Becky threw herself to the side as Mikey slammed into Caleb's back. Both of them disappeared. Caleb's shotgun clanged to the ground.

Becky scurried over and grabbed it. Then she backed up and pressed herself against the wall. She waited, shotgun leveled and ready to fire the moment Caleb showed himself.

It had been foolish of him to Fade, but she understood the instinct. They'd been trained since they got to Wakefield to Fade when in danger. He probably hadn't even thought about it. He'd just done what came naturally.

Becky cast a worried glance Baughman's way. He was flickering even faster now. She knew what kind of a toll Fading even once took on the human body. What was happening to him... he might not recover. And if it didn't stop soon, he'd drop dead of a heart attack.

She remembered what Merle had said about the Fade being unstable in those not born to it, but she had to try something. For better or for worse, Baughman had been employed by her father. In a roundabout way, it was her fault he was here.

"Baughman," she said. "Baughman, you have to get control. You have to..." She drew a deep breath, trying to remember how Merle had explained it to them when they'd first been learning. "Picture a stillness in your mind. Even a tiny dot of stillness is okay. Then slowly expand it. Take back your mind a little at a time."

She had no idea if her words were getting through to him. For all she knew, his brain was already mush.

And yet, it seemed his flickering might have slowed, just a little.

Her focus was still on Baughman when Caleb appeared in front of her. He grabbed the shotgun with two hands and forced the stock upward, slamming it into her chin. She cried out in pain, and he yanked the shotgun from her hands.

No sooner did he have the weapon than Mikey reappeared three feet away, a look of fury on his face. Caleb was ready. The shotgun let out a devastating boom, and Mikey flew backward. He landed on the ground, a ragged hole in the center of his chest.

"No!" Becky shouted.

Without thinking, she surged forward and slammed into Caleb. He stumbled sideways, trying to keep his feet. He took one more step and staggered to the spot where Baughman had been standing a split-second before.

Baughman rematerialized, and his suddenly corporeal body tore Caleb's apart. It was like a bomb had gone off inside Caleb's torso. Blood, brain matter, and bone sprayed across the room.

Baughman disappeared again. Caleb's body balanced there for a horrible moment. His left side was mostly intact, but his right side was another story. His arm had somehow avoided the destruction, but it hung from a mangled shoulder. The leg was gone—Becky would later find it on the other side of the room. The right side of his torso was destroyed, and the innards from his left side were drooping, threatening to spill out. Before they could, Caleb toppled over. His corpse landed with a wet *thwap*.

Becky sank to the floor, shotgun clutched to her chest.

She was the last one alive in the cabin except for Baughman, and she had a feeling it wouldn't be long until he joined Caleb and her brother.

32

Eric sprinted down the trail through the woods, not daring to look back over his shoulder. He knew what was behind him. He knew what was coming.

With the pure Fade swimming in his mind, the woods looked even more vibrant. The greens practically glowed. It hurt his eyes to look at anything too closely. Human eyes weren't meant to see colors this way.

As he ran around a bend in the trail, he saw something. A ghostly man floating about a foot off the ground. He had a long mustache, and his clothes looked like they were from the seventies. Another Faded. How long had Merle been doing this? Since he was a boy? Since he first bathed in the glowing waters of Lake Stano on a summer night way back then? Eric didn't know. Not only had Merle torn babies from their mothers' arms and kidnapped twelve-year-olds from their homes, but he'd trapped dozens of people in a limbo state between life and death. And why? What was the end game? Spreading the Fade?

Merle's words came back to Eric again and a chill ran through him. *Why does any species try to replicate itself?*

And suddenly, Merle stood ten yards in front of him on the trail, an unworried expression on his face, his hands folded neatly in front of him. "Eric, the work we're doing is important. We have the ability to open people's consciousness in a completely new way. We're talking about helping people evolve into something greater than human."

Eric stopped and glared at the man. The words were uncanny, as if Merle had been reading his mind. And maybe he had. Maybe their shared possession of the pure Fade gave them a mental connection. Eric hoped not. The thought sickened him.

He took a step toward Merle. "Helping? The Fade kills nearly everyone infected. You said so yourself."

"For now, sure. But humanity adapts. It's what we do."

That rang false to Eric. Merle didn't believe a word of what he was saying. It wasn't humanity's interests he had in mind, and Eric was done listening. He raised his pistol.

Merle disappeared.

Good. Eric didn't want their final confrontation to happen in the woods. For Eric to have a chance, it had to happen somewhere else. He thought about initials carved into a baseboard, and he kept running.

When Eric reached the house, Merle was already standing in front of the backdoor. He still wore his casual expression, but there was concern around his eyes now.

"I don't know what you're hoping to accomplish," he said. "This running, it's counterproductive. Embarrassing even. Is this really how you want to start our working relationship?"

Eric strode toward the door. "I notice you're doing a lot of talking and not knocking me out of my body. You can't do it anymore, can you? The power you put into my head protects me."

"Oh, I can," Merle said. "But it would not be easy. It would severely damage your mind, and I'd prefer to avoid that outcome. Besides, what would be the point? Can't we just talk it out?"

Over Merle's shoulder, through the window into the kitchen, Eric saw a floating woman. The same one he'd seen in the bathroom mirror. He wondered if it was Nancy.

"No." He raised his pistol.

Once again, Merle vanished.

Eric charged onto the porch and threw open the back door. When he stepped inside, he froze for a moment. Three Faded floated in the kitchen. They stared at him with hollow eyes. They made no attempt to speak or communicate with Eric. He wondered if they even knew he could see them. Either way, their hopeless expressions served as stark reminder of what Merle was capable of, what he'd done to so many others, what he might do to Eric.

Except Eric didn't think he would. Merle had spent a long time searching for him, and then he'd patiently waited thirty years while Eric's mind grew strong in its resistance to the Fade. He'd lost Lewis in his attempt to bring Eric home. He wouldn't risk damaging Eric's mind by knocking him out of his body. Not unless he absolutely had no other choice.

Eric charged through the kitchen and into the living room. He wasn't surprised to find Merle sitting in a chair, his left leg crossed over his right, an easy smile on his face.

"This is silly. How about you sit down and we have a chat?"

Eric ignored him and hurried past, only glancing at the two disembodied Faded occupying the room. He wondered what they'd done to deserve their hellish punishment. Disobeyed Merle? Posed some threat to his power? No, in the end, their real crime was the same one Eric, Becky,

Mikey, Caleb, and Lewis had committed; they'd been born in Wakefield. Their parents had been infected, so they were too.

He headed up the stairs, rushing past the second floor. When he reached the third level, he ran for the door with the three deadbolts. It wasn't locked this time, and he charged into the room that had once, for three terrible weeks, been his own.

And then he waited.

After a moment, Merle appeared in the doorway. "Are you finished running away?"

"I was never running away."

That gave Merle pause. "Okay. So here we are. What happens now?"

Eric's eyes scanned the room. It took a moment, but then he saw what he was looking for floating in the corner. "This was your room, wasn't it?"

Merle looked amused. "Yes. I grew up in this house. And this was my room. How'd you know?"

"Becky mentioned that you let her and Mikey live in this house, which implies you own it. Then I remembered the initials carved into the baseboard. M.N. Your initials, right?"

Merle just nodded.

"You know, when you had me locked in here, I used to stare at those initials for hours, wondering who carved them. I thought maybe it was some other kidnapped kid. They gave me hope. I'm wondering what happened to the boy who carved those initials."

A slow grin spread across Merle's face. "Is this the big plan, then? You bring me back to my childhood bedroom and what? Help me remember the boy I once was? Appeal to my humanity?"

Now it was Eric's turn to smile. "No. You don't have any humanity."

The smile disappeared. "What are you—"

"Back at the cabin, you said, *Why does any species try to replicate itself?* You were talking about your species. The Fade." He took a step forward. "Merle's not in there anymore, is he? I'm guessing he hasn't been for a long time."

"No," the thing that wore Merle's skin answered. "He hasn't."

Eric glanced at the corner where the Faded Merle, the real Merle, waited. It was the Merle that Eric had seen as a child. The one that had somehow managed to grab his throat with its non-corporeal features.

Then Eric looked back at Merle and stared at the center of his forehead. And he pulled.

Merle's hand went to his temple. "Ow! What are you..." Then he understood, and his eyes filled with panic. He began to fight it, but Eric was almost there.

It took everything inside Eric's mind, every ounce of the pure Fade Merle had shoved into his brain. Eric tapped into all of it as he pulled. The resistance was massive. Merle's body hadn't been occupied by a human spirit in many years, and it fought him. Eric ignored the pain ripping through his mind and kept pulling as hard as he could with the Fade.

The Faded Merle began to move toward his body as if he were being pulled on a string. Eric pulled even harder. In an instant, the Faded Merle disappeared into the body.

Merle staggered backward, both hands on his temples now. He looked up at Eric and snarled. Eric could see the conflict in his eyes. Two presences were fighting for control.

But Eric wasn't done pulling. His original plan had only been to put Merle back in his body, but he felt the other Faded out there. He knew how he could help them.

The pulling was easier now, as if whatever mechanisms existed in Merle's head had been lubricated by the return of his spirit. Eric pulled hard and fast, imagining himself yanking huge arm-lengths of rope with each tug. In a moment, the Faded he'd seen in the living room came rushing through the door and into Merle's head.

Eric still wasn't done. He pulled harder, and the Faded from the kitchen came next. He saw the woman he'd spotted in the mirror earlier, the one he thought might be Nancy, disappear into Merle.

The work was becoming even more painful now. Eric knew he was damaging his mind, but it didn't matter. There were more Faded out there. In the woods. In the cabin. Who knew where else? They might be all over Wakefield. So Eric kept pulling. He pulled for what felt like hours. Three dozen Faded disappeared into Merle's body, and Merle grunted in pain with each one.

Eric didn't know exactly how this all worked, but he was confident the many Faded he'd shoved into Merle's head couldn't co-exist in there long. He needed to end this.

One last Faded slid through the door. This one looked like a kid of no more than fourteen, and he had a large scar across his cheek. Eric pulled one more time, and the kid disappeared into Merle.

Eric tried to pull again, but it was as if there were no more rope. There was nothing left to pull.

Merle staggered back and forth, head in his hands. He let out a long, inhuman groan.

Eric raised his pistol. "You're all free now."

And then he fired.

The round hit Merle in the center of the forehead, the same spot Eric had focused on when he'd been pulling.

Merle fell backward. He was dead by the time he hit the floor.

Eric stood there for a long moment, waiting. He half-expected dozens of spirits to come rushing out of Merle, but they didn't. It was a true death. A natural death. He'd killed three dozen people with one shot. Their bodies had been destroyed years ago, and now their souls were finally free.

Eric walked back to the cabin, wondering who he'd find alive there.

When he entered, he saw Becky huddled in the corner, clutching a shotgun. Mikey lay dead near the door, and pieces of a mangled body Eric assumed had belonged to Caleb lay scattered throughout the room. Baughman was unconscious not far away, but he appeared to be breathing.

Becky flinched when she saw Eric, leveling the shotgun at him. The light of recognition came into her eyes, and she lowered it.

"What happened here?" Eric asked, crouching down beside her. "Are you okay?"

"Mikey's dead," she said flatly.

"Are you hurt?"

She blinked slowly, as if this were the first time she'd considered that question. "It's gone. The Fade is gone. I can't feel it anymore."

Eric put an arm around her shoulders. "Good. That's good, Becky."

She looked up at him. "Did you kill it?"

He swallowed. "Yeah, I killed it."

It wasn't a lie. Not exactly. He had killed Merle, who'd

been the source of the Fade, and that should have destroyed the Fade in almost everyone who'd been infected.

But the pure Fade—the true Fade—wasn't gone. It burned in the back of Eric's mind like fire.

EPILOGUE

Marsha Crawford answered her door and found Eric Partin standing in the rain. Despite the cloudy day, he wore sunglasses.

"Hello, Mrs. Crawford. May I come in?"

She hesitated for a moment. Then she moved aside.

He stepped through the door and paused in the entryway, looking around the home as if he were seeing it for the first time.

"Are you all right?" she asked. "I see your FBI friend isn't with you today."

"I'm fine, thanks. Baughman left Wakefield. He has a job out of town."

"But you haven't left."

"No."

He took off his sunglasses, and Mrs. Crawford stifled a gasp. His right eye had two pupils.

It wasn't the first time she'd seen something like this. Every now and again, she spotted someone at the grocery store or in church with a black spot in their eye. And her own husband had a speck in his eye. It had grown into something more than a speck toward the end, before his heart attack.

"I'm staying in that old cabin by Lake Stano now. You know the one I mean?"

She nodded. "Merle Neuman's cabin."

"Yes."

Mrs. Crawford waited to see if he'd say more, but he didn't. "Is there something I can help you with, Mr. Partin?"

"Yes, maybe. I was wondering if you might have some pictures I could look at. Of you and your husband. I'd like to see the two of you as you were then."

For a moment, she didn't answer. She had to swallow the lump in her throat before she could. "How long have you known?"

"I've suspected for a while. It made sense that you'd be motivated to see me again. And Merle would use that. But also, I felt something when I was here the first time with Baughman. It felt familiar."

She shook her head. "That's impossible. You were just a baby. You only stayed in this house a month."

"I didn't mean the house. I meant you."

Marsha Crawford wasn't one for tears. She kept her emotions in check, especially in front of people she barely knew, but she couldn't stop the tears that filled her eyes now. "I'm sorry. Sorry we gave you up. Sorry I called Baughman and asked him to bring you back. I knew Merle's intentions were bad, but I did it anyway. I needed so badly to see you."

He smiled and put a hand on her arm. "I'm here."

She let out a noise that was half sob, half laugh. "I've wanted this for so long, and now I don't know where to begin."

"Then let me." Eric gently squeezed her arm. "My

parents—my other parents—died. Dad fifteen years ago, Mom eleven. I'm divorced. No children. No siblings."

He paused and looked into her eyes. She saw something familiar there. For just a moment, she remembered what it had been like to hold him the day he was born. That was a memory she hadn't allowed herself to revisit in a very long time.

"I don't have very many people in my life," he continued. "It strikes me that if two people find each other, even after a very long time apart, they can still be a family. It strikes me that maybe those two people should try to love each other."

She let the tears roll down her cheeks now. She put her hand over his and felt the warmth of it on her skin. Her son was finally home.

"Come with me," she said, "and I'll tell you about your father."

ON A WARM AFTERNOON in early October, Becky Talbot pulled her car into the parking lot of an elementary school in Durango, Colorado.

She'd spent three days over the past week watching the school. She knew what time the children went to recess. She knew that if she parked her car in this part of the lot, she'd have easy access to the playground while being blocked from the view of the teachers who congregated near the door. And she also knew that the first few minutes of recess were the most chaotic. The teachers would be so involved in the chaos that they might not notice a woman walking into the playground and approaching the boy who always played left field in the daily kickball game.

After careful consideration, Becky had decided this was

her best opportunity to get to the nine-year-old boy who now went by the name of Jimmy Hughes.

She waited nervously, eyes flickering between the clock on her dashboard and the side door where she knew the children would emerge at ten for morning recess. When the door didn't open at precisely ten a.m., she started to grow concerned. At one minute after ten, crazy thoughts began racing through her mind. What if recess was canceled today? What if it wasn't even a school day, and all the cars were just teachers attending an in-service or something.

She took a deep breath and tried to calm herself. If any of those unlikely events occurred, she could always return tomorrow.

But she didn't want to return tomorrow. She needed to get this done. Today.

At two minutes after ten, the side door flew open and a teeming mass of children exploded onto the playground. As they scattered, forming smaller groups that headed to various parts of the yard, Becky opened her car door and stepped out, her heart thudding wildly in her chest.

She spotted Jimmy trudging to his spot at left field as his friends took their positions to start the kickball game. Her gaze shifted to the teachers near the door. They were gathered in a clump, talking with each other as they sipped their coffee. Only one was even facing her direction, and his view was partially obstructed by another teacher. This was her moment.

Walking as fast as she could, she stepped onto the kickball field and headed straight for her son. A few kids glanced her direction, but none of them seemed to pay her any mind.

When she was three feet from the boy, she crouched down. "Hello, Jimmy."

The kid stared at her, not speaking, clearly freaked out. But that was okay. She'd expected this to be a little uncomfortable. The important thing was his eyes.

She stared into them, inspecting first the left and then the right. Then she checked one more time. She'd never get another shot at this, not ever, so she needed to be sure.

Her hand went to her mouth, and she let out a laugh of relief. There was no speck in his eye. Eric had been right. The Fade was gone.

She hadn't planned to touch him, but she couldn't help herself. Her hand grazed his arm, and he took a big step back. A pang of sadness shook her, but she pushed it down.

"Bye, Jimmy." It was all she could think to say.

She stood up and started toward her car, forcing herself not to look back. If she looked back, she might run to him, grab him, and that wasn't why she was there.

"Ma'am?" an adult voice called. "Ma'am, can I help you?"

Becky fumbled with her keys as she opened her car door.

"Ma'am, you can't be here!" the voice called.

But Becky was already in the car. She backed out, careful not to look toward the kickball field, and drove away from Durango, Colorado, never to return.

THAT AFTERNOON, Eric was swimming in Lake Stano, something he found himself doing more and more often lately. It calmed his troubled mind.

Other activities helped, too. He often hiked the nearby Appalachian Trail, just as the man named Claude had suggested on his first plane ride to Wakefield. He'd hiked

Rook Mountain and visited the ponies of the Grayson Highlands, though he'd obeyed the signs cautioning him not to feed them. But wherever he went, he always found himself drawn back to this lake.

He was doing the breast-stroke, working hard, when he noticed someone standing on the dock in front of his cabin. He paddled his way over and climbed onto the dock.

Baughman was dressed in a polo shirt and blazer, the same ensemble he'd worn on their first day in Wakefield. He had a manila folder wedged under his arm.

The two men shook, despite the water dripping from Eric's hand.

"You got your watch back, I see," Eric said.

"I only had to ask Becky three times." Baughman glanced warily toward the lake. "You actually swim in there? That's where the Fade lived, right?"

Eric picked up his towel and dried off. "Not exactly. It lived inside Merle. But yeah, the lake appears to have been the source of it. But it's gone. There's only one place the Fade lives now." He tapped his own temple.

Baughman laughed. "Better you than me, buddy. I didn't take to it very well."

"No, you did not. Come on. You look like you could use a beer."

Baughman had slept nearly two solid days after Merle's death, but he'd emerged Fade-free and mentally intact. Though the experience had certainly affected him. The few times he'd discussed it with Eric, he'd had a haunted look in his eyes.

Eric led Baughman up the trail to the cabin. Over the past two months, he'd slowly gotten rid of Merle's things and began accumulating his own. The massive desk and filing cabinets were gone, replaced with a couch, an easy chair, and a television set. The contents of the filing cabinets had gone to Baughman.

Baughman sat down in the easy chair while Eric got a couple Yee Haw Dunkels out of the fridge. He tossed one to Baughman, then sat down on the couch.

"So you live here now?" Baughman asked, a smile on his face.

Eric shrugged and cracked open his beer. "No one's complained yet. Merle didn't have any family left alive."

"Squatters' rights then?"

Eric had discovered that the Wakefield Police were well practiced in turning a blind eye. Their official report of the recent incident declared that Merle had killed Caleb and Mikey before going back to his childhood bedroom and killing himself, despite the lack of evidence to support that theory. If they were willing to look past three bodies, Eric doubted they'd give him much trouble about squatting in an abandoned cabin.

"If anybody can figure out who actually owns the place, I'd be happy to buy it from them. I like it here."

"You like Becky."

Eric didn't bother denying it. "Like I once told you, there's nothing wrong with making new friends." He leaned forward, his face suddenly more serious. "And your work? How's it going?"

"It's going. And it will be for quite some time." Baughman was slowly working his way through Merle's files, checking on each kid who'd been adopted out of Wakefield. He posed as a representative of the adoption firm doing a follow-up visit, but he was actually checking to make sure none of them had the Fade. Eric was funding some of his travel. Becky was handling the rest. It turned out

Albert Wilson had amended his will before coming to Wakefield, and he'd left her a rather tidy sum.

"Anything I should know about?"

Baughman took a sip of beer before answering. "Eric, you've been through a lot."

"We all have."

"Sure, but some of us were more equipped to deal with it. I never saw anything like the Fade in my time with the FBI, but I'm no stranger to intense trauma. Becky was raised with the Fade. But you? You're a lawn-care guy from Wisconsin who suddenly got thrown into this crazy situation."

Eric chuckled. "Didn't you hear what Merle said? I'm the *most* equipped to deal with it."

Baughman shifted in his seat. "I guess what I'm saying is, I'm not sure the Fade has to be your responsibility."

Eric looked down at his hands. He suddenly felt very alone. "I've got a constant fiery pain in the back of my head telling me otherwise. It's the first thing I feel every morning when I wake up and the last thing I feel before I go to sleep. It's trying to push me out of my body the way it pushed Merle out of his. I can fight it back, but I'm in constant fear that someday I'll slip, just for a moment, and it will push me out. So when you say the Fade isn't my responsibility, I have to disagree."

"I'm sorry, Eric. Sorry this happened to you."

"I'm sorry too. I hate the pain and the fear. I hate that people died. But I spent so long pretending the kidnapping was just a weird thing that happened to me, that it didn't matter. I got a divorce. Sold my business. And I pretended that those things didn't matter too. I never really let myself grieve for either of them. I'm done with that now. I wish it hadn't taken something like this to wake me up. But now that I'm awake, I'm not going back to sleep."

Baughman nodded slowly. "If I found someone infected with the Fade, would you want to know?"

Eric considered that, but only for a moment. "Yes, I would."

"Okay," Baughman said. "Because I have."

Baughman handed Eric the manila folder. Eric opened it and started to read.

AUTHOR'S NOTE

Thanks for reading Found Shadows.

It was a lot of fun returning to the haunted region of Eastern Tennessee. Wakefield, like Rook Mountain before it, is fictional, but this part of the world does have a magic all its own. I've spent many days hiking the mountains around these parts, and Found Shadows was born on those solitary walks. If you get out to this part of the country, take Claude's advice and hit the hiking trails.

As you may have guessed from the Epilogue, I'm not finished with Eric Partin yet. The concept of the Fade is just too interesting. Besides, Lewis mentioned the other experiments Merle had attempted. Eric's going to learn quite a bit about those in the near future.

If you liked this one and want the next Eric Partin book, leave a review and let me know.

In the meantime, consider checking out my book REGULATION 19. It takes place in Rook Mountain, Tennessee, and if you enjoyed Found Shadows, I think you'll really like that one as well. I've included the first chapter here to give you a little taste of the story.

PT Hylton

AN EXCERPT FROM REGULATION 19

I.

Frank Hinkle was staring at the murder weapon in his hand when Correctional Officer Rodgers called his name.

"Hinkle!"

Frank squeezed his eyes shut and muttered a near silent curse.

He had been standing in the prison yard, drifting. Not even thinking. Just drifting. It had been happening more lately, the sense that his mind had become un-anchored from reality. He would find himself standing in the middle of the yard with no idea how long he'd been there. The old timers said the longer you were inside, the more it happened. You would find yourself losing bits of everything —time, your personality, even the reality of the prison walls around you. Still, common or not, it was damn unsettling.

If he had seen the Newg striding toward him, he would have turned and walked the other way. But he had been drifting hard, and he didn't see the Newg until the other man was up in his face.

The day Jerry Robinson arrived at NTCC, one of the

men in the yard called him 'the New Guy'. As a reward for this burst of wit, Robinson punched the inmate in the throat. In spite of the throat-punch, the nickname had stuck. Over the years, it had morphed from 'the New Guy' to 'the Newg.' and somewhere along the way the Newg had come to embrace his new name. He even had it memorialized on his right bicep in prison ink.

While the Newg wasn't opposed to a good old-fashioned throat punch when the need arose, he now preferred to repay perceived slights with a shank. He'd doled out one such repayment only two days ago, and the COs were in an unusual hurry to find out who had stabbed the kid in the shower.

The Newg gave his shoulder a gentle squeeze as he spoke. "Man, I need your help. I know I ain't paid you back for what you did before, so I feel real bad asking. But I ain't got no choice."

Frank blinked hard. His mind snapped back to reality, but he still felt like he was playing catch up, jumping into the middle of a conversation he didn't fully understand.

The Newg must have taken Frank's silence as permission to continue. "Need you to hold on to this for me."

Something slipped into Frank's hand. He didn't have to look to see what the Newg had handed him. Frank's mind, and his pulse, sped to life.

"Whoa, Newg," he said. "I respect you, and you know I'd love to help. But you also gotta know I'm not putting a murder weapon in my bunk."

The Newg's face scrunched up in desperation. The man wasn't handsome to begin with and the look did nothing to improve the situation. "You were at the laundry, right? They got you signed in at the time of death, and at least three guards laid eyes on you while you were working."

"It doesn't matter where I was. They're going to keep tossing bunks until they find something. How did they not find this already?"

The Newg glanced around and lowered his voice. "I got a hiding spot in the yard. But it's not the kind of spot that's gonna withstand a full sweep."

That was the moment the voice came, shouting his name like it was a cuss word. "Hinkle!"

The Newg looked up and the color drained from his face. He backed up. "Looks like Rodgers wants a word."

"Newg!" Frank whispered as loudly as he dared. He still hadn't turned to acknowledge the CO's call. "Get back here and take this thing!"

The Newg wiggled his head back and forth, his eyes never leaving the figure behind Frank. "I appreciate this. I owe you double." He turned and hustled away.

Frank remained frozen. There was nothing to do but wait for the inevitable. He snuck the shank into the waistband of his pants and pushed it down as far as he dared. If he shoved it down too far, it would fall down his pant leg and onto the ground. Guards tended to notice stuff falling out of the leg of an inmate's pants. It was an all too common, last resort option for getting rid of contraband in the loose-fitting, pocketless prisoner's clothing.

"Hinkle! You got shit in your ears? I've been calling your name for two minutes."

Frank felt a hand on his shoulder, this one from behind him, and he grimaced. He turned and saw Correctional Officer Rodgers standing there, the light hint of a smile on his face. When CO Rodgers smiled, it was never a good sign.

Frank had most of the guards figured out, but Rodgers...Rodgers was different than the others. Rodgers was smart. He was good looking. He was an athlete. Fifteen years ago, Frank had been in the stands the day Rodgers had led the Bristol, Tennessee High School football team to a stunning victory over Virginia High. The kid had been a natural athlete.

Rodgers went on to play for UT his freshman year of college before being cut from the team as a sophomore. He finished school and got his degree in criminology. And then, for some reason, he had come to work with a bunch of dunces and thugs who'd barely made it through high school.

"Sorry about that," Frank said. "I was spacing out. Didn't hear you."

Rodgers grunted. He nodded his head toward the Newg who was now halfway across the yard. "Having a little conversation with Robinson?"

Frank nodded, not quite meeting the other man's eyes. "Yes, sir."

"Every time I give you a little bit of credit and start thinking maybe you're an actual human being with a functioning brain, you gotta turn around and prove me wrong. Why is that? Did you have to train hard to act so stupid or does it come naturally?"

The shank in Frank's waistband felt huge. Rodgers had to see it. Any moment he would blow his little whistle and ten guards would sprint across the yard and tackle Frank to the ground.

Frank said, "I guess it comes naturally, boss."

The smile faded from Rodgers's face. "That was a rhetorical question, Hinkle. See what I'm saying? You just proved my damn point." He grabbed Frank's right arm and marched toward the administration building. "Come on. Warden wants to have a chat."

"What?" Frank asked. He struggled to keep up without

dislodging the shank from its precarious position. "What's the warden—?"

Rodgers stopped and spun to face Hinkle. He leaned in close to the prisoner's face. "Do me a favor. Keep your feet on that side of the yellow line and don't speak unless you are asked a direct question."

Frank may not have understood the inner workings of CO Rodgers's mind, but he did know enough basic guard psychology to understand that Rodgers had no idea why the warden wanted to see him.

They stopped outside the door to the administration building. "Hands in front."

Frank held out his wrists, and Rodgers clicked the handcuffs into place. "Okay, let's move," Rodgers said.

They entered the administration building and walked down a long, institutional gray hallway. It didn't look much different from the other buildings in the NTCC except for the doors. They were standard office building doors with nameplates instead of the heavy metal monstrosities found in the rest of the prison.

Northern Tennessee Correctional Complex wasn't a terrible place, at least as far as maximum security prisons went. The bizarre rule changes during Frank's nine years inside had made things worse, but the location was still hard to beat. The prison was located in Rook Mountain, Tennessee, and the prison yard views of the Smoky Mountains could be outright breathtaking. Still, even after nine years, the sight of the administration building unnerved him.

He had been in this building once before. He had been scared that time, but at least he had known why the warden wanted to see him. He could reveal or withhold the facts as he wished. That little bit of power had been something to hold on to, something to savor. Even though they had him in handcuffs, he chose whether to talk. This time, he had no power.

Also, last time he hadn't had a murder weapon in his elastic waistband.

Rodgers led Frank into a room with no windows. The warden sat in a chair behind a large metal table. The fluorescent overhead lighting gave his already weathered face a sickly hue. He looked uncomfortable, like maybe he was suffering from a bout of gas. He nodded to Rodgers, and the guard moved Frank to the lone chair on the near side of the table. Frank sat down, and Rodgers locked the handcuffs in the latch built into the table for this purpose. Then Rodgers took a few steps back until he was out of Frank's field of vision.

The warden leaned forward and folded his hands on the table. "We've only got a few moments, so listen to what I am about to tell you."

Frank shifted in his seat.

"An hour ago I got a call from Rook Mountain City Hall. They told me Becky Raymond needs to meet with you. I know you haven't had the chance to keep up with politics lately, but Ms. Raymond is the city manager of Rook Mountain."

The warden stared at Frank for a long moment.

Frank had the feeling that he was supposed to say something. He couldn't quite keep the smile off his face. "This the same Becky Raymond who used to work at the Road Runner gas station out on Dennis Cove Rd?"

The warden leaned even closer. Frank saw beads of sweat forming on the big man's forehead. "Ms. Raymond is going to be here any minute, so don't be cute. I need

An Excerpt from REGULATION 19

answers. What the hell does the city manager want with you?"

Frank shrugged. "I have no idea."

"Come on. Think!"

"I...I guess it could be something to do with my brother. He works for the city. Maybe he's up for a promotion, and they want to interview me for some background check or something."

Rodgers snickered behind him. "I'm pretty sure your brother isn't up for a promotion."

The warden smacked the table. "You expect me to believe the Rook Mountain city manager would come down here and walk into this prison about a background check?"

Frank paused, unsure of how to continue. "All due respect, but it seems like you may be thinking about this a little too hard. We're going to find out what she wants in a few minutes, right?"

The warden shook his head. "You don't understand. Things have changed in Rook Mountain. The city manager represents the board of selectmen, and the Board..." The warden paused. He glanced at Rodgers as if looking for an assist, but the CO remained silent. The warden continued. "The Board has done amazing things since you've been inside. Wonderful things. But there are rules –"

If Frank hadn't been looking at the door behind the warden, he wouldn't have seen it. But he was, and he saw a flash of blue light through the crack below the door.

The door opened and a tall, sharply dressed woman in her early fifties marched into the room. She moved toward the table and held out her hand to the warden. "Warden Cade?"

The warden leapt to his feet and shook her hand. "Yes ma'am. It's an honor. Thanks for coming down. I think you'll find what we are doing here is in keeping with the Regulations."

"Fine." She slid into the nearest chair and looked at Frank. Her face was all sharp angles. Her deep brown eyes perfectly matched her hair color. "Mr. Hinkle," she said, "how would you like to get out of prison?"

2.

Will Osmond drew a deep breath and concentrated on putting one foot in front of the other. They were hiking through a dense stand of pine trees, but it wouldn't be long now. In a few moments, they would step out of the trees and onto the round bald top of the mountain. The view would be worth it. It always was.

Henry Strauss said, "You holding up okay?"

Will stopped and glanced back at the other man. Henry was red with heat and slick with sweat. Both men were in their late thirties, but, when Will compared his own stamina with that of the six twelve-year-old boys hiking with them, he felt much older.

The two men held up the rear of the procession. Ostensibly, this was so that they could keep watch on the boys in front of them. In truth, it was so they could go at a non-lethal pace without the kids stepping on their heels.

Will grunted in reply.

"Yeah, me too," Henry said. "It sure was easier when we could drive up."

Will ignored that last comment. Sometimes it was better to let things slide.

He said, "We made it. That's the important thing. Almost made it, anyway."

Two years ago, the board of selectmen had decided vehicles were not allowed past the old ranger station on Rook

Mountain. Before that, you could drive all the way up to the parking lot at Carter's Gap. A stroke of a pen turned a fifteen-minute hike into an excursion that took a whole afternoon. Will had no idea why the board had passed the change or what danger a vehicle near the summit of Rook Mountain might pose, but he had long ago stopped asking those types of questions out loud.

When it came to the board of selectmen, trust was a must.

Will stopped for a moment and waited for Henry to catch up to him. Then he fell in step with the other man. When he spoke, it was quiet enough that only Henry could hear him. "Did you see what I saw half a mile back?"

Henry nodded. "Under that boulder by the overlook?"

Will smiled. "Good eye. We have to deal with it on the way back."

Henry arched his eyebrow. "What about the boys?"

"The boys are the reason we have to deal with it," Will said. "What if one of them saw the backpack wedged under that boulder? The hiker wasn't even trying to hide what he's doing."

Henry nodded. "So the kids might have seen it. That's not the end of the world. We'll report it when we get back to town and let the boys sign the testimony. It'll be good for them."

Will snorted. "We're supposed to be teaching these kids to be men, right? How's it look if we just go back and report it? Sure, we're fulfilling the letter of the Regulations, but we aren't doing our duty. Is that what you want to teach Carl? 'Cause it's sure as hell not what I want to teach Trevor. By the time we go to town, file our report, and the law gets back up here, the hiker could be long gone."

Henry squinted at him. "What are you suggesting we do?"

"You know what I'm suggesting. I'm suggesting we teach our boys to uphold the Regulations."

Neither man spoke again for a few long moments. Only the call of distant birds and the excited chatter of the boys on the trail ahead cut the silence.

Finally Henry said, "You're right. We don't have a choice. We need to take care of it on the way back down."

Will nodded. "Good man."

Henry was the leader of their Rook Mountain Scout troop. Henry's son Carl was Trevor's best friend, so Henry and Will saw a lot of each other. The two men weren't close. It was mostly a quick hello when dropping off the kids at some activity or a little chat around the dessert table at a school function.

It had come as a surprise when Henry invited Will to help out with this camping trip. Will knew Henry wouldn't have called if he wasn't desperate. The Scout troop's usual co-leader had come down with a case of something or other, and Henry had nowhere else to turn. People got a little nervous around Will because of his job. Combined with his wife Christine's job and...well, they didn't get invited to a lot of cookouts. Sometimes he thought it wasn't fair the way they were cut off socially just because they served the community. Other times he felt like it was a necessary evil.

Truth be told, he had been a little thrilled at the invitation. Things between Trevor and Will had been strained recently. It was natural. The kid was growing up and finding himself. He was feeling the need to rebel and he was just starting to discover what form his rebellion might take. So far it was a lot of moping around and disdainful glares when he thought Will wasn't looking. Will could deal with that, and he thought he would be able to deal with whatever rebellion came in the next few years. Still, he couldn't help hope that the weekend would be a time to reconnect, a time to teach the kid a thing or two about nature, about being a man. It hadn't worked out that way so far. The kids had kept to themselves, and Trevor had interacted with Will only when required.

And now the thing with the hiker. He hoped it wouldn't embarrass Trevor too much. Either way, it couldn't be helped. The Regulations were the Regulations. Trust was a must. Will was a leader of the community, and he was expected to uphold the Regulations. Appearance was everything in Rook Mountain.

The kids had disappeared around a corner, but Will could still hear them talking and laughing. They were out of the dense part of the forest and surrounded by bushes. A few months earlier, this spot had been covered with the blazing purples and reds of rhododendrons. Now, the season of the flowers had passed and the bushes were bare, spindly as a tangle of fishing line left unattended.

The pitch and volume of the boys' conversation went up a couple excitement levels.

"Sounds like they made it to the clearing," Henry said.

Will rounded the corner and there it was—the summit.

Rook Mountain and the surrounding peaks were grassy balds—blunt rounded mountain tops covered with dense vegetation. The balds of the Southern Appalachian Mountains were unique because they were well below the tree line. The peaks' lack of trees was a scientific mystery. Some researchers cited long centuries of grazing by a wide variety of large animals, many of which had gone extinct. Other scientists said it was the composition of the soil. There was no conclusive verdict.

Just another damn Rook Mountain mystery, Will thought. Add it to the list.

The thought snuck into his mind before he could suppress it. He was usually good at blocking those kinds of thoughts before they took shape.

Whatever the origin of the grassy balds, the end result was a clear three-hundred-sixty-degree view of the surrounding landscape. From up there the land looked untouched, an endless sea of deep green forest. Will had lived in the town of Rook Mountain for sixteen years. It had been the center point of his whole adult life. At the summit, it seemed tiny, just a series of small gaps in the thick trees that blanketed the landscape below.

When Will first moved there, the town of Rook Mountain had been a small village to the north of the mountain. The town limits had been expanded eight years ago, and the mountain itself was part of town now, all the way to where it bumped up against the North Carolina border. The prison was in the town limits too. But regardless of what the maps said, the mountain top had always been the real Rook Mountain for Will. It was his favorite place on Earth. The view, the crushingly beautiful, endlessly green view below him, was a large part of the reason he had settled there while most of his college friends had migrated to cities like Chicago, Denver and Phoenix. Up there, more than anywhere else, Will felt like he was home.

But there was a job to do.

The boys were gathered on top of a large boulder near the summit. Just a couple of years ago they would have been playing King of the Mountain, the boy at the top of the boulder fighting to keep his position as the other boys struggled to take it. Now they were too cool or too proud. Or maybe they were just growing up.

Will and Henry stopped a few feet from the boulder.

"You wanna tell them?" Henry asked.

Will nodded.

"Guys," he said in a voice full of hard-won authority from sixteen years standing in front of a classroom. "Listen up."

Their roar of conversation diminished to a soft murmur.

"I have something important to tell you. On the way up here Mr. Strauss and I spotted something."

The boys turned to look at him. They went silent.

"Before we came up, we checked with City Hall. There shouldn't be anyone on this mountain but us. Unfortunately, we saw someone. They appeared to be camping. Maybe even living up here."

"Regulation 11," muttered the boy at the top of the bolder.

Will nodded. "That's right, Russ. This individual is in violation of Regulation 11."

There was a long silence. Finally Carl Strauss said, "What are you going to do?"

"Not me. We. We are going to do what we have to. We are going to find this Regulation breaker, and we are going to carry out his sentence."

3.

Frank looked at the city manager for a long time before speaking. "I'd like to get out of prison very much, but I guess you already knew that."

Becky Raymond smiled. "I guess I did. Let me restate that. I have it within my power to release you from prison today."

Frank sat up a little straighter in his chair. The shank in his waistband dug into his side as he moved, reminding

Frank of its presence. Was that what this was about? Did they want Frank to give up the Newg?

His palms were sweaty. They always got sweaty when he was nervous. He wished he could wipe them on his pants the way he always did back in the day before reaching for a girl's hand, but his wrists were handcuffed to the table.

He waited to see if Ms. Raymond would continue. She didn't, so Frank said, "What do we need to do to make it happen?"

Her lips curled into a smile. "When was the last time you saw your brother?"

Frank recoiled under the pressure of her cold brown eyes and the unexpected question.

The warden spoke before Frank could. "Ma'am, as you know, our prisoners have not been allowed any contact with the outside since Regulation Day."

Regulation Day. That was a term Frank hadn't heard before. He could infer its meaning from the context: the day eight years ago when everything had changed at NTCC.

The first year of Frank's stay at NTCC had been difficult, but there had been contact with the outside world. The prisoners were allowed regular visitors and TV time. There were phone calls and magazines and letters. It had been a lot like the versions of prison Frank had seen in movies, only noisier and smellier.

Then, eight years ago, everything had changed. With no explanation, televisions were removed, mail was cut off, and the phones were taken out. The prisoners were told there would be no more visitors. They had reacted with predictable fury. They'd threatened lawsuits, but since they weren't allowed contact with lawyers that hadn't gotten them far. There had been a series of riots, but the guards had violently put those down.

Eventually, the prisoners had come to accept their new circumstances, taking out their anger on each other more than on the prison leadership. New prisoners were kept in a separate cell block, cut off from the prisoners who had been inside before the day everything changed. Except for the occasional new guard, Becky Raymond was the first new person Frank had laid eyes on in eight years.

Ms. Raymond ignored the warden's comment about Regulation Day and kept her eyes fixed on Frank.

"My brother came to see me once," Frank said. "Right after the trial."

"Only once?"

"Ma'am, I'd be happy to pull the visitation records if you'd like to verify Hinkle's story," the warden said. "We could get the exact date for you. Wouldn't take but a moment."

Ms. Raymond shook her head. "Why didn't he visit you more?"

Frank shifted in his seat again and the shank wedged deeper into his side. If they were serious about letting him out, what would happen if they found the shank?

"I killed a friend of his," Frank said. "Jake didn't take it very well. He didn't have much to say to me after that."

"You look like him."

Frank couldn't help but smile. "I've been hearing that my whole life. It's been a while, though."

"A lot has happened while you've been incarcerated. With the town. If you get out of here today, you won't believe the changes we've made. The things we've been able to do."

"The warden mentioned something about that. I think he called it wonderful."

The warden practically glowed at the comment, but Ms. Raymond didn't seem to notice.

"That's an accurate statement," Ms. Raymond said. "And I don't say that out of pride. It's the simple truth. I think it's fair to say you won't find a town like Rook Mountain anywhere else on Earth. It is truly a marvel."

"What's this have to do with me getting out?"

Ms. Raymond reached forward and touched Frank's hand, a casual gesture that made him flinch in surprise. It had been a long time since a woman had touched him.

"I'm sorry to tell you this," Ms. Raymond said, "but your brother killed three people."

Frank drew a deep breath. "That's not possible."

"I'm afraid it is."

Frank let this idea, this horrible idea, roll around in his mind. Sure, Jake had hit a rough patch and got in some trouble as a teenager, same as Frank. Unlike Frank, Jake had met a nice girl and made a solid life for himself. Jake was a husband and a father. He was the only person Frank knew who could accurately be described as content. The idea that Jake could have taken three lives was absurd.

Something wasn't right about this. Something seemed off in a big, bad way. The sudden meeting where even the warden was caught off guard. The way Ms. Raymond had walked through the door as if she owned the place. All this talk about the board of selectmen like they were the President's Cabinet or something. And now this lady was saying Jake was a killer? Had she come to prison just to deliver this horrible news?

Why was Becky Raymond really there?

Frank's hands were dripping a fair amount of sweat onto the table. He really wanted to wipe them on his pants. "Okay. So my brother's a killer. You still haven't told me what I need to do to get out of here."

"After the killings, your brother realized that we were on to him, and he ran."

A chill went through Frank. He pictured Jake on the run, living out of hotel rooms and dying his hair unnatural colors. "When was this?"

Ms. Raymond smiled her hollow smile. "Seven years ago."

"What about his family?"

"He left them behind."

Frank's stomach felt like lead. Christine and Trevor had been going it alone for seven years? "I don't understand. Why didn't anyone tell me?"

The warden cleared his throat. "We discussed it. But the selectmen decided, and I agreed, of course, that telling you wouldn't serve any purpose. Time in prison is hard enough without that on your shoulders. Besides, Jake had only been here the one time. We assumed you two must not be close."

The smoldering lead ball of emotion in Frank's belly was growing hotter by the moment. He wanted to lash out at them, to scream. Not close? A thousand childhood memories flashed through his mind in an instant. A hundred inside jokes. A dozen secrets. Not close? Frank had been closer to Jake than to anyone else in the world. Jake and his wife and son were the only real family Frank had. Maybe things hadn't been friendly since the trial, but this went deeper than that. This was family.

Frank took a deep breath and reminded himself of what the city manager had said. He could get out of here today. He couldn't help Christine from behind the walls of this prison. Whatever emotions he was feeling, he had to remain calm and figure out what the city manager wanted to hear. Whatever he needed to say, he would say it.

"You still haven't told me how I get out of prison," Frank said.

Ms. Raymond leaned forward and took a deep breath before speaking. "We have reason to believe your brother is still in town. We believe he's been in Rook Mountain all this time, deep in hiding. We have used everything we can think of to ferret him out. We've failed. We are not one step closer to finding Jake than we were seven years ago. We've turned over every stone in this town. There is nowhere we haven't looked. We've investigated every angle. And we have nothing."

Frank spoke cautiously. "And you think I can help?"

The city manager nodded. "We're hoping you can."

"You must be pretty desperate."

"Watch your mouth!" the warden said.

"It's okay," Ms. Raymond said. "We are desperate, but we also have our first clue in seven years."

Frank cocked his head and waited for her to continue.

"Do you remember Sally Badwater?"

Frank nodded. Sally had lived a few doors down from the Hinkles when Frank and Jake were growing up. She was two years younger than Frank, but the boys spent a fair amount of time with her because of the trampoline in her backyard.

"Sally claims that your brother came to see her three days ago."

"Why would he go see Sally Badwater?" Frank asked.

Ms. Raymond reached into her briefcase, pulled out a stack of paper, and slid it to Frank. Frank repositioned the pages as best he could with his restrained hands.

"Top of page four," Ms. Raymond said. "Jake approached Sally in the Food City parking lot. She was putting her groceries in the trunk. She turned around and there he was."

Frank flipped over the first three pieces of paper and looked at the text on the top of the fourth page.

OFFICER DENSON: What did Mr. Hinkle say to you?

SALLY BADWATER: It was about that brother of his. Frank. The murderer.

OFFICER DENSON: Do you remember exactly what he said?

SALLY BADWATER: Yeah, I remember. He was real intense. Got up in my face. He said, 'Tell my brother to meet me at the quarry.'

OFFICE DENSON: The quarry? Does that mean anything to you?

SALLY BADWATER: No, of course not. He was talking nonsense.

"What did he mean by 'the quarry'?" Ms. Raymond asked.

Frank thought for a long moment. There was no quarry in Rook Mountain. "So that's it, huh? Decipher my brother's cryptic message for you and I can walk free?"

Ms. Raymond nodded.

Frank paused. This was the most power he'd had in nine years. He couldn't waste it. "I think I'd like a lawyer."

"Jesus, Hinkle." The voice came from behind him. Rodgers. Frank had forgotten the guard was in the room.

A cold smile crossed Ms. Raymond's face. "The whole point of a lawyer is to get you a better deal. I'm offering you the ability to walk out of prison today. You think a lawyer is going to get you something better than that?"

Frank licked his lips, trying to decide how far to push this. "No lawyer means no paperwork. No paperwork means maybe you don't hold up your end of the deal."

The woman shrugged. Her face was unreadable. "I understand your concern. Your choice. If you want to go back to your cell, ask for a lawyer again. If you want to get out of prison today, answer the question. What's the quarry?"

Frank weighed the options and then answered. "You're right. I couldn't ask for anything more than what you're offering. The thing is...I have no idea what Jake was talking about. I've never heard of any quarry around Rook Mountain."

Ms. Raymond sighed. Then she did something unexpected. She reached out and she took one of Frank's hands. For a moment, he felt the old familiar shame at their sweatiness, but then she looked into his eyes. And when she did, all other thoughts slipped away. Her gaze had a force to it, a weight. There was nothing intimate about it; in fact it was the opposite. Her stare was cold and clinical. She looked into him like he was a math problem. He felt her gaze squirming into him. It was a feeling he had felt only once before.

After an endless moment, she released his hand. She didn't look away, but her stare lost its weighty intensity. She had an odd look on her face, a surprised look.

"I believe you," she said, and she stood up. "Thanks, warden."

"Wait," Frank said. This was it. His freedom was about to walk out of the room, and he was about to go back to the world of the Newg and mentally drifting and shower stabbings. "Maybe I can still help you."

"I don't think so. But I appreciate your willingness to try."

Frank's mind was spinning. He had to say something. He had to find the right words to stop her from leaving. Jake needed him. Christine needed him. "Jake wants to see me, right? That's what he told Sally. He can't do that in here. But if I were out there maybe he would make contact."

Ms. Raymond picked up her briefcase from the table and put it under her arm.

"And in the meantime, I could do some digging. I've lived here all my life. I know everybody and they'll talk to me. And I know these mountains. I know them as well as Jake does. If anyone can find him, it's me."

Ms. Raymond paused for a long moment, then looked at him. "Thirty days."

Frank's heart almost stopped as he waited for her to finish.

"You have thirty days to find him. If you do, you're free. If you don't, you come back here and serve out your sentence."

Frank felt himself nodding.

"You meet with me each week to discuss your progress. You don't leave town. And if I even suspect you aren't following through, your little leave of absence ends."

She reached into her briefcase and pulled out an envelope. She slapped it onto the table in front of him. "This is enough money to get you some clothes and a week of food. I assume you can find somewhere to stay?"

Frank nodded again. He looked at the envelope. She'd had it ready.

"Okay," she said. She looked at the warden. "Get him released. He has work to do." The warden looked as shell shocked as Frank felt. He nodded to Rodgers.

"Ma'am," Frank said. "How do I find you? For the weekly meetings."

Ms. Raymond smiled. "You don't. I'll find you."

Rodgers moved back into Frank's field of vision and unhooked the cuffs. Frank felt a smile growing on his face, and he was powerless to stop it. He had a feeling it would be there for a long while.

Ms. Raymond turned to the warden. "He's carrying a weapon. Tell the guards to overlook it."

Warden Cade nodded. "Ms. Raymond, I'm not sure how to do the paperwork on this thing."

"Jesus, Cade. Figure it out. Do it fast. If he's not a free man in the next sixty minutes, I will not be happy."

As Rodgers led Frank out of the room, Frank heard the warden say, "Shouldn't we tell him?"

Ms. Raymond said, "No. Let's see how he does. He'll either figure it out or he won't."

4.

The walk down to the boulder took much longer than it should have. The boys were quieter, and they walked behind the men. There was an energy in the air, part nervousness, part anticipation. The things the boys had been taught in school, the things they had been trained to do in the Scouts, the stories they heard the men telling, usually after a few drinks, they were about to see them up close. They were about to carry out their duty. They would soon take down a Regulation breaker.

Will leaned close to Henry. "You bring a gun up here?"

Henry nodded and patted the pocket of his thick jacket.

"I got mine too," Will said.

"I've got plenty of rope. Enough to tie him up and also tie a lead around his waist for bringing him to town."

The men had spent almost an hour talking to the boys on the summit of Rook Mountain. They had talked about the boys' responsibilities in capturing the Regulation breaker. They had told them to stay out of the hiker's reach and to stay alert. It was all review, stuff they had heard a thousand times before in the classroom, but the boys had listened with focus. There hadn't been any laughter or side conversations. Not this time.

Will held up a hand to stop the group before a curve in the road. He waived the boys in close. "The boulder is about a hundred yards ahead. From here on out, we are silent. Stay as quiet as you can and follow me and Mr. Strauss. Stay behind us and don't do anything different than what we discussed. Nod if you understand."

Will looked around the group, making eye contact with each boy. They all nodded when he looked at them, a silent vow that they understood, that they would perform their duties.

Will reached into the front pocket of his backpack and pulled out the pistol. It was a 9mm Glock. It had been a couple years since he had fired the thing at the range, but that was okay. He didn't intend to use it today. He just wanted to have it ready in case things turned bad. There were six boys here to think about after all.

Will slung the pack onto his back and began creeping down the road, the gun held loosely in his right hand. He stepped lightly, but he knew any effort to be silent would have been futile. A group of eight was sure to be noticeable. They walked down the center of the road to minimize the noise, but bits of gravel still crunched under their feet.

It didn't matter. Will could see the boulder. Most likely, there would be no one there. The backpack could have been abandoned, or its owner might have left it for the day while he went foraging for food. They would probably find nothing, the Scouts would file a report when they got back to town, and that would be that.

The lump of ice in Will's stomach told him there was another possibility. There was a possibility that someone would be there, and it would fall to Will to take the lead. Scout leader or not, Henry had already shown that he didn't have it in him. Try as he might, Will couldn't help but hate Henry a little for that. The way things were, there was a burden that had to be borne. For every person like Henry, too squeamish or indecisive to do their part, there had to be someone like Will to pick up the slack. It wasn't meanness on Will's part; it was just the way it was.

Will was fifty feet from the boulder. Henry was a few steps behind him, and the rest of the group hovered back a bit farther. Will reached down and shifted the pistol to a two hand grip. He looked at Henry one more time to make sure the man was ready. Henry nodded.

"Step out from behind the rock," Will said. He spoke in the calmest, most authoritative voice he could manage.

He was met with silence.

He tried again. "Come on out. We don't mean you any harm."

Another long moment of silence.

Henry spoke softly. "I don't think—"

Will held up his hand to quiet him.

Will said, "I take your non-response as hostility. We are moving in."

"Wait!" The voice came from behind the rock. It was a hoarse, throaty voice, but it was also higher pitched than Will had expected.

"Step out onto the road," Will said.

A shadow moved at the edge of the boulder, then it grew until it revealed feet, legs, a body. The figure moved into the sunlight. Will heard a boy behind him gasp.

"Don't shoot!" the woman said. Her eyes were glued to Will's pistol. Her hair was a tangle of blonde and black. Her t-shirt featured the faded logo of the band Phish.

Will kept his gun trained on her. He concentrated on keeping it steady.

"Ma'am, you have broken Regulation 11. We need to escort you back to town."

The woman's voice trembled when she spoke. "Please. I haven't hurt anyone. I just want to be left alone."

"Jesus," Henry said. "That's Jessie Cooper."

Will felt a surge of anger rising up. The last thing he needed was Henry complicating matters.

"Jessie Cooper," Henry repeated. "She works at the Food City. And before...she was my accountant."

"Henry Strauss?" the woman asked, squinting into the sun.

"I don't care what she was in the Before," Will said. "Get out your rope and tie her hands. Boys, go collect her things."

Henry paused only a moment before reaching into his pack and pulling out a coil of nylon rope. He moved toward the woman.

Will kept his gun trained on her while Henry bound her hands.

"Mr. Osmond! Come here!" The voice came from one of the boys behind the boulder.

Will looked at Henry. "You got her?"

Henry nodded. "Go."

Will pocketed his gun and trotted around the boulder. On the other side, he saw the boys huddled around something on the ground. They parted as he approached, and he saw the oversized piece of paper that held their attention.

It was a map. And not just a map of Rook Mountain. It was a map of the county. A red line had been drawn straight north from the town of Rook Mountain to Elizabethton.

Russ said, "Mr. Osmond, was she planning a route to leave town?"

Will didn't respond. He stood up with a grunt and then took a deep breath. This was not good. He tried to steel himself for what was next. What had to be next.

Will walked back around the boulder. Henry stood a few feet away from the woman. Her head was down, and her shoulders were slumped.

"Ms. Cooper," Will said. "Are you familiar with Regulation 1?"

She raised her head. Her face was a bitter mask of contempt. "Yes, I think I've heard of it."

"Were you planning to leave Rook Mountain?"

She kept her eyes on him, but she did not speak.

"Ms. Cooper, were you trying to leave town?"

"It's not fair what they've done to us," she said. "It isn't right and I'm done with it. Done with all of them!"

"Jessie, are you leaving Rook Mountain?" Will asked.

"Yeah," she said. "I'm leaving. Now let me go."

Will fired, and the sound echoed off the side of the mountain. The bullet hit Jessie Cooper in the chest, and she staggered backwards. She made it three wobbly steps before collapsing. She landed with a thud.

Will walked toward her, not rushing, but careful not to hesitate either. He couldn't lose his nerve. He stood over her, staring into her vacant eyes. A sick wheeze came from her chest as the breath leaked out of her.

Will fired again, this time hitting her near the center of the forehead. There was no mistake now—the woman was dead.

He turned and saw the group staring at him. He looked from one to another, making eye contact with each of them just as he had done before they approached the boulder. He saw looks of shock, horror, revulsion, and terror. There was even a look of awe from Carl Strauss. But they were all present behind their eyes. Whatever feelings they had about what had just happened, none of them were going to lose it. At least not now.

Will spoke softly and calmly, as if his tone could counteract the violence. "We did what we had to do. This woman was a Regulation breaker. Not only that, she was a Regulation 1 breaker. She was going to leave Rook Mountain and go elsewhere. At best, she would have been killed by the Unfeathered. At worst, she would have led them back to Rook Mountain."

The boys remained still.

"There was no shame in what we did here," Will continued. "We protected ourselves. We protected our families. We did our duty, no more and no less. Everyone understand?"

The boys all nodded, some more enthusiastically than others. Things would be different now, for Trevor and for all of them.

"Don't touch anything," Will said. "Leave her things where they lay. When we get to town, we will report what happened. The police will come up here to investigate. They'll want to ask you all some questions. As long as you answer honestly and tell them exactly what happened, everything will be fine."

Will looked at Henry and waited for the man to say something. If Henry took charge, it would go a long way toward getting things back to normal. But Henry said nothing.

"We want to get to the ranger station before sundown," Will said. "Let's get moving."

As Will turned, he heard Carl say, "Hinkle, your dad is a badass."

"Don't call him that," Trevor said.

"Sorry," Carl said. "Step-dad. Whatever. He's still a badass."

"Yeah," Trevor said. "I guess he kind of is."

Will angled his way through the group until he stood next to Trevor. He put his arm around his stepson's shoulders and started down the mountain.

CONTINUED IN REGULATION 19.

CPSIA information can be obtained
at www.ICGtesting.com
Printed in the USA
BVHW071357230722
642850BV00004B/574

9 781087 811598